T0365259

DIANE AT
FIFTEEN

DIANE AT FIFTEEN

Richard McGowan

To order additional copies of this book, contact:
Xlibris Corporation
1-888-795-4274
www.Xlibris.com
Orders@Xlibris.com

[1]

Diane, at fifteen, moved into the old green house on Orchard Street. At the turn of the century it had been a farm house, and the only dwelling for half a mile in any direction. But by the time Diane moved in, nearly seventy-five years later, it was only one of many large, old houses along a rather narrow street lined with maple trees. It was distinguished by being the largest house on the block, with a back yard that went on and on, containing fruit trees and roses and separate little gardens where, had she been a few years younger, she could have played a really good game of hide-and-seek. She was too grown-up for that now, and would leave it to her younger brother Bobby and his playmates.

She first saw the house, before her parents bought it, from the back seat of the family car. Her father drove and she leaned forward over her mother's shoulder to see out the windshield. When the house came into view between two huge maples, she thought of it at once as sprawling, though not in the sense of rambling on horizontally ranch-style. The front facade, with a large covered porch that wrapped completely around one side, was overgrown with flowering vines that nearly reached the second storey, and the whole sprawled not so much out as upward. It had a full basement with a few three-paned windows just below ground level, each with its own little cubby-hole dug into the ground and lined with bricks. Above the stone foundation stretched two floors of living quarters with high ceilings, and above those a full stand-up attic. The ground floor contained a true farm-house kitchen with acres of tiled counter space, dark wooden cabinets with old-fashioned ceramic knobs. And beneath a wrought-iron chandelier, there was an oak table large enough to feed a dozen field hands. The table

came with the house since it proved too large to remove by any of
the doorways. Everyone concluded that it must have been built in
the room.

On the ground floor were several rooms that Diane did not
care much about, including a dining room, two studies, a laundry
room that led to a screened back porch with a walk-in pantry.
With her mind on other things, she glanced at the front rooms
only briefly, and hurried on. She wanted to be the first upstairs to
stake out her own room. Since she had seen two telltale windows
high up in the front beneath the steeply peaked roof, she already
knew the house had an attic. Up the dark, narrow stairway she
ran, barefoot with the hem of her granny skirt bunched in her fist.
The first landing was also high of ceiling with its own dusty
chandelier. Further up she continued, almost out of breath,
thinking she must find the attic. Always she had wanted an attic
room. A huge, empty attic all her own.

The stairway to the attic—not a flimsy pull-down ladder—
was at the back of the house, and so narrow that Diane immediately
wondered how she could manage to get a bed or any other furniture
up there. But she pressed on, and at the top of the stairs, which
ended with not so much as a landing, she found a door with cracked
and peeling varnish. The door was locked, but opposite it was a
small window that gave dusty light to the passageway. It had a
pane of rippled glass in the center, outlined by stained glass in
little rectangles. To peer through it and see anything but sky, she
had to stand on tip-toes and stretch her neck. But the view outside
was magnificent. The window looked directly over the back yard,
which ran far away toward a stone fence covered in ivy—and behind
it she could see the neighbors' yard. Beyond that orchards stretched
away, stopping abruptly where the brown hills leapt up. They
were almost at the edge of town. In the spring, they could probably
find wildflowers and grasshoppers all over those hills—and maybe
rattlesnakes. She already knew there were rattlesnakes in Central
Washington. But rather than seeming fearful, the hills looked almost

inviting with soft golden grass and clumps of sagebrush. Here and there were outcroppings of dark, shattered basalt.

Initially Diane had greeted news of their impending move with anger, and when she heard the specifics of where they were going, she had gagged. "Apple Basket of the World?" she had screamed at her father. "It's a stupid one-horse ghost town on the most god-awful boring stretch of the Columbia!" But on the way there, when they drove through Leavenworth, a quaint Bavarian village at the mouth of the Tumwater Canyon, she began to warm a little to the area. And maybe the town was not too small. The main street was rather long and lined with stores and businesses that seemed livelier than she had expected. The hills were dry, but rather scenic, and there were lots of green orchards, even in town. And now—if she could only have the attic room—maybe it would not be so bad after all.

"Ah!" came her father's voice from the bottom of the stairwell.

Diane dropped from her toes and turned to see him, looking so small at the bottom of the steps. "You can see the whole yard!" she said, and stood again on tip-toes.

Her father laughed to see her cheerful oval face framed in wild curls—the result of her recent experiment with 'frizzing'. He was relieved to see in her face no trace of her former outburst against moving. A move at her age was always hard, leaving friends she had known since grammar school.

"I knew I'd find you here," he said, starting up the steps after a pause.

"The door's locked, though." She turned again to rattle the handle.

"Try this," he suggested when he reached her. In his hand he held a tarnished skeleton key attached to a ring with several other keys and a big fob bearing the real estate agent's mark.

At once Diane grabbed the key and pushed it into the lock. Bursting into the room, she ran to the center and flung out her arms. "Look at it!" she yelled, smiling at how her voice echoed. "Isn't it fantastic?"

Her father knew she had always dreamed of having the attic room, and stood leaning against the door jamb, smiling at her while she ran to and fro. There were six windows, each in its own alcove, dormitory style, and at the front of the house two windows side-by-side overlooked the front yard and the street.

The room was filled with fine brown dust that billowed up when Diane ran, and cobwebs hung from the rough-hewn rafters. Plaster showed through the slats, mixed with old straw. In floor-area, it was by far the largest room in the house.

"Oh, Daddy!" she shrieked. "We just *have* to buy this place. Please?"

"You like it, huh?" he asked, walking toward the center of the room.

"It's fantastic!" she repeated. "I can put my stereo there, against the back wall, or maybe my bed with a light above, and bookshelves here . . . You could almost dance in this room." She clasped her hands and pleaded. "We're going to buy it aren't we, Daddy?"

"We're thinking about it," he answered. "But—" he glanced around with a half-smile and chuckled, "we'll have to pull in some electricity. Probably do some other work, too." Probably a lot of work, he thought. And it really should be made into a playroom, or simply left for storage. But if he let her have it, maybe she would take the move better. Having one dream come true, at least, would help her settle more quickly.

Diane looked around in every corner, and her face dropped as she did. There was not a light or electrical outlet to be seen anywhere. Immediately she brightened and turned to catch her father's hands. "It'll be a cinch, though, right?"

"Perhaps," he said, and started walking back toward the door. "When you're finished admiring the attic, come on down and see the rest of the place. You missed all the bedrooms."

"OK," she said, and turned away, stepping over to the front windows. For a few minutes she sat, just looking out the smudged glass into the front yard. The sun played through the row of tall trees lining the street. Across the way were other houses, with white picket fences in a row halfway down the block. Some children a few doors down rode around a driveway on their bicycles, and she could faintly hear their shrieking voices. The youngest had training wheels, and rode in circles, almost tipping over each time she yanked the handle-bars. Diane turned away with a sigh, and sat with her back to the windows, resting on the frame between them.

How romantic it would be, and secluded, to live in a room like this. She could have all her friends over and talk about whatever they wanted—nobody anywhere could hear them all the way up here. At night she could read peacefully and write in her diary. She smiled and closed her eyes, hugging her knees close to her chest. If she had to move—she must have this room! It would be almost like having her own apartment—and she would even have a lock on the door. She could invite boys in, too, and make out on the bed in this huge room of her own—when her mother was out.

Sitting with her eyes closed, she squeezed her legs together, feeling warm and suddenly wet—so wonderfully blissful. Just a little, she wanted to slip her finger into her panties and think about how it would be . . . She could have her first lover in this room. He would have to be the handsomest boy in the school, but a poet too, and she would write about it—unexpurgated—in her diary. Someday when she was about twenty-five, but still beautiful, they would discover her, and she would be in all the literary magazines—sought after for lectures and talk-shows to give her frank and uninhibited views.

When a faint sound reached her, she shook her head and her eyes came slowly open. If she did not appear soon downstairs, they would come looking for her. With a sigh, she wiped her fingers on the front of her panties, then got up and went down the narrow stairway again. She found her parents on the upper floor, looking at the bathroom.

"Do you think we can buy it?" she asked as she approached her mother's back.

Nancy laughed when she heard that. It was precisely the

question she had asked her husband just before Diane appeared. "It's that kind of place isn't it?" she said. "The first time you see it, you just fall in love with it—huh Tom?" They had seen the place together a week before, and she had said the same thing then. She looked at him expectantly and slipped her arm into his.

"I guess that's four out of four," agreed Tom. "I'll make an offer today."

"Where's Rat?" Diane asked casually.

"Your brother *Robert*," said Nancy, with a narrow-lipped glance at Diane, "is playing in the yard."

"Sorry," Diane whispered. She rolled her eyes and tagged along behind her parents as they went down the hall to the next little room.

"This will be Bobby's room," Nancy announced as she pushed open the door. Diane peeked in on the way past. The room was painted pale yellow with white trim. It had a beautiful wooden floor and a set of built-in bookshelves along the inner wall.

"And this will be the baby's room," Tom announced when they stopped at the door next to the master bedroom. Nancy began to smile but said nothing.

"The what?" Diane asked a moment later, looking from her father to her mother. "You're kidding, right?" she said, but her heart leapt with excitement. "You're pregnant?"

Nancy bit her lip, grinning, giggling. "Uh huh."

Diane fell into her mother's embrace, laughing. "Mom, that's wonderful! When's it due?"

"In about six months. Do the figuring yourself."

Standing back, Diane hesitantly touched her mother's stomach, then looked up into her eyes. Even without makeup her mother's face looked fresh. She seemed even prettier than usual and her blue eyes caught the light, sparkling. Diane decided it was true that pregnant women looked more beautiful.

"November?" she said tentatively.

"Bingo," Nancy laughed. "It's due mid-November."

"So we have to buy this place now, Daddy," Diane observed, "otherwise we'll have no place to put the baby. Right Mom?"

"That's the idea . . ."

Diane held her mother's arm while she looked happily into the baby's room. It, too, had a wooden floor, as did all the bedrooms. Only the hallway was carpeted, with a long burgundy carpet that might have been Navajo. The wallpaper in the baby's room was off-white with little pansies and ribbons in lavender and green. It was the only bedroom that had curtains, and these were gorgeous thick lace, tied back with big bows to let sunlight stream in.

"It'll be nice and bright for the baby, won't it?"

"I think it's the brightest room in the house," Nancy agreed, "but that might just be an effect of the wallpaper."

"Do you think so?" Diane said.

"Could be the light; it faces southwest . . ."

"Come on," called Tom from the doorway. "If you want to put an offer in, we'll have to run."

They all turned out into the hallway and hurried down the steps. Bobby was in the front yard stacking jagged little pebbles along the walkway. Tom scooped him up quickly in one arm and they all piled into the car, then drove to the nearest pay-phone, and put in their bid.

[2]

About a month later, in July, Diane's family left Seattle. For weeks she had been saying good-bye to all of her friends, vowing to write constantly and call at Christmas. But by the time she really left, Diane was looking forward so much to her new room, that she did not mind leaving as much as she thought she would. It was true that she cried with her best friend Helga who came to see her off. Yet an hour later, she felt nothing but anticipation for the future. Who would she meet; what would the school be like; how would she decorate her room? She had a thousand ideas for that, and while the car crawled slowly over Stevens Pass and began to descend toward her new home, she began to make some idle sketches in her diary.

Diane spent the first night in her new room with a sleeping bag, a flashlight with extra batteries, and a thick romance novel stuffed into her overnight bag. Past midnight, she lay under the front windows where she had hung a sheet in place of a curtain. Her pillows were propped up against the frame between the two windows. Moonlight shone from one of the side windows, making a pale silver streak on the floor. She hung the flashlight from a rafter with some string so she could see to read, but reading was a bit difficult until the flashlight stopped swinging, pendulum-like on its string. A while later, she felt too warm, so she turned onto her stomach and pushed her sleeping bag down below her knees, leaving her legs bare. She stopped reading long enough to pull the hem of her short nightgown down over her bottom. The book was simply too absorbing—gushingly romantic and delightfully sexy. Practically every few pages there was a man with strong arms, handsome and brawny, rescuing or pressing his body into, or pulling open the heroine's bodice. Of course it was full of lace and taffeta and luscious silks and satins. What it lacked in literary merit, she decided early on, it made up for in raciness. She felt wet between her legs, and squeezed them together during love scenes, keeping her hands away for the longest time. Finally she turned on her side, holding the book in one hand, and put her other down into her panties where she could stroke the hair very lightly and slowly run her finger along the cleft . . .

"Is that the sort of thing young ladies read these days?" said a soothing man's voice at her shoulder.

Diane's hair stood on end with the sudden shock, and she jumped up, struggling to get her sweaty feet out of her sleeping bag. The book dropped, and she vaguely felt herself step on it.

"Who's there!" she yelled. Pouncing on the flashlight, she ripped it from the string and held it to her chest, flashing it all around the attic. Slowly she edged over toward the corner, shivering in fear. At that moment she was so scared—filled with more sheer terror than she had ever known—she had to concentrate on not peeing all over herself, and her face began to sweat. It must have been a dream. She had been dozing over the book and was having a nightmare.

"Is anyone there?" she whispered, still slowly waving the light into all the corners. When there was no answer, she tried to calm herself, but kept sweeping the light around the room.

"I didn't mean to startle you, Miss," said the voice again, in a low whisper. "I won't harm you at all, I promise." The voice seemed normal, and was rather pleasant to Diane's ears, despite her terror.

"Where are you?" she asked, her voice a bare squeak. She coughed to clear her throat. "Who are you?"

"Turn out the light, and I'll show you."

"Oh no!" she yelled, backed against the rafters. "Not a chance, Mister!" Pleasant voice or not, she was caught in the room with a prowler—maybe a rapist. She wished she had a gun or a knife, feeling her stomach knot with fear. "I'm going to scream if you don't tell me who you are and how you got in here. And keep your distance," she warned, "I've got a knife."

"Won't you try shutting the lamp off," the voice pleaded. "I'll stay way over here," it continued calmly while receding until it seemed to come from near the doorway. "Right here."

"Forget it."

"Turn it the other way, then, or stop it with your hand."

He must be just outside the door, Diane decided, and his proximity had been an aural illusion. Slowly she covered the flashlight with the palm of her hand, and then stood in the darkness for a second. The moon must have gone down, for there was little light from outside and the sheets covering all the windows glowed faintly. She tried drawing the sheet aside from the front window, but it got no brighter. All the street-lights pointed downward, not into the front windows, where she had drawn it aside. She peeked outside and could see the empty street.

"Can you see me yet?"

Faintly at the far end of the room, she did see something, but she could not quite believe it. Again, her hair began to stand on end, rising slowly from her neck. All across her scalp she could feel each and every hair rising.

"You're scaring me," she whined hoarsely, feeling tears welling in her eyes.

There was a luminous presence beside the door: the outline of an older man, perhaps in his mid-twenties. As her eyes adjusted, she could see that he was clean-shaven, with dark, short hair parted just off center. He wore an old-fashioned suit with a high, white collar, and a narrow bow-tie. He was seated, as if in a chair, but several inches off the floor, with his booted feet propped up before him.

"You're a ghost," she stated, feeling stupid as soon as she did.

"As your mother would say—Bingo."

Denial was simple, and she tried it. "This is not happening. I'm dreaming."

"Hardly," he said. "May I come closer?"

She clutched the flashlight tighter. "Stay there. How did you get in here?"

"I live here," he said, sounding mildly affronted. "Where else should I be?"

"Oh God," she whispered as she collapsed trembling to her knees. "This is the worst nightmare I've ever had." It was her first night in a new house, and she had had nightmares sometimes in the past when she slept away from her own room. She wished she could wake up, and tried hitting herself with the flashlight.

"Are you that scared?" he asked. "You don't seem so terribly frightened to me. Your aura has shrunk considerably, but it's a healthy color."

"My aura," Diane said simply. She sat quietly with her legs crossed and regarded the ghost. Then suddenly self-conscious, she pulled the sleeping bag over her bare legs. "Oh God!" she swore in a hiss, "You're not real. I don't believe in ghosts."

"Nonetheless," the man said. "Aren't you going to ask me the usual questions?"

"What usual questions?"

"Oh," he said enthusiastically. "I don't know. How did I die? What's my name? How can you get rid of me? What's it like?"

"Do people always ask those questions?"

"I don't know," he laughed. "Usually they faint if they're real ladies. Men usually bolt for the front door. Children sometimes talk, but they're hardly stimulating company. Actually, I've hardly had a conversation this long in fifty years."

"That's funny," she said.

"Do you want me to leave?"

Diane thought about that for a moment, and found that she was not really scared any longer; she simply felt strange. Despite the late hour, she was suffused with adrenaline, and not the least bit sleepy. He seemed rather personable, and somehow charming even. It was not exactly her typical nightmare.

"Are you going to kill me or anything? Drive me insane?"

"Whatever for, young lady?"

"Isn't that what ghosts do?"

"Not in my house they don't."

That satisfied her that he was at least benign. "So—what's your name?" she asked finally. "My name's Diane. Kolansky."

"Warren Brannigan," he replied. "Pleased to meet you, Miss Kolansky. Sorry I haven't a hat to tip. Died without it you know. Now I'll never live it down."

Diane laughed and tilted her head, smiling warmly. His demeanor had relaxed her already, and she found herself talking almost normally to him, though a part of her kept repeating that he was a ghost. It really seemed a wonderful dream.

Without seeming to move, Warren stood and walked about as he talked. After a while he sat in the air close enough for her to perceive his face, almost as if he were living—though she could see the gray outlines of the rafters and windows through him. After nearly half an hour, she learned to see him so well that he was almost as visible and opaque as anything else in the room. She supposed he might seem brighter with some practice, and he confirmed this conjecture. After all, it was her first supernatural experience, and she could be expected to improve as she became accustomed to it.

Some time later, Diane suddenly burst out to say that he looked and talked more like a David than a Warren.

"Really?" he answered. "I had a cousin named David. We didn't look much alike though."

He went on in an amusing way to recount some facts about his cousin, by way of demonstrating how a David would behave, and how different they were. Diane was fascinated—especially by his voice, but eventually she yawned and stretched her neck, throwing back her head and rolling it around.

"Are you tired?"

"Huh?" she asked. "A little. But I've never met a ghost before or anything."

"Of course. Would you like me to tell you a bedtime story?"

She twisted her mouth to the side. "I'm a little *old* for that."

"If I might ask," he asked tentatively, "Just how *old* are you? I'm not very good with ladies' ages."

"Sixteen," she lied instantly.

"Ah ah," he scolded with a wagging finger and broad smile. "I can tell when you're lying—your aura goes all dark and fluttery for an instant."

She began to blush and admitted, "I'm fifteen."

"Still, you're a young lady and I shouldn't keep you awake any longer. You've got a picnic tomorrow, and you must get your rest."

"How do you know that?" she ejaculated in surprise.

"I live here," he replied. "I hear it all . . ."

"Oh, God," she moaned. She felt indignant—as if her bedroom walls had turned to glass, and she was naked. "So you can spy on us all the time?"

"Only until I get to know you," he said quickly. "After a while— it's like any family, and one ceases to be quite so interested in every detail. Then I only look in when something interesting happens."

"Oh." She bit her lip thoughtfully. "If I promise to talk to you sometimes . . ."

"Yes?"

"Will you promise not to spy on *me* when I want to be alone?"

Warren grinned and sat upright. "Will you really talk to me?"

"I'm talking to you now aren't I?"

That was a fact, and he readily agreed to her terms. It would be wonderful to have real conversations again. "All right, Miss Kolansky—"

"Call me Diane," she interjected.

"Diane. I guess we have a pact." Her smile fell somewhat, and he regretted the choice of words. "A deal, I mean. When you want me to be gone, just say so." He held his hand out solemnly, and she reached to shake it, closing on air. "Hah!" he laughed, "It works—just like in the movies." With a wave, he bid good-night, and faded away through the floor.

Diane, left in darkness, remembered the flashlight. It had long been turned off yet remained in her lap. She switched it on long enough to rearrange her sleeping bag, then stowed it behind her pillow and lay down, deeply tired. She was too sleepy to keep her eyes open, but at the same time, her mind was racing, filled with incredible thoughts. She had her very own ghost. What could she do with a ghost? First, off, she could write about it in her diary— but who in the world would believe it? Nobody need believe it if she had some hair-raising adventures to tell. Maybe he knew all the haunted mansions in town, or could take her to the graveyard on Halloween . . . With her thoughts skipping along romantic, adventurous lines, she drifted to sleep, curled up with one hand between her thighs and the other beneath her head.

[3]

The morning after meeting Warren Brannigan so abruptly and unexpectedly in her new bedroom, Diane awoke with a vaguely puzzled feeling that something was wrong. She remembered a dream—a nightmare, in fact. But it could not have been a dream, since she usually awoke from dreams with a feeling of disappointment in their unreality; or from nightmares with a feeling of relief and safety. Her feeling that morning was different from either of these; rather one of curiosity and expectance. She had never had such a vivid dream before and it seemed much too tangible to be unreal. No, it could not have been only a dream.

As the reality of her meeting with a ghost—in her own new bedroom—began to work its way into her consciousness, she had a rising, irrational fear. Her heart raced as she lay on her back, the sleeping bag pulled up around her shoulders. Only her face poked out, and she lay quietly looking and looking around the room. If she actually had met a ghost she had no idea what to expect. Of course nobody would believe her if she told them. She lay staring at the ceiling watching dust motes in the air, churning in the shafts of light that peeked from the edges of the sheets along the eastern windows.

When she heard voices downstairs, so far away they sounded like faint bees buzzing beneath the floor, she finally stirred, then got up and dressed in the same clothes she had worn the previous night. She had almost nothing else, as the family's belongings had not yet arrived, and she was conserving to avoid having to do her laundry. Her mother would probably make her change if she noticed, but she had so much on her mind, too, that she might not.

Warren sat on the roof and watched the sun rise. When he noticed Diane awaken, he waited a decent interval before greeting her, until he was sure that her fluttery aura was back to normal. She had awoken with start, and such a thin, wavery presence that he could tell she was in a state of keen anxiety with a thousand questions running through her mind. She had admitted as much as never having seen a ghost before, which was strange, to him, considering that those who saw them at all usually had such experiences from a much younger age.

After descending from the roof, he went to her doorway. She sat on the floor brushing her hair while she looked out the window onto the street, and after watching her for half a minute, he called softly.

"Diane?"

She turned with a start to whisper in a thin wobbling tone. "Hello?" Maybe it really was not herself dreaming or going crazy. "Warren?" she inquired softly as she stood up.

"Good morning," he said. "How are you feeling?"

"Relieved that I'm not going crazy. That it wasn't a dream." She stood with the brush in her hair. After making a couple of strokes through her hair, she held the brush at her side.

"Are you sure you're not?" he asked. "Normal people don't hear ghosts—and certainly don't see them."

"I saw you last night . . ." She lifted the brush again and started brushing her hair more vigorously. "No, really, I am going crazy. I'm so crazy I'm not jumping out of my skin—and any normal person would faint, or run screaming downstairs."

"It shows you've got the gift," he replied with conviction. "Can you see me this morning?"

"No," she answered, "I can't."

"Concentrate. I think you can do it."

She tossed the brush on her pillow and looked toward the door, not sure what she was looking for.

"Think to yourself how real I am," he said. "Maybe that will do it."

She crossed her eyes and tried to focus in the air, but her vision only blurred. He slowly faded into visibility as she concentrated not on focussing but simply feeling there was something to be seen. Suddenly, the door opened behind Warren and her mother stepped through him into the room.

"Mom!" Diane screamed.

"What is it?" asked Nancy. "Did I give you a fright?"

Diane let out a sigh and walked toward her mother, trying to smile. "No—I mean yes, you scared me."

Laughing, Nancy said, "I thought I'd have to wake you up. Come on down when you're ready. We're going out to breakfast this morning."

"OK," Diane answered, then sat cross-legged and gave her hair a few more strokes until her mother closed the door behind her. "Warren?" she whispered when Nancy's footsteps faded down the stairs. "Are you OK?"

"Couldn't be better," he said, standing right where he had been before.

"She stepped right through you."

"Didn't feel a thing."

"She didn't see you, did she?"

"Obviously not."

"So it's just me?" Diane asked hesitantly.

"Unless Rat or Tom have the gift, I suppose it is. A good thing, too," he mused. "If everyone could see me there'd be no end of trouble. I'd be everyone's message boy and have no time left to wander around and haunt anything."

Diane laughed, then put aside her brush. Warren patiently answered her questions while she rolled her sleeping bag, then sat on it. She was full of questions, and since he had not talked so much for so many years, he was cheerful and animated, pouring out such witticisms as might amuse a young lady, until he did have her giggling delightfully. Finally, remembering that her mother was awaiting her, he shooed her off to breakfast.

"We've got all the time we need," he said as she departed.

"I'll see you later, won't I?" she asked.

"Of course," he replied. "I'm not going anywhere. Give my regards to Broadway, won't you?"

She smiled and closed the door behind her.

[4]

In the following days, Warren appeared to Diane frequently. Usually he came in the evening, and at first he always appeared by the door. From there, he would call softly to her and ask permission to enter. Only once in the first week did she ask him to come back to see her later. That time, though, she was already in bed. She had been reading and during a passionate love-scene, had gradually let the book slide and drop to the floor. With her fingers in her panties, she had almost reached orgasm when he appeared.

"Uh, I'm busy reading," she pleaded breathlessly, sitting straight up when he called to her.

After he left, she lay still for a moment then picked up her fallen book and found her place, but she kept wondering whether he had seen her before he called her name and it took her a long time to get the mood back again. She really wanted that romantic feeling to continue, and loved the way it mounted up in her, tingling until it penetrated every nerve in her body. Maybe that would be how it was to have sex, and she practiced sometimes pushing her finger partly inside—it felt good, too, but it was better just to rub slowly, and let her other hand wander between her thighs and over her belly, softly with her fingertips.

She rose toward orgasm very slowly while playing through a fantasy of the previous summer's boyfriend. He had loved to French-kiss her so much they constantly had chapped lips. And she imagined him pressing against her behind the house, leaning against the wall when he brought her home at night. His arms around her, holding tightly and whispering love . . . while he tweaked her bra-strap open, and she felt her chest suddenly expand and he caught her up just before she flew away. The memories of his hands on her breasts, feeling her up; once or twice sucking her nipples until they were hard as pebbles; his hand slipping into the top of her jeans, down into her soft hair. She came at last with a slow dissolution, pressing both palms against herself and when it was over, she relaxed, feeling sleepier and sleepier.

When Warren did re-appear she was asleep and he came to stand by her, simply looking at her and smiling. He was so happy to have a new friend that it almost did not matter to him that she was asleep. Looking at her shallow breathing, her hands soft against her cheek, knowing she would be his friend—that was enough to last him half the night. And she was such a warm, attractive girl, too. Even in sleep her aura waxed and waned, large and yellow with her breathing. The rest of the night he spent wandering in his usual way, making the rounds, checking on the mice in the cellar and the birds under the eaves. He took a turn about the garden later and checked the flowers.

Diane's furniture and things arrived a couple of days later, and she spent a busy week unpacking and settling in. Warren was delightful company while she unpacked. They talked and she told him about all of her belongings. She even showed him some of the less private parts of her diary.

In their first week together, Warren would most often sit on the edge of the bed after she climbed in for the night, speaking in his deep, dreamy voice and lulling her to sleep while she lay with the covers pulled up to her neck, feeling little flushes of excitement while he talked. Sometimes even while he was there, she would slide her fingers down into her panties, always surprised at the dampness there, right in the plump cleft. He made her feel that way, all the time. Everything about him was interesting and made her feel wonderful—but she had this little uneasiness about her feelings. She thought she might be starting to fall in love—but that was ridiculous, because he was a ghost. He could not even touch her. She had to do that for herself, but still it felt comfortable to wiggle her fingers, letting the warmth spread through her, getting more sleepy as he kept telling whatever story he had. A few times, she fell asleep while he was talking. Then in the morning when she woke up and opened her eyes, he would be there, right where he had been, asking how much of the story she remembered.

He began to tell funnier stories as they got to know each other. Diane was not a prude by any means, and there were times when he skirted across some point, being somewhat careful of her sensibilities, until she would blurt out something that, had he been living, would have caused him to blush. It was not that he was embarrassed about what he was saying, or even the innuendo of the story, it was merely that he had never said things quite like that to such a young woman, and had them all acknowledged and understood for what they were—blatant flirtation. It was a fright to him, sometimes, how societal norms had changed—but then everything had been vastly different since his day.

While talking one evening, Warren said something in passing about Bobby.

"How could you know that?" Diane asked.

"What, that he took an extra doughnut?"

"Yeah. Were you watching him?"

"No, actually I wasn't. But when your mother confronted him—and that I did see, because I happened to be in the living room—he went all wobbly and dark."

"You mean his aura?"

"Yes. It's a good indicator—that's probably why people have them, I've always thought. I think people can sense them quite well if they take the time to practice. Most people don't, you know, they just—" He stopped in mid-sentence, abruptly noticing that her aura had taken a huge leap outward and brightened suddenly. "I'm rambling again aren't I?"

Diane nodded, laughing. "It's OK, I like it."

"I know," he said enigmatically. Her liking for him was lavishly apparent in her aura, and he loved to watch how she blossomed when he flirted with her. "Anyhow, she asked him if he took a doughnut, and he said no. But I could tell."

"Can you tell what he's thinking?" Diane asked.

"Of course not," Warren replied vigorously, "but through observation, I fancy that I know all kinds of things that people never mention."

"Like what?"

He smiled and looked into her eyes quietly, then after a moment began to sing almost in a whisper:

> Maxwellton's braes are bonnie
> Where early falls the dew
> And it's there that Annie Laurie
> Gave me her promise true.

After the first verse he stopped, and watched her aura shrink very slightly from a brilliant and gauzy shimmer.

"Like what?" she asked, remembering that he had not answered her question. "Give me an example."

"For instance," he said rather slowly, watching her eyes with great care, "I can tell when you're playing with yourself."

Her aura shrivelled to darkness, and she made a slow movement under the sheets. While Warren burst into laughter, she blushed hotly and looked away.

"Embarrassed you?" He was still chuckling. "I'm sorry. I guess that was a mean joke."

Abandoning any thought of secrets, surrendering everything, with an outburst of passion she turned back to face him squarely and answered. "I just like to. It feels good."

"I know," he whispered, staring into her eyes. "And I like it too—I like to watch you and talk to you when you're doing it."

"You do?" She parted her lips and inhaled softly.

He nodded, and continued. "You look so blissful and content—your aura waxes huge and shining, all yellow and white like sunlight; as big as a full moon. It's like a big harvest moon around you sitting so prettily. And I'm happy just watching you. Is that all right?"

She tingled all over and was half tearful when she nodded slowly, and pulled the sheets up around herself with a shy smile.

Her feeling was very much like love. "I like it when you're watching," she whispered.

Soon, she felt sleepy, but kept her heavy eyes open long enough to listen to the end of the story he had been telling earlier. When he finished, and she had said good-night, she closed her eyes and tiredly yanked down the corner of her pillow the way she liked it. "Can you sing me to sleep?" she asked sweetly.

"I'll sing anytime you want," he said.

"Thanks."

Warren began to sing again in his soothing baritone, wishing so much that he could reach out to touch Diane's lovely hair. The last bit of awkward tension in their relationship was gone that evening. He had felt everything snap and they both breathed more easily at the instant she admitted—so vulnerably—that she liked to play with herself. And his presence was a catalyst. After that beginning, he foresaw wonderful things for them, wishing dreadfully that he could take her into his embrace. Perhaps she might even help him in ways very close to his heart. His thoughts turned to a bright, summer's day, long ago, when he had felt that way about another woman. She had been very much like Diane in some ways. After a while, he got up to make his evening rounds, humming as he walked.

[5]

One's first meeting with a person who becomes one's closest friend is often recorded lucidly in the memory. But the initial process of knowing them—that delightful, drunken wooing that, when it happens, seems to go on forever—somehow becomes colored by all the things that happen afterward. And by the time one realizes it, one is deep in a comfortable friendship that seems always to have been there—and may not be quite sure how one got there, except that it was natural and inevitable. It was like that between Diane and Warren. She was not sure precisely how their deep friendship happened—though it was, when she looked at it, abrupt. It took them the remainder of July and half of August to mutually acknowledge that they were fast friends. Had he been alive, and perhaps closer to her own age, she would have been drunk with love. As it was, she felt giddy half the day—it was so much more than friendship. By the time the new school year was threatening, she felt closer to Warren than she had to anyone, ever.

Warren was a breathtakingly handsome man by anyone's standards—by the standards of any age, even—and she found him immensely attractive in that way. But even more, she loved his amusing way of looking at life—and in his case, death—through continual jests, yet with a kind of insight and good-sense that awed her. And this comfortable feeling led, she was not sure how, to her sharing the deepest kind of confidences with him. Though he was a man, and she would never, before him, have considered dropping such confidences on anyone but her closest girlfriends—and sometimes not even them—she felt absolutely safe with him. He was a ghost, after all, and if she talked of kissing, he could not kiss her, or pressure her, or be physically rude; of course he never would be, he was simply too nice and understanding a man to be anything but wonderful. If she mentioned something sexual, he pointed out the change in her aura and they could joke about it. And if he could see that far into her, though he could not actually read her mind, there seemed nothing she could hide from him. Presently, there seemed no need to hide anything, and before she knew it she had intimated to him nearly everything she had ever thought upon the subject of her own sensuality, her urges, and her passions—even the most secret parts of her diary. To him, she opened completely.

In that endearing way young blooming women have, the feeling of being attractive and important to a man gave her such confidence and charm that even the prospect of beginning the school year without a friend in the world did not affect her in the least. Hardly more than twice had she written to anyone back in Seattle, and only a few lines. She was as cheerful as she had ever been, and her parents were delighted that, for whatever reason, she seemed thrilled with the town, the house—and with the prospect of starting in a new school.

Diane's friendship was important to Warren as well. As he told her, he could certainly not boast a great quantity of friends— and they were all dead, he would always add. It was a rare living person who could see him, and in his eye, the ability to see beyond life into the hazy world of the spirit was always a special gift. He presaged great things for Diane—though he realized that she would have to mature a little first. He was in luck that she had been raised well, so far, and only required a modicum of finishing, in his view, to rise as the cream of what these days passed for the crop. Had she been a child, he could certainly never have had quite the friendship he did have with her. She was at the most delightful age of discovering the world, when everything was interesting and love was everywhere. Her emotions sang like crystal at his tap. She also knew her body probably better than any woman he had known during his lifetime—his death-time was a different matter entirely.

When her things arrived, Diane hung from the ceiling two

beautiful African print fabrics that had been a going-away present from her friend Katrina. She had a huge rattan chair with a kind of canopy over it, and from the rafters near the center she hung a hammock on one side. Her two chests of drawers were against the back wall where she had also put up a full-length mirror. She had no closet, but near the drawers her father had put in a double rack for all her dresses and coats. He had also built her some standing bookshelves about the height of a kitchen counter, and they divided the room into a kind of sitting room with a table where she could work, and a bedroom proper, with almost a hallway out to the door. It was the coziest place she had ever dreamed of living, and she thought if she only had her own bathroom, it would have been as good as having her own apartment.

Warren and Diane sat talking one evening in her room after she had fully settled in and had her familiar furniture about her. A few days before that she had finally pronounced the interior decorations finished. Nancy had taken her to the mall that day, along with Rat, to buy a few new things for the school year, but she was not thrilled with the new fall fashions.

"Why not?" Warren asked. He had believed that young ladies were supposed to be all goggle-eyed over fashions, no matter how ludicrous, and he told her so. He was in a jovial mood, and felt like teasing mercilessly, which she always really loved. "So are skirts getting too long for you this year? You prefer to show a bit more leg?"

"No," she said, "They're just not *me*."

"Ah, they're too short then. Your butt sticks out, and if you don't keep up your diet, you'll have two fat buns flapping around your knees."

"No!" She began to giggle.

"Around your ankles then—it's all those Twinkies you know—and you'll have to carry them about in a wagon behind you. They'll think you're six! 'How much for your hot buns?' the old ladies will call."

"No!"

"Why not open a bakery? Miss H. C. Buns and Co."

"No!" she laughed hysterically.

"Their motto? Get thee to a Bunnery!"

Diane sobbed with laughter.

"I'm just envious," he remarked. "I haven't been out of the house in fifty years."

"Fifty years?" she asked when she had time to finish laughing. "Why don't you go somewhere? Can't you just float away and visit any place you want?"

He was at that moment floating in his usual position, mid-air, and leaning back as if reclining in an immense easy-chair, but he sat upright to answer.

"It's not that simple just because I'm a ghost," he said. "I can't leave."

"Why not?" It seemed to her that all he had to do was walk out through the walls. It had not occurred to her that he might not be able to leave.

"The front door is trivial," he continued. "It's after that. You see, the further I walk, the harder it gets. It's like walking under water. But the water gets thicker and thicker." So he explained—thinking that he must have mentioned this all to her before—that he was stuck within a rather short distance of the house.

"How far can you go?"

"A good eight inches if I'm really horny," he said straight-faced.

"No!" she yelled, laughing again. "I mean from the house!"

"I've been out to the edge of the block a couple of times. Years ago."

There was a shrill call just then from the bottom of the stairwell. "Diane!"

"Yes mother!" she called, rushing to open the door.

Nancy stood at the bottom of the stairwell and had just begun to ascend slowly. She carried a towel over her shoulder, and her hair was damp, as she had just come from the shower. "Are you all right?" she asked.

"Huh? Yeah, I'm fine, Mom. What's wrong?"

"I just heard you screaming," Nancy said, still ascending the stairs. "I was wondering if something had happened."

"Oh that!" Diane chuckled. "I was just reading . . . and laughing . . ."

"Oh." Nancy stopped and turned around. "Well, next time laugh a little more quietly. I thought the house was on fire or something."

"Just her pants, Madam," called Warren from behind her. "Nothing that can't be remedied with a good douche."

Diane shut the door, giggling, and heard her mother's steps die away below.

"You, Mr. Brannigan, are incorrigible."

"And you, Miss Muffet—"

"Have a hot little tuffet?"

"So I've observed," Warren said in a sensual tone, and lounged back in the air, with his hands behind his head.

"Where were we?" she asked, settling down in the hammock.

"My not leaving the house," he reminded her.

"So, you said you can't leave the house, but why?"

"It's because of the ashes," he said, as if that explained it.

"What ashes?"

"Why—haven't I told you all this before?"

"Nope."

"Oh," he said, reclining on his side near the hammock. "Well, there's a limit to my mobility—governed by an inverse square-law, actually, rather in the same way gravity works. You know how, if you drop a ball from some height it—" He stopped speaking when she rolled her eyes with great exaggeration.

"No interest in physics," he said, pretending to jot a note to himself. "Wouldn't want to hear about love-making in space or anything like that."

Diane laughed at that, but said, "I really want to know."

"I can't go very far from where my ashes are kept," he said, setting aside his jests. "The ashes of my body, that is."

"And where are they?"

"In an urn, which is buried in the cellar."

"What? How come you never told me you're buried in the house!"

"You never asked about that. I guess it didn't occur to *me* that you wouldn't know that. But, you've never been dead, so how would you know . . ."

"So how would you know," she mocked, thrusting out her shoulder. "Let's go dig you up, then."

"Dig me up?"

"Sure," she said. "If you can't get far from your ashes, maybe you can come with me if I carry them."

Warren already knew that he could follow where his ashes went, for their whereabouts fully governed his mobility—and he had been out of the house that way before—but he was so pleased by Diane's suggestion that he nearly fell over, and had he been susceptible to floors, he would have hit it. "From the mouths of babes," he cried, and toppled backwards in a mock faint. His head grazed through the floor into the room below, and he popped back up to resume his seat. "You're brilliant, Diane!"

"All in a day's work—for H. C. Buns and Co."

[6]

In darkness, Diane would not descend to the cellar despite Warren's solemn assurance that it harbored nothing fearsome whatever, but she promised him she would dig him up first thing in the morning. It was after midnight when Nancy knocked on the door to kiss Diane good-night and make sure she was getting ready for bed. All summer, she had been up late, and with school approaching, Nancy wanted her to start going to sleep earlier, because it would ease the transition back into the school routine. Diane lay in the hammock with a book in her hand and assured her that she was only going to read to the end of the chapter. In reality, she had not read a chapter all evening and had picked it up just before her mother walked in.

Nancy took the book from her hand and glanced at the cover. "Really," she said with a sigh. "You might try to read some history or something."

"This *is* history," Diane insisted. "Read the back cover."

"Prairie Love?" Nancy smiled, and sat down on the hammock. "It's a western."

"Oh, I can see that," said Nancy. The front cover showed the usual rugged mountain man with open rawhide vest and a horsewhip in one hand, a breathless woman in red with low-cut bodice enfolded in his arms. "Is it any good?"

"Yeah, it is. I'm learning all about the the westward expansion."

"Hopping from bed to barn to riverbank," Warren added.

Diane bit her lip to keep from giggling.

"Penis ahoy!" Warren yelled. "Look out astern! He's diving mates!"

Vaguely, Nancy flipped a few pages and looked at the bookmark, then set the book down on the hammock with a tender smile. "Good-night," she said, and kissed Diane's forehead. "Don't stay up too late, OK?"

"I won't. Good-night, Mom."

When Diane awoke in the morning, Warren was hovering nearby, sitting forward with his hands on his knees, blinking rapidly.

"It's daylight," he said hopefully.

Diane jumped out of bed and threw off her nightgown. She had long since become comfortable doing that in Warren's presence. The first few times he had been present when she wanted to change, she made him turn his back, but after a while that seemed ridiculous, and she stopped doing it. He never stared, and never tried to touch—which he could not do in any case—so now, she simply changed and kept talking.

"Do you ever talk about sex with your mother?"

"With Mom?" Diane said, slipping on a T-shirt. "No. I mean, I had the 'Functions of the Human Body' and 'Where Babies Come From' lectures years ago, but . . ." She flipped her hair out of the T-shirt and started to run a brush through it with a few quick strokes. "She's not as easy to talk to as you are."

"Thank you."

"She tends to stay technical, and you can't talk to her about *feelings* or anything. It's like learning to screw from Popular Mechanics. Why?"

"I was just thinking," Warren mused. "If you want to learn how to really enjoy sex—something you should learn from a woman, by the way—you should talk to her."

"Why? Because she's pregnant?"

"No."

Her face brightened. "Because she likes it!"

"Bingo," he said with a smile. "And pregnancy doesn't stop them from having a good time, it just means he enters her from behind more often."

"God, you mean my parents do it doggy-style?" She stopped with her jeans halfway up her thighs. "When? Last night?"

"Crude, Diane . . ."

"Classic rear-entry position," she corrected, then buttoned her jeans and sat down on edge of the hammock. "So you watched them?"

"I happened to be loitering around their bed. They really enjoy each other. Did you know that?"

"Huh," she laughed. "I never thought about it."

"I'll tell you about it over breakfast," he suggested.

Diane's parents were already up, so instead of grabbing a Pop Tart and milk on her way to the toolshed, she was forced to sit through breakfast, trying to keep a straight face while Warren kept up a monologue about the positions Nancy and Tom liked best. Diane could hardly believe what he was saying, until he kept pointing out little things about Nancy. The way she moved, or gestured. Diane watched her out of the corner of her eye while eating a bowl of cereal. What he said seemed to be true. Nancy was in a pretty good mood, and Warren said that was because they had lovely sex the night before—and she was still thinking about it.

"She likes sex when she's pregnant," he said. "It makes her all soft. Of course your father likes it too because he can grab onto her ass and rub her from the front. And she gets especially wet when she's pregnant . . ."

"Wet," Diane said under her breath.

"What dear?" Nancy called from her place by the stove where she was minding an egg for Bobby.

"Nothing Mom, I just got my T-shirt wet."

"You mean your pants, don't you?" said Warren.

"Uh huh."

"I suppose we'd better talk about something less exciting?"

"Uh huh."

Warren continued with some comments on how breakfast foods had changed since his day when everyone had two eggs and big slices of bacon. "Pop Tarts," he said in conclusion with some amusement. "Pop Tarts! Sounds like something you'd find in a red-light district."

After breakfast, it did not take long for Diane to dig up the urn. It was buried, just as Warren had said, in the only unfinished part of the basement. There was an old root cellar, and the place where the cellar door opened to the outside had been walled off into a separate storage room. Part of the floor was still dirt. Warren pointed her to a spot in the corner near the outside foundation, and she began to dig with a small garden trowel.

"Who buried you here?" she asked while carefully laying aside a tiny shovelful of dirt.

"Ah. That's a long story," he said.

He was eager to have the urn unearthed and sensing this, Diane looked at him for a moment and went back to her digging, thinking she could ask him again later.

"I'll tell you some time," he offered.

"OK."

Diane kept shovelling. Six inches below the surface, her shovel struck wood. She carefully dug around it and after some time hauled up a wooden box about eight inches across, with a small ceramic urn inside.

"Wow," she whispered when she had it opened and held the urn in her hands. "This is *you*."

"Don't drop it, please," he implored. "Yes, it's most of me, anyhow."

She put it back in the box and set it aside, then filled in the hole and patted the dirt back down. Taking the box with her, she went to put away the shovel. Once back in her room, she opened the box again and took out the urn. Putting it in the middle of the floor, she sat cross-legged to look at it.

"Where would you like to go?" she asked.

"The church on Fourth street," he said without hesitation.

"A church?" she said, wrinkling her nose. "Why?"

"That's where we were married."

Even as Warren said the word, Diane's aura shrank. "You were married?" she whispered slowly.

"Oh, didn't I tell you about that either?"

"No." Her heart suddenly pounded and almost stopped. "I didn't know you were married."

"Well, it was very brief." Seeing how her mood had darkened, he came close and put his arm around her—though she could not feel it. In a moment he took his arm away and sat upright with his hands on his knees.

"Do you have other secrets?"

"Secrets?" he asked incredulously. "It's not a secret, I just didn't realize I hadn't told you. Look, when you've been dead as long as I have, your memory isn't what it once was. I've been a ghost longer than I was alive, you know. Does your grandmother remember everything that ever happened to her?"

"Being married is different," she said, moving away.

"It's not that I wouldn't have told you," he said, "it's just that it slipped my mind. I wasn't trying to hide it."

"Really?"

"Of course not," he said. "We're such good friends—that sometimes I forget whether I've told you things or not."

She seemed cheered by that, and smiled a little, but Warren could tell she felt hurt, and was sorry he had mentioned the church at all.

"What was her name?" Diane asked.

"Priscilla."

"Oh."

"Anyway, there's nothing to worry about," he said standing up, "because the marriage was never consummated."

"It wasn't? You mean you didn't—"

"No, never. I was killed the same day."

"On your wedding day?"

"It's a long story," he said. "I'll tell you some time."

"But not now?" she asked.

"I thought we had a date . . ."

"Oh, yeah," she replied, her cheerfulness returning, a little reluctantly. But if he said it just slipped his mind, she was ready to believe him—and that was that. "It'll only me take a minute to get ready."

After brushing her teeth, consulting Warren about which pair of jeans to wear, fussing to get her frizzy hair tied back to keep it out of her face, and putting on some make-up Diane was ready to go out. She slipped the urn carefully into her back-pack and rode her bicycle a few blocks. Warren was still with her, sitting on the handlebars, his smile growing broader the further Diane pedalled. Suddenly at a corner she stopped her bicycle and jumped off.

"By Jove, it works!" Warren cried. "It's unbelievable! I'm a free man again!"

"Now we can go anywhere!"

Diane picked up her pace riding down Buchanan and turned onto Fourth Street, following Warren's directions. He was certain the church was at the corner of Fourth and Pierce, but they found an apartment house instead. Diane obligingly rode from one end of the street to the other twice over but they never found a church. Warren suggested asking in the neighborhood, thinking that perhaps he had mis-remembered the location, but Diane had a better idea. They stopped in the public library, which Diane had seen on the way, and asked how they might go about finding a certain building.

"How about the phone book?" suggested the librarian. She sat with her hands folded on her desk, a pencil stuck behind her ear, partially hidden by graying hair, tied up in a bun behind.

Diane turned to Warren and almost asked what the name of the church was, but thought better of it, and turned back to the librarian, with her mouth open hesitantly. "I don't think it has a phone," she said.

"Which building are you looking for?" the librarian asked. "Do you know the building's function? Or the address?"

Warren sat on the edge of the librarian's desk, pushing his finger through the tip of the pencil behind her ear. "How do you think she keeps this from falling out?" he asked Diane, who bit her lip to keep from giggling. "Chewing gum?"

"A church on the corner of Pierce and Fourth," said Diane.

"Oh, land sakes, honey," the librarian answered, suddenly in her element. "I can tell you that. They tore that old place down twenty years ago. The city condemned it—the roof leaked something terrible and the foundation was cracked under the pulpit. The congregation couldn't raise enough money to rebuild it, so they sold the land."

"So my memory's not failing me after all," observed Warren. His tone was sullen, though, and Diane noticed it.

"I used to go there when I was a little girl," the librarian continued, beginning to smile a little, almost looking through Diane. "My mother sang in the choir. I remember it like it was yesterday . . . I'd close my eyes and listen to the heavenly voices, straining to hear mother's sweet soprano rising above the rest . . . We always had prim white dresses on Sunday with pink bows on the sleeves . . . They always sang *Ein' Feste Burg* . . . in English of course. Pastor Phillips loved it so much . . ."

Warren had already stood up to leave. Diane dug her fingernails into her palm, politely thanked the librarian very much for all her help, and left her to her reverie. With Warren ambling silently beside her, she went out the door. He seemed downcast for the rest of the afternoon, and it was not until late evening that he perked up again.

"After all," he said, feeling resigned to the inevitable, "everything changes, and I can't expect it to last. It was rather a blow, though, to hear they've torn it down. Makes me think how long I've been dead."

"I'm really sorry, Warren."

He laughed a little then, finally breaking the layer of ice that had settled over their evening. "It's not your fault, Buns. I'm sure you'd have stood in their way."

That evening Warren told Diane a lot of things about himself, not quite from the beginning, but from the time he decided to make his own way in the world and left his parents' home in Spokane. He found work in the railway station as a clerk in the days when the railroad was bustling rather than rusting. But he actually preferred tinkering with motor-cars. He had had grand ideas of setting up his own mechanical shop, catering to the transport of the future, and had saved all his money to that end. Priscilla, his bride-to-be, was the daughter of a tailor who lived nearby. They had fallen in love almost as soon as they met, and he proposed to her within months.

By the time Warren got through telling her about the town and the railroad and the rise of the motor car—with numerous digressions—and had come finally to the cusp of his betrothal in 1911, Diane was asleep. With a gentle look, he bid her good-night. In a way, he was rather glad to save the story for another time.

School started in September, and immediately much of Diane's energy was consumed with studying. While she did her home-work in the evenings, she tried to think of things for Warren to do, and finally hit upon the idea of letting him read. He could not turn pages, so she would prop books open with paper-weights or other books, and turn pages for him while he sat across the table from her. The experience of reading again—and not over anyone's shoulder, but whatever he wanted when he wanted to—was excit-ing to him. One of the first things Diane suggested was 'Catcher in the Rye'. She had read it the year before, and since everyone was reading it, thought he should too. That way, they could have a common reference point in contemporary literature. He rather enjoyed it for its unabashed raciness. Generally, however, he pre-ferred older, more cerebral literature, and thought he might like to begin a kind of survey of twentieth century literature. Diane then paid her second visit to the public library and let him choose his own books. He began, naturally enough, where he had left off—with the works of Sir Arthur Conan Doyle—and moved forward. Some evenings they played chess and discussed Bobby Fischer's games. Other times they played cards, and often they simply talked, especially about Diane's classes or whatever books they had read recently. Diane also set aside time—at least a few minutes every day, and preferably more like half an hour—to make entries in her diary. Only rarely did she join her parents and Rat downstairs around the television. Her parents noticed this change in her hab-its almost immediately, but neither of them breathed a word, since they found it a relief to see her lose interest in television.

On weekends, especially Saturday mornings, and whenever

the autumn weather was good enough, Diane began to take Warren places on her bicycle. She turned out his ashes into a cone made from newspaper, and put them into a large thermos she bought at the Salvation Army store downtown. She thought it would be much less suspicious if she carried a thermos than if she carried his ashes around in the urn. At first, they would not all fit, and in the end she opened the bottom and poured the remainder around the glass lining. When she ended up with a small handful still left, she stood holding the thermos in one hand and the newspaper cone in the other.

"Pour the rest in the garden," he suggested.

Skeptically, she looked at him. "Is that OK?"

"I'll be fine," he replied. "You have the bulk of them, and that's what matters most."

Warren did not mind the change of residence at all, and remarked on their way out to the back yard that, in fact, the thermos was rather an appropriate update. "And it'll certainly keep me warmer in the winter won't it?" he joked.

"Do you get cold?" she asked.

"It's always chilly. But that's no concern of yours," he added. "I'd rather go places than stay home."

In biology class Diane met Janet, who befriended her early in September. Neither was the social type who went out for sports or cheerleading, but they had little else in common. Diane was more studious, Janet a bit more flirtatious—and she seemed to know a number of boys. After Diane's first week at school, the socialites lost any mild interest they had in her. She had worn a plaid mini-skirt and a low-cut sexy top the first day—Warren had really admired it when she showed him. She continued her nice dressing unfailingly for a week or two, but even so, they began to see through her and gradually found excuses to exclude her and decline the tentative invitations she made. Janet took her up immediately, and they sometimes did their homework together—more to Janet's than Diane's benefit.

Warren was always pleased to hear about Diane's school days, and one morning she asked him if he would like to spend the day with her. He jumped at the chance, literally sending himself through the roof, and somersaulting down through the floor.

He had never seen the new high-school building, though he was aware the old one had been retired, and he was endlessly fascinated by the modern touches, especially the auditorium and the audio-visual lab. Diane took him on a tour of the entire school—including the locker rooms, both before and after her P.E. class. There, he admired the fresh, young bodies at length.

"The last time I saw this many women bathing," he remarked walking among them, "was at a mass baptism in the river." Diane paused in washing her hair to glance at him with a smile. "They were clothed, however, in long white gowns. This is much nicer."

There was a pop-quiz in her geometry class that afternoon, and she whispered to him halfway through. "Do you know the answer?"

"I could probably figure it out but I won't," he said firmly. "You won't always have me at your elbow, and you'll have to learn it yourself."

She saw the sense of what he was saying, even if he did sound like a typical adult right then. "What the hell am I going to use geometry for?" she asked under her breath.

"You never know," he said. "I used to think the same way, but some time it may come in handy. Say for instance, you have thirteen dinner guests and you're trying to cut a pie into so many equal trapezoids."

"Thanks," she mumbled, and quietly finished the test without Warren's help.

On the way home from school, she stopped at the corner store. It was a small place built inside an old house, and delighted Warren when she stopped her bicycle in front of it.

"The East-Fourth market!" he cried when he saw the sign swinging in front. "I didn't know it was still here."

She laughed, "has it changed much?"

"It's a completely different building," he answered. "I wonder if that old lady with the beak still works here?"

"After how many years? She's probably dead if she was an old lady in your day."

The man in the store was in his late forties, Diane guessed—maybe a bit older than her father. When they entered, a little bell rang over the door.

"It's the same little bell," Warren observed happily, walking in behind her, directly through the plate glass.

Diane let him look around, then picked a can of Dr. Pepper out of the refrigerator and set it on the counter.

"Ah!" Warren crooned, leaning over her shoulder. "Will you do me a favor?"

She nodded in the furtive way she had learned to do when answering him in public. A few times, she had seen people look quite strangely at her when she stood on a corner talking to herself.

"Buy me a Playboy?"

"God no!" she shouted.

"I beg your pardon?" asked the storekeeper.

"Oh," she mumbled, as if flustered. "I thought I lost the money. I guess I can't get it . . . Oh wait . . ." She dug into her purse.

"What?" the man asked.

"Playboy," she piped cheerily. "My Dad asked me to get one, and I thought I lost the ten!"

"I see," he said. "One Playboy." He pulled one from the rack behind the counter and punched the price into the register, then slid her Dr. Pepper over next to it and punched that in. "Will that be all?"

"Ask him for a box of rubbers," Warren suggested.

"No way," she laughed, looking over her shoulder at him, then turning to the storekeeper said, "Oh, yes, sorry—that'll be it."

The man gave her a rather strange look, then licked his thumb and taking a paper bag from his stock beneath the counter carefully rolled the Playboy into it and slid her Dr. Pepper down inside, without jiggling it too much. "Thank you," he said handing over the bag with a smile. "Come again."

"You see?" Warren said as they ambled out of the store. "He never even asked. I'll bet girls come in here all the time and get their father's Playboys."

"Right," she said, kneeling down to put the bag into her pack. She pulled out the Dr. Pepper and opened it right there, taking a seat on the wooden stairs. "Bet he'd have popped his wad if I asked for a Playgirl."

"A what?"

Diane laughed at his expression. "Never heard of it? It's just like Playboy, sort of. For women."

"They look at pictures of scantily clad ladies?"

"No, they look at studs with big cocks."

"Ah. For a minute I was worried about future generations of Americans."

After taking the last gulp from her Dr. Pepper, she tossed the can into the trash barrel. "Ready to go?"

"I can't wait to read the Ribald Classic," he said, rubbing his hands together. "You have lots of homework to keep you busy this evening?"

"Sure," Diane said agreeably, then hopped onto her bicycle and peddled away from the store.

It had been years since Warren had seen an issue of Playboy. When they brought it home, Diane insisted on setting it aside while she finished her chores. It was her day for dusting, and to her mother's surprise, she did not have to be told even once to do it. Warren hovered at her side during the procedure.

"Ah, you missed a spot," he would say, always pointing to someplace practically inaccessible to Diane.

"Forget it," she would reply as often as not.

He pointed to the shelf. "How about here?"

"Nobody can even see back there. I'd have to take all the pictures off the shelf and put them all back again."

"But wouldn't someone be surprised if they *did* look back there?"

"Ha, they might. How much you want to bet nobody looks there between now and next week?"

"A dance," he replied at once.

Diane could see that something was on his mind. "You want to go to a dance?"

"Sure," he said. "I haven't been to a dance for . . ."

"Right, fifty years," Diane replied.

"Longer than that," he said.

"All right. Keep your eye on that spot. If anyone looks there, you're on." She would have taken him anyway, if someone would ask her to a dance. There was a boy named Paul, whom Janet insisted liked her, but she had hardly spoken to him. He was always hanging out with Ron Blankenship—a boy whose locker was next to hers, and whom she had detested on first sight. But Paul was all right, she kept thinking while she methodically dusted her father's bookshelves. There were tons of law books, half of which she thought he had never even opened.

"Penny for your thoughts?" Warren asked, hovering over her. "Missed a spot there . . ."

"You haven't got a penny," she said, smiling. "I was thinking that if Janet could get Paul to ask me, I could take you along."

"Why don't you ask him out?"

"Huh?"

"In my day," he remarked, "women had just gotten the vote in Washington."

"What's that got to do with anything?"

"Times change. Schweet-haart!" he exclaimed, in a very bad imitation of Humphrey Bogart. "You're living in the seventies! The age of bra burning and women's lib. If you ask him and he doesn't go, he's a male chauvinist pig anyhow, so you can leave him for Janet."

"You think he'd go?"

"Have I met him, or not?" Warren asked.

"Huh-uh. I didn't see him today."

"Oh. Well, are you finished dusting yet?"

"Almost."

She finished the living room and had nothing left but the family room. By the time she finished with that, it was almost dinner time. Rat was watching a re-run of Gilligan's Island, and Diane got caught up in it. She had seen it before—what episode had she not seen?—but it was always hilarious.

"I think the professor's cute," she said. Rat looked at her and rolled his eyes, but the comment was for Warren's benefit.

"You like the studious type . . ."

"Sometimes," she answered.

Through the rest of the show, Diane was laughing so hard she could hardly hear the television. Rat told her to shut up, but with Warren's running commentary, it was impossible to keep from laughing. When the show was over, Nancy called them for dinner, and Warren mercifully went off to inspect a new nest of baby mice in a hidden corner of the store room. He and Diane had been leaving food for the mother because the babies were so cute. The mice were fine, and after a round of the house, he joined Diane in her room. She had already unrolled the Playboy and was leafing through it.

"Can we start at the first page?" Warren asked.

"Don't you want to see the pictures?"

"Of course, that too. But the anticipation makes it better. If you start at the first page, and try to actually read some of it . . ."

"OK," she said, perfunctorily flipping back to the beginning. He had been averting his eyes to keep from catching an accidental glimpse of the centerfold.

"It's not like I thought it was," Diane observed sometime later. They had not yet reached the photo layouts, but were bogged down in articles that Warren wanted to skim. Half the time, he read aloud, and Diane was moderately interested despite herself.

She flipped a page, and Warren exclaimed. "Ah, the fun part."

"You think she's pretty?"

"Quite."

"Don't you think her tits are too big?"

"They're not that big. Look at her proportion. She's quite nicely built."

"I don't like her mouth."

"Nobody asked you," he teased.

"But I bought it." She flipped to the next page, and they continued through the layout.

At the centerfold, a little gasp escaped from from Warren. "Unbelievable!"

"What?"

He pointed. "Had I not lived through the sixties," he said, casting a glance at Diane—"I'm speaking figuratively, of course . . . I would have called *that* indecent." The photo showed a fair bit of the model's pubic hair, and the rounded furrow leading to her treasures was rather clearly visible.

"What, her cunt?" Diane asked.

"I wouldn't have used that word either."

"Indecent, huh? What would you call it now?"

"Sexy," he replied, then dropped into silence, staring. Indeed, times did change—in his youth the entire magazine would have been scandalous.

"I was a child in the sixties," Diane offered, flipping the page.

He laughed quietly, patting the air above her head. "You're still a child."

"Only until I'm sixteen."

"Oh? Then what?"

"I'm planning to lose my virginity, remember?" As soon as she said it, she wondered if she had told him that.

"Oh, yes. And that makes you not a child anymore?"

"Uh huh," she nodded, with a satisfied smile.

"Have you found your stud yet then?"

She laughed and swatted her hand through his. "Not yet," and then with a little grin, "Maybe it'll be Paul." She turned pages slowly until she found the Ribald Classic, and left the magazine open for Warren to read. "I gotta do my homework," she moaned when she looked at the clock. It was nearly nine.

Warren adjusted himself comfortably to read. After witnessing what went on in his house during a few summers in the late sixties, the classics were tame. But that did not make them any less amusing, in his estimation, and he spent a pleasant hour lingering over the story, not wishing to disturb Diane too often by requesting that she turn the page.

[8]

As if by some miracle, Paul called one evening and asked Diane to the next dance. She thought it was Janet's doing somehow, and after she hung up the phone she called Janet, and they ended up talking for an hour. Warren stood by for ten minutes, waiting to find out what happened with Paul, but Diane shooed him away.

"I'll tell you in a while," she said, covering the mouthpiece. "I want to find out how Janet did it." It was not such a miracle after all, as Janet explained, at great length, and with any number of digressions about her cousin Liz and the guy she was dating. Paul had had his eye on Diane, and when Janet finally convinced him that if he asked, Diane would accept, he called her right away.

On the evening of the dance, her first date since moving to town, Diane spent over an hour in the bedroom with Warren checking every aspect of her attire.

"You think I should go bra-less?" she asked at one point.

"Heavens, no," he said, covering his forehead as if about to faint.

"I'll look too flat, huh? Should I stuff it?"

"Don't even think about it. There's nothing a boy hates more than to put his hand over a little wad of tissue. And it would be all over school by noon the next day."

She knew he was right about that, having heard enough rumors about who stuffed and when, and who found them out. "But I should wear the bra?"

"Wear the lacy black one."

She found it and held it up. It was a thin one that provided no padding, with a wire beneath. Its chief virtue was that one could see her nipples through it. "You think it's sexy enough?"

"It's marvelous," he said. "But the best part isn't how it looks."
When Diane gave him a questioning glance while starting to fasten
it on, he explained. "All your other brassieres fasten in the back,
and that's typical. Any sixteen-year-old with a few chances to
practice can undo it with one hand."

She had already discovered that for herself. "What's the
difference?"

"It's in the excitement," Warren explained. "He'll have his arms
around you like this, and he'll be going to feel you up (as you say),
right?"

"Uh huh . . ."

"And there he'll be, fumbling in the back, and kissing you,
moving down your neck. But he won't find the catch at the back.
So what you do is part your lips like so," he demonstrated, "and let
him slip his tongue into your mouth—if you really want to get
down to business, I mean. Then—"

"Not yet," she answered, "but I might let him feel me up."

"All right. Anyhow, you take his arm, and pull it around. At
that moment, he'll think you don't want him to undo your
brassiere—but you'll out-fox him by moving his hand around to
the front, and saying 'here honey' or something like that. He'll be
ecstatic."

"Are you kidding?"

"You have my positive guarantee. I've seen it happen."

Having chosen the bra, she put on the pair of frilly black panties
that had come with it—they were not crotchless, but did have a
long slit up the center. The intimate ensemble had been a present
from a previous boyfriend, and she had only worn it a few times—
never for him, because they broke up about a week later. She usually
wore them when she ran out of everything else.

Warren thought she should choose a blue dress, or something
with flowers to highlight her eyes, and was hovering near her dress
rack. Diane curbed his impulse with a word.

"Nobody wears dresses to these things," she said. "This isn't
the prom. It's gotta be jeans. If I'm going to dance, I don't want to

be constantly wondering if my slip is showing, or who can see up my dress."

She chose a pair of wide bell-bottoms with a little patch over the rear pocket, and a long-sleeved work-shirt, which she tied up to show off her midriff. Her black lace-up platform shoes completed the ensemble.

"I see," was Warren's comment, delivered with rather a dejected tone when she twirled around to show him. "Well, if that's the style."

"But I'll wear a dress to Homecoming," she said to cheer him up. "And if someone asks me to the prom, too. Then I'll be your little doll, OK?"

During the final touches in the bathroom, he insisted her make-up was too thick, and made her take off the foundation.

"You have beautifully clear skin—let it show. You haven't had more than half a dozen pimples—or 'zits' as you call them—in your life," he said. "But if you keep putting that stuff on, you'll ruin your complexion."

"Huh? This is supposed to be good for it."

"Unless they've improved this trash since my day," he answered, "it does nothing but clog up a woman's freshness. I've always thought it looked monumentally hideous. And I'll let you in on a secret," he said leaning over. "Boys hate it too."

Diane had been under the impression that make-up became her. Her girlfriends had always said so. But the more Warren talked, the more she began to believe he was telling the truth—at least as far as he saw it. Still, she could not go out without some kind of make-up, or everyone would wonder if her mother had forbidden her to wear it. Warren agreed after more fussing that a rather thin layer of green eye-shadow actually did become her when she wore it in combination with a pair of dangling turquoise earrings. They disagreed again over the lipstick. Diane wanted a bright, kissable red.

"Kissable my left toe-nail," he said, feigning a gag. "It'll rub off all over him."

"But if it doesn't rub off—how will anyone know he kissed me?"

"If they can't tell by your aura," Warren answered, "they don't deserve to know. But if you insist on lipstick, try this one," and he pointed to a pale pinkish one.

"It makes my lips look cold."

"And he'll be dying to warm them up for you."

"You think so?" she asked, meditatively holding one lipstick in each hand.

"Try it and see."

"OK." She applied a thin layer of the pink lipstick, using a brush the way her mother had taught her. ("If you glop it on straight from the tube," Nancy had always said, "it looks terrible— you know how Aunt Caroline always looks? You have to do it carefully, and stay just a millimeter away from the very edges, thinning it out like this . . ." And of course she had demonstrated more than once, and always got much better results than Diane could manage.) "How's this?" she said, closing her eyes and puckering for Warren.

"Stunning," he said. "You look marvelous . . ." He really did mean it—about her face anyway. Her outfit left something to be desired, but her breasts looked very full with the shirt tied off tightly below them, and with the skin of her abdomen so visible, he had to admit she had great appeal, rather after the manner of a belly dancer. "He's bound to kiss you, I'd say."

"Great," she said, and plunked the lipstick down on her dresser.

Even if she had school books with her, Diane often carried a huge purse instead of a pack. Her pack was practical for activities like bike-riding, the purse was for everything else. Warren remarked that her purse was so large he could hardly tell the difference, and often commented on how much junk she carried around. But more than once, he admitted that something or another had come in handy, and she hated so much to transfer things between purses that she almost always used only the one purse. She even carried the rubber her mother had once given her during one of their first conversations about the Facts of Life. "God knows why she gave me this," she had remarked to Warren the first time he saw it, and he had replied, "Perhaps she thinks it'll come in handy on your sixteenth birthday."

Before leaving her room to bounce down the stairs, the last thing Diane did was slip Warren's thermos bottle into her purse, after pulling out a good load of her precious things—a couple of paperback novels, her poetry notebook, a handful of pens, and some tampons.

"Let's go," she chimed. While they waited on the porch for Paul, who was due at seven-thirty in his parents' car, Warren wandered around the front yard.

"You're supposed to make him wait, you know," he said when he had circled the yard once.

"Yeah, but then he'd have to come in, and Mom will say something stupid, and Dad will have to act all responsible and ask him about what he's going to study in college and what his father does and all that shit."

"Ah, best to avoid all that shit," Warren agreed, bubbling. "Plenty of time to meet the in-laws after the baby's born . . ."

Paul arrived precisely as scheduled, yet after they got to the dance, he all but lost her for an hour while he hung around with some of his buddies. Ron Blankenship was among them, and as Diane could not stand even the sight of Ron, she sat out a few dances alone, then danced by herself for a couple more before sitting down with a Dr. Pepper, no ice. Paul seemed to suddenly remember her later, and held her hand while showing her off, as if she were a great catch. Diane was puzzled, since he seemed not very like himself. Warren insisted he was himself then, and maybe he had not been before; but since she hardly knew him anyway, it was difficult to tell.

The band stopped playing at eleven, and after hanging around in the parking lot, they drove out to Western Avenue. He offered to show her the view from Skyline, and she accepted that. There, when he did kiss her, which she allowed simply because she really wanted to be kissed and held, it was not a very enjoyable kiss. He pushed just too hard, and his teeth tended to get in the way. He smelled very nice, though, and she did like the way he kissed her neck and brushed back her hair. She tried to talk, but he was insistent on the making out and she abandoned herself to whispering at him while his lips dallied around her neck and shoulder. He almost got to her bra.

Warren whispered into Diane's ear at the moment Paul's fingers touched her bra strap that, much as he hated to interrupt her when he could see that she was enjoying the physical sensations, he had a rather bad impression of Paul's aura.

"It's too dark and clammy," he reported flatly. "This fellow wants to be right into your pants."

"Really?" she mumbled.

"Absolutely. I would bet Janet made him think you'd be eager for a romp in the hayloft."

Diane managed to mumble her way through something about not going too far on the first date, though she continued to kiss Paul's lips lightly as she extricated herself from his embrace. Cooled rather quickly, Paul smiled and said it was all right, and that he respected her feelings. Then after admiring the view of town for two or three minutes, he started the engine and took her home. He was polite enough, but his manner seemed strained and disappointed, though he continued to smile and say nice things. When they got to her house, he told her with some restraint what a great time he had had. Neither Warren nor Diane believed him, and they both concluded that he would not ask her out again.

"Did I do anything wrong?" Diane asked while they sat on the front porch analyzing the evening.

"Not at all," Warren assured her. "I think you had a good time for a while—even if I'd call your dancing more of a lunatic romp— but he's not the type you're looking for. He's immature. He's more concerned with his friends—or showing you to his friends—than with you. And when it comes to you, he wants to dive right into your black-lace panties. I certainly wouldn't recommend him to my sister."

By the time she trudged upstairs with Warren to go to bed, Diane decided that the evening had been a complete flop and foreshadowed the end of her incipient social life. She could probably never get Janet to recommend her to anyone again. Warren pointed out that on the other hand, if every boy Janet knew were like Paul, that might be for the best.

[9]

Nancy's baby arrived within a few days of the expected birth date. She and Tom had discussed names, but had not yet reached agreement. Diane had asked a few times about names, but her parents insisted they would have something ready when the time came, and it never paid to think of names beforehand. When she first got to hold the infant girl while visiting her mother in the hospital, Diane discovered that in fact they had no name ready. While they were thus busy blurting out possible names for the baby, Diane suggested Priscilla, at Warren's urging.

"Priscilla?" Nancy said making a sour face that turned to laughter. "No thanks."

"How about Prudence?" Diane went on.

"Ludmilla," Warren suggested in her ear.

"Or Ludmilla," Diane echoed aloud.

"Where do you get these names?" Nancy laughed. "Too much history, is that it? We were almost settled on Victoria. How about that?"

"No," Diane said, a little crestfallen. "Victoria? It sounds like Queen Victoria."

"It's after one of your father's great aunts," Nancy replied.

"Oh."

"Well, that's that," Warren chimed in, taking a seat behind Nancy. "You can't argue with Tom's great aunt Victoria."

"Actually, Victoria sounds fine, Mom," Diane said.

"I'm glad you approve—Can I nurse her now?"

"Sure," Diane said, handing the baby back carefully.

After baby Victoria was a few weeks old, Warren became rather interested in her and could hardly stay away from her crib. Being still so small she did not use her own room, though it had been furnished in readiness, but slept with Tom and Nancy in a crib on Nancy's side of the bed. Warren constantly looked in to make sure the baby was all right during her naps, and he almost never missed a feeding or a diaper change. He watched the diaper changes only out of curiosity, because he had never had the experience himself. He liked baby's bath times as well. He not only liked to watch the baby suckle and coo, but he liked the prolonged view of Nancy's breasts, which gave him a feeling of satisfaction and tenderness, even though it all reminded him terribly of Priscilla and what they had missed. Nancy's bosom had swollen tremendously, and he found it delightfully erotic to watch her pumping out the excess milk, which she sometimes left in bottles with Diane when she had to go out for some reason. That gave her much more freedom than she had had with either of her previous children. Diane did not mind watching the baby either because she adored Victoria, her very own baby sister. And as Warren pointed out, it was good practice for her if she planned on having children. The crying and burping part he considered especially realistic preparation for motherhood.

Tom also took tremendous pleasure in suckling at Nancy's breast late at night. At first, she would tease him about not taking too much, lest the baby have none, but Tom pointed out that she was already having to pump the excess out. She seemed to get more milk with each child and had never had so much to waste when Diane had been born.

"There's plenty," Tom said, running his tongue around Nancy's nipple. The baby was suckling the other one, and looked up, letting the nipple drop out of her mouth whenever Tom said something.

"Shh," scolded Nancy, putting the nipple back into the baby's mouth. "She's almost asleep. If you can't be quiet, I'll roll over the other way."

"All right," Tom said, and after a few more mouthfuls, he let her change the baby to the other breast. In a moment Victoria was asleep, and the nipple gradually popped from her mouth.

"Want some?" Tom asked with a smile.

"Probably tastes the same as last time."

Tom pulled her nightgown apart and took a mouthful to share with her, dribbling it slowly into her mouth. His other hand slid toward her belly, and she made a soft little moan.

"How is it?" Tom asked.

"Thin and sweet," said Nancy.

"I didn't mean that . . ." His hand reached the top of her panties, and she adjusted herself a bit to let him pull up her nightgown. She was feeling warm and amorous.

"Gently," she whispered.

"Uh huh," he replied in a whisper, kissing her. "I'll be very gentle."

Warren went back upstairs, allowing them at least one night of privacy. They had not yet had sexual relations, to his knowledge, since the baby. Nancy was still tender, but he could see she was getting over her discomfort.

"I think she sees me," Warren told Diane later.

"The baby? Come on," Diane replied. "She's about a month old—she's hardly got her eyes open."

"No, I'm serious," he said. "I think she's quite bright."

"How can you tell?"

"She curls her fingers, and make noises, too."

"All babies do that. What makes you think she sees you?"

"You know how she follows your mother's face? She follows me with her eyes when I'm in the room."

Diane was not yet convinced, but a few days later she had to watch Victoria while Nancy was out, and she had Warren come around to perform for her. It did seem as if the baby knew he was there, and she sometimes stopped sucking her bottle to look at him and gurgle.

"She's got the gift," was his pronouncement. "You should take care of her specially when she gets bigger."

"Oh, I will anyway," Diane said, rocking Victoria against her shoulder. "She's my precious, too. Aren't you, Vicky?"

Victoria burped loudly, dribbling milk down Diane's shirt.

"She left you a calling card," Warren said. "You'd better wipe it off at once." He began cooing at Victoria, and she made some faint noises for him while Diane wiped her shirt.

[10]

To the immense delight of Warren, Diane had a slumber party once in the first week of December. It had been some years since he had seen that many young ladies in the house at once. He hung around the whole evening watching Diane's friends and listening to their multiple conversations. They leafed through fashion magazines and flitted among topics. Their conversation was frequently side-tracked and they would break into two or three different groups until someone overheard someone else, then they would mix together again. After midnight he decided they spent entirely too much time talking about cute boys, make-up, their tangle of feminine rivalries, and musicians he did not care for. Rock music he knew something about, since it had first tiptoed into his home in the fifties, made itself comfortable with the coming of the Beatles a few years later, and finally blasted itself into every corner of his home in the late sixties. Never one to allow his musical tastes to stagnate—especially after death—he had long since found that he tended to follow only a year or so behind the rest of America. By the time he developed something of a taste for Jefferson Airplane, Diane had arrived, with quieter tastes. In a way, it was a mild relief. Nonetheless, the stream of top-forty hits that jangled from the radio all evening left him moderately cold, and he found himself growing slightly bored, especially with Susan. She looked pretty enough, with clear skin, sparkling icy blue eyes, and light blonde hair that she wore in child-like braids for the occasion.

Susan was not a close friend of Diane's, but she had wanted to invite as many people as she could think of, and since Janet knew Susan pretty well, Susan ended up there, along with a couple of other girls who seemed to be her proteges. She was a little more of a socialite, so she tended to talk, rather domineeringly, about cheerleading and boys who played football. She also had what Janet termed 'really big boobs' and she seemed to appeal to boys more than any of the others. Janet maintained that *everyone* knew she was not a virgin, and when the conversation drifted close to such questions, she asked directly—on Diane's behalf.

Susan replied as she always did: "That's for me to know, and you to find out."

"She's discreet, at least," Warren observed when he accompanied Diane to the bathroom later. "But I'd wager she's either a virgin, or ashamed of the extent to which she's not, if you take my meaning."

"Her aura, huh?"

He smiled his affirmation. "She's not that good looking, either—but that's only my opinion." He did not, however, strongly disfavor her looks.

"Her tits are really big, though aren't they?" Diane asked.

"Only moderately," he answered, adding diplomatically, "and yours have a prettier shape." This was absolutely true; Diane had much lovelier proportions.

"Thanks," she said, with a quick downward glance, and bit her lower lip. "That's really sweet."

They went back upstairs to rejoin the party, but a while later, Warren decided he had had enough of Susan for the evening. "I'm going to make my rounds," he said in Diane's ear.

"OK," she whispered under her breath.

Janet looked over and asked, "What?"

"Nothing," Diane said, "just clearing my throat."

"Oh." They both turned back to listen to a scary story called 'The Leavenworth Nurse' that Susan was telling. Warren could tell Diane was a little bored herself, even though she had never before heard the story.

After Warren left the party, he stopped in Diane's parents' room for a few minutes to see if there was any romantic action there. The baby was asleep, but Tom and Nancy were both reading in bed, and Tom had one leg over the top of Nancy's leg. They leaned together shoulder to shoulder. While reading, though, they were carrying on a conversation with occasional comments. It seemed to Warren that he had arrived well into it.

"It's not just her talking to herself," Nancy said.

"Oh," Tom said after an interval.

After a few more pages Nancy said, "She carries some really strange junk around in her purse, too."

"Nance," Tom said, looking up from his book, "I thought we agreed we wouldn't snoop. She's old enough to have some privacy."

"I just opened her purse to see what she had," Nancy insisted. "It's not like I was snooping. She left it on the couch, and I just moved it. It was so heavy, I just peeked inside."

He refrained from asking how that differed from snooping. "And?"

"She carries a diary—and no, I didn't read it. I *do* respect her privacy. Her poetry's a bit mushy, but I think she's pretty talented . . ."

"Nance . . ."

"I don't think she's smoking at any rate."

"No cigs, huh?"

"Nope. No lighter or tobacco flakes either."

"That's good. Does she carry a condom?"

"Tom!"

"Well—you're the one that gave her her first one."

"Yes, and she's still got it," Nancy said.

"So maybe she isn't screwing anyone yet. That's a relief." He turned the page in his book, which he had not been reading for several minutes. "So, what's strange about her purse?"

"She had a thermos in it. I'd never seen it before. It looks like a pretty old one."

"So?"

"So, I opened it up. And you know what she has in it?"

"What?"

"Ashes. Tom—" She tossed her book aside. "The damn thing's filled with ashes."

Tom laughed and pinched the bridge of his nose for a second. "That's great. Nance—didn't you ever carry something incomprehensible that would have puzzled your mother, had she ever snooped in your purse?"

"You're right," Nancy said, and picked up her book again. "Probably none of our business, huh? But don't you wonder what the hell she carries a thermos full of ashes for?"

Warren had heard quite enough of their conversation to be alarmed, so he drifted back up to Diane's room and motioned to her. "Diane, I have to talk to you. Meet me in the powder room?"

She nodded. "Back in a flash," she said, and stepped over Janet who was lying down in a sleeping bag next to her. "What's up?" she asked when she got to the bathroom downstairs.

"I heard your parents talking," Warren said. "I think you should be a bit more careful about where you leave your purse."

"What? Why?"

"Your mother peeked into it when you left it on the couch yesterday."

"Oh, shit," Diane said.

"She found your diary."

"Oh, really holy shit," Diane whispered, covering her mouth.

"She says she didn't open the diary, and I tend to believe that," Warren said. "Otherwise she might have—"

"Found out about you," Diane said, completing his thought. "Jeez, I'm glad she didn't . . ."

"She'd think you most peculiar. She also found my thermos."

"Oh, God . . . what did she say?"

"She just thought it was damned peculiar. Anyhow, I think your father had a pretty good retort, though. He asked her if *she* had ever kept anything in her purse that her mother would have found incomprehensible."

"What did she say?"

"She said he was probably right. I think she was a bit

embarrassed about looking, because they seem to have had a long-standing agreement about not prying into their daughter's private life."

"Really?" Diane asked. "That's a relief."

Warren laughed. "Exactly what your father said when your mother reported that you still carry the condom she gave you."

"Jesus . . . So she figures I'm still a virgin?"

"And she's right. Your father thought that was a relief."

"Right," Diane said, opening the door to go back upstairs. "I'll be more careful. Thanks for telling me." On the way upstairs, she had the thought that now her mother knew she was a good girl. Maybe she should throw away the condom—or get a new one. That might keep her mother guessing if she snooped again.

[11]

Nancy had somewhat more cause for concern a few days later. Warren learned about it only because he started taking special care to listen to Tom and Nancy's late-night conversations.

Diane had purchased another Playboy magazine for him. She did it in the morning on the way to school, and stuck it in her backpack. To her dismay, while she was opening the pack in the hall to put her things in her locker, someone bumped her from behind. Her pack slipped and spilled onto the floor. Before she could grab everything, Ron Blankenship spotted the magazine.

"Playboy, huh," he said with a smirk, kicking her other books aside. Turning to his friend he said, far too loudly, "Look, Diane's got a Playboy. Christmas issue, too!"

"Shut up, Ron," Diane hissed at him, fumbling to put everything into the locker before anyone else saw it. Ron tried to grab at it, but she stomped on his foot and sent him jumping back in pain.

"What did you do that for?" he yelled.

"It's none of your business," she said, grabbing up the last of her books. She threw it in and slammed her locker shut. At least four or five other people had seen the magazine, too. "God, I hate you," she whispered at Ron. With a dirty look, she stalked away, her face bright red with embarrassment.

"Lezzie!" he called behind her. His friends began to cackle.

The story was all over school by afternoon, and Diane ran home almost in tears to tell Warren. Going directly to her room, she slammed and locked the door. Warren was there to greet her with a smile.

"Here's your stupid magazine," she said and threw it right through him onto the floor.

"My stupid magazine?" he asked with great surprise. "Is there a problem?" He could see that there was and sat down beside her, wishing he could put his arm around her; do something to stop her tears. "Shhh," he whispered. "It's all right, Diane. Stop crying and tell me about it. Did I do something to upset you?"

"I bought it for you," she sniffled, "and now everybody in the damned fucking school thinks I'm a *lezzie*!"

"Aren't you?"

"Oh, fuck you Warren!" she screamed.

"All right, he said backing away. He knelt down on the floor in front of her and tried to look contrite. "Forgive me, that was a heartless remark. I know you're not a Lesbian. What happened though?"

Diane told him the story, and by the end, he had made enough crude comments to set them both to laughing about it.

"Next time, buy yourself a nice Playgirl," he suggested.

"Yeah, right," she laughed. "Then they'll think I'm a nympho."

"How about Sunset? Ladies Home Journal? Better Homes and Gardens?"

"How about Seventeen?" she suggested. "Or Cosmopolitan— that's got lots of juicy stuff you'd just love."

"I'll try it," he agreed, having never seen Cosmopolitan. The name alone appealed to him, hinting of the big city.

That evening during dinner Nancy had nothing particular to say to her husband about Diane. When Warren stopped in after she and Tom retired to their room, just to see if they had anything to say privately about Diane, he was pleased to find that they were in an amorous mood. He sat comfortably at the foot of the bed and watched them make love. They enjoyed each other so much that the sight made him not only terribly lustful himself, but really homesick for Priscilla. Finally he left them sitting together, Nancy on Tom's lap, and took a turn around the garden. It had snowed recently, and there was a light fog. The moon's halo gleamed with the ice crystals in the air.

A couple of days later, Nancy did have something to report to her husband, and Warren was hovering nearby to hear their conversation.

"Tom," Nancy said when they finally closed the door to their room and began to putter around in the bathroom while getting ready for bed. "I heard a silly rumor about Diane today."

"What was that?"

"Susan's mother told me that she heard from Susan that Diane was carrying around a Playboy magazine in her pack—at school."

"Playboy? Where would she get that?"

"I'm sure I don't know," Nancy said, tightening her lips and giving him a long glance.

"What?" he said, throwing up his hands. "I didn't give it to her."

"I'm not saying you did, sorry," Nancy said, turning back to finish wiping her face with a cotton ball. "But I did a little snooping again." Directly she glanced at him, wondering if he noticed her choice of terms.

"Nance . . ."

She tossed the cotton ball into the wastebasket. "Well, it concerned me, Tom. If it's only a rumor, that's fine—I know as well as you how that kind of stuff spreads around a school."

"Yeah," he laughed, remembering fondly rumors he had helped spread when he was in high school.

"Well, this isn't a rumor," Nancy concluded, turning to face him.

"Oh?"

"Nope. I went up to her room—on the pretext of putting some of her laundry away."

"You never put her laundry away," Tom replied, squeezing toothpaste onto his brush.

"I know that, I just had to have an excuse."

"Was anyone else home?"

"Just the baby."

"Then why did you need an excuse? To ease your conscience?"

He stuffed his toothbrush into his mouth and began brushing carefully.

"I guess. Anyway, I did. And I found—three issues of Playboy under her mattress."

"Three, huh," he mumbled.

"Tom," she said rather slowly, as she leaned against the open door. "Do you think she might have . . . Lesbian tendencies?"

"Oh, hell," Tom cursed, and spit his toothpaste into the sink. "She's probably got a good excuse for it. She's had boyfriends before. Come on, Nance, she dates now, once in a while. No," he said seriously, "our daughter does *not* have Lesbian tendencies. She's perfectly normal."

Nancy laughed despite herself. "You look like a rabid dog with toothpaste dripping down your chin."

"Aaargh!" he snarled, and grabbed her around the waist.

"Keep away from my clean face," she said, turning away from his protruding lips.

He kissed her anyway, on the cheek, then took out a tissue to wipe the toothpaste off. "Shall I have a talk with her?"

"No, I will," said Nancy. "I'll talk to her tomorrow."

"You're probably right. She'd never tell *me* the reason."

The following afternoon, while Nancy was nursing the baby, she cornered her daughter in the kitchen after school.

"Diane," she said quietly, "I've been meaning to have a little talk with you."

Diane had already heard about her parents' conversation from Warren, and knew what she was in for. As if clairvoyant, she looked directly into Nancy's eyes, and said, "No mother, I'm not a lezzie. Ron gave me the Playboys so I could read the Ribald Classics, and I have to return them anyway."

"Ron who?" Nancy replied, too stunned to think of anything else worth saying.

"Ron Blankenship," Diane said calmly. "His locker's next to mine."

"Oh," mumbled Nancy, shooting up her eyebrows in

puzzlement. "Well, if that's all . . ." She had nothing further to ask, and fell silent.

Diane ducked past her to leave, then turned around. "Oh, yeah—and the thermos."

"I was going to ask about that," Nancy said, surprised that she should mention it. "Are those Mugsie's ashes?"

"Mugsie's? No. We buried those in the yard, remember?" It had been a long time since Diane had thought about the cocker spaniel her mother used to keep, and wondered why she would have thought the ashes belonged to Mugsie. "I'm just keeping it for a friend," she said.

Nancy started to open her mouth, but Diane spoke up hurriedly before she said anything.

"Please, don't ask, OK Mom? I told her I wouldn't tell anyone."

"OK," conceded Nancy, holding up one palm. "I won't ask."

Diane murmured a thank you and went to her room.

Later, Nancy asked Tom if he had spoken to Diane, and when he replied that he had not, since he had hardly spoken to her all day, she became even more confused, and reported their curious conversation.

"I'm not surprised," he answered, "but it's usually boys who're interested in that kind of stuff. She must have just had it on her mind—and that was the one thing she'd think you just *had* to ask her about."

"And you still think she doesn't have Lesbian tendencies? She's just reading Ribald Classics?"

"Probably some boy was bragging about them," Tom suggested.

"She says the boy in the locker next to hers gave them to her."

"I wouldn't doubt it. She's just at that curious age, Nance. You know the kind of stuff she reads—"

"Right," Nancy said grinning at him. Prairie Romance in one hand and D. H. Lawrence in the other?"

"Or Catcher in the Rye? I wouldn't be shocked if she actually *was* reading the Ribald Classics. It shows she's got taste anyway," he teased.

"I still wonder what she's doing with that thermos."

"She's probably got some friend who was supposed to throw the ashes away or something," said Tom, trying to think of a zany excuse. "Didn't you ever do anything like that? They're probably some dog's ashes, and they have a big secret about it."

"Yeah, it's just so weird," said Nancy, unable to suppress her curiosity. "I can't imagine why she'd being doing that. Tom, she carries that thing with her all the time."

"Forget it, Nance. I don't think she's doing anything sick or illegal, and she'll probably tell us when she's good and ready."

"Maybe you're right," Nancy said with a sigh. "But don't you just wonder why?"

Tom only laughed faintly. "I'm content to wait until she's ready to tell us."

Nancy tilted her head and smiled, thinking that men really had so little curiosity about some things. At least he had not accused her of snooping—and when she thought of it, neither had Diane.

Thereafter, Diane kept Warren's magazines hidden more carefully in her room, but she did not stop taking him with her on outings. She took him to school only rarely, but otherwise, she put his thermos at the bottom of her pack or deep in her purse, and almost never left him at home when she was going anywhere interesting.

[12]

Over Christmas vacation, Tom's parents came to visit. He had to drive all the way to Seattle to pick them up at the airport, and to be sure he could meet their plane on time, he left the previous day and stayed at a hotel. Steven's Pass closed completely for several hours the next afternoon while snowplows worked to clear the highway, so he was unable to return with Grandma and Grandpa until well after midnight. The grandparents stayed in Tom and Nancy's room, while they put out sleeping bags in the baby's room and took the crib with them. Tom's parents had never been to Central Washington before, so family outings were planned for almost every day following their arrival.

For the duration of their stay, Warren kept out of the way after his first encounter with Diane's grandmother. The day after their arrival, he came downstairs while the family was eating and stood at the kitchen door for a moment, intending to listen to their conversation.

"I'm so glad we'll have a white Christmas," Grandma was saying. At that moment she happened to glance up, and stopped with her fork halfway to her mouth. Though she did not scream, Warren knew instantly that she had seen him, and he backed away from the door.

"Tom," she said, setting her fork back down on her plate, and casting an inquisitive eye at her son. "Do you take the children to church at all?"

"Mother," he stated. "Let's not start that again."

"Yes, yes," she said irritably, dabbing her mouth with her napkin before pushing it onto her lap. "But it's Christmas time."

Tom and his father exchanged glances, the latter shrugging almost imperceptibly.

"And if you're going to celebrate the occasion," Grandma continued sternly, as she adjusted her napkin on her lap again, "it seems the least you could do is teach them the meaning of it."

"We know Santa's not real," said Bobby. Nancy smiled sheepishly at Tom, and put her hand over Bobby's, giving it a pat.

"They know the meaning of Christmas, Mom," Tom said, with a quick glance at Diane, hoping she would refrain from blurting out something about pagan winter festivals.

"Trudy," Grandpa said quietly but with evident finality, "let it rest. Please?"

"Well it just seems a shame," concluded Grandma. She picked up her fork and began to push peas into her mashed potatoes. "You weren't raised that way, and I should think you'd want to share some of your own upbringing with your children."

The talk continued, with Tom and his father trying to steer the conversation another way. At the earliest opportunity, Diane asked nervously to be excused and helped to clear and wash the dishes. Tom and Grandpa retired to the living room, and on the way out, Grandpa turned to whisper, "I don't know what's gotten into her, Tom. Sorry. I made her swear she wouldn't bring it up again."

"It's all right," replied Tom. "I know. Let's just forget it."

Wood had already been brought in. They set about building a fire, and when it was finally roaring in the fireplace, Grandpa took out his pipe and knocked it against the bricks.

"Still smoking that thing, eh, Pop?" Tom chided. "Thought you were going to give it up."

"Just a pipe after dinner," Grandpa said, grinning. "Keeps your mother on her toes. If she didn't have anything real to bitch about, she'd have to invent something."

Tom laughed—it was the same argument his parents always had.

After dessert was served around the fire, Diane said she was tired and made her way upstairs after planting kisses on the cheeks of her grandparents.

"Warren," she called when she had closed the door of her room. "I saw you come in, what happened?"

"I know precisely where you get your gift," he said.

"Where?"

"Your Grandmother saw me as soon as I peeked in the doorway—why do you think she suddenly started talking about going to church?"

"She always does that," Diane said. "Are you sure she saw you?"

"I'm positive she did," he said. "She's got the gift too, but—"

"But what?"

"I don't know. She thinks it's evil or something."

"Let's not talk about that, OK?"

Warren agreed, and they dropped the subject. Instead, they played a game of chess, and Warren told her another story.

On Christmas Eve a few days later, Grandma managed to henpeck Grandpa into looking up the nearest Episcopal church, and out of a feeling of obligation, Nancy agreed to accompany them, persuading Diane to come along with her.

"All right," Tom hissed at her under his breath when it was apparent that resistance would only aggravate everyone. "If it'll make Mom happy, let's all go."

Diane reported afterward to Warren that she had been bored stiff through the sermon—but that the organ music was moderately fun, and loud enough to keep her awake at strategic moments. She snuck a glass of wine later on the pretext of getting some juice, and they played cribbage for the rest of the evening.

"I have something for you, too," she said suddenly, just after midnight. "Wait here." She opened her door and picked up a package from the stairwell. "It's Christmas now, so I can give it to you," she said setting it on the table.

"A Christmas present!" Warren exclaimed. "That's so thoughtful—you know, I haven't received a Christmas present since—well since I died, in fact." He sat and simply gazed at her, sighing. "You're wonderful, Diane. Thank you."

"Aren't you going to open it?" she asked.

He blinked at her twice slowly, his smile spreading.

"Oh yeah," she said breaking into a girlish grin. "I'll do it." After untying the ribbon, she turned it over and began to undo the tape, being careful not to tear the wrapping paper. The package looked heavy, and he wondered what could possibly be in it.

"It's nothing expensive," she said, "but I hope you like them."

"Delightful!" he exclaimed when she had opened it. Inside were a dozen different automotive magazines, and a thick engine repair manual.

"You told me you liked to tinker with cars," she said. "Are they OK?"

"I'm sure they'll be really educational," he said seriously, then added with a smile, "Yes—they're great." After she spread the magazines out on the table, he pointed to the engine manual. "I haven't seen anything like this for a long time! And never this modern. Can I take a peek?"

"Read all you want," she said. "I'll turn pages, OK?"

They settled down to look at the manual, Diane resting her chin on her hand as she turned pages, simply watching Warren's smiling face while he read and glanced over the diagrams, his eyes flickering along the lines, sometimes mumbling numbers in an awed tone of voice. After a while he looked up and turned to Diane with a sigh.

"I wish I had something for you," he said, with great sadness. "I'm really sorry I don't."

"It's OK," she said, chewing on her lip while her eyes blurred for an instant. "I'm just happy having you for a friend."

"You *are* wonderful," he whispered.

Before turning in for the night, Diane spread several magazines open on the table and left a lamp on so he could see them while she slept. Touched deeply by her gesture, Warren sat and contemplated them. A single page of each held his attention for a while, but he gradually turned his eyes toward Diane, whose serene face always fascinated him, no matter how long he watched.

[13]

The crisp February snow crackled under Diane's feet. She and
Warren were out for an evening walk in the apple orchard two
blocks up the street from her house. Over one shoulder she had
slung her pack with his thermos safely tucked inside, wrapped in a
sweater. He insisted the sweater made no difference to him, but
she always liked to at least pretend he would be warmer.

"You never did tell me how you ended up buried in the
basement," Diane said. She had asked him the question several
times, but it always seemed like they got side-tracked before he
managed to answer completely.

"Oh, that," Warren mused, looking up at the brilliant moon.
The night was very cold and there was a huge halo around the
moon, which was nearly full and high overhead. "It's a long story."

"You've been saying it's a long story for months," she said.
"Just tell it. It can't be that long."

"Well, it all goes back to how I was killed."

"So start there."

"I've told half of it before," he said. "Bernie Hawkins was mad
as a hornet when he found Priscilla and I were engaged, because
he'd had his eye on her since they were about seventeen. He had
proposed to her two or three times—according to her—and she
refused him each time. But that seemed to only aggravate him,
and he continued to pursue her."

"So he shot you as you came out of the church," she said. "We
got that far."

"He was drunk as a skunk, of course, otherwise I don't think
he'd have done that. He claimed later he only wanted to scare
me—but he was really far too late for that. He never did have

much in the way of brains, and that was one reason Priscilla couldn't stand the man. Anyhow, he shot me through the heart." For a moment Warren stopped walking and opened his coat to show Diane the blood-stained hole in his shirt. She looked closely at the dark patch on his white shirt, almost fluorescent in the moonlight.

"He hung for it later," Warren said, adjusting his coat and resuming his walk again, "much to my satisfaction."

"How'd you end up in the house, though?"

"The house belonged to Priscilla's grandparents, who built it about 1897 I believe. Before we were married, they told us they'd leave us the house as their wedding gift. They were rather aged, and knew they'd soon be going, so we expected that within a few years—by the time we had a family at least—that the house would belong to us. That would have given us a lot of savings to play with in other ways, like opening my mechanical shop, so we were both quite pleased about it. Anyhow, right after I was killed, Priscilla moved in with them. When they died within two years, her sister moved in with her."

"Her sister?"

"Oh, yes," he said. "Didn't I mention that? Priscilla had a younger sister—her name was Ludmilla."

"Ludmilla!" she exclaimed, recalling his suggestion of a name for the baby. "Shit that's worse than Priscilla."

Warren was mildly offended and turned away.

Diane looked sheepish—but only for an instant. "I'm sorry," she said. "I didn't mean it that way. It's just that they both sound so old-fashioned."

Warren stopped walking. "I understand," he said curtly.

"Will you tell me the rest of the story?"

With the mist of her soft breath curling away as she talked, she looked so eager and ruddy-faced, he could not possibly hold anything against her, and in a moment was smiling again. Presently he began to walk, and Diane kept pace at his side.

"Their grandparents died, as I said, within two years after I did. Grandfather went first, and Grandmother wasn't far behind him. So Priscilla and Ludmilla took up housekeeping together."

"What about their parents? Where were they?"

"Oh—I never saw much of them after I died. They had a younger brother, too, so—"

"What was his name?"

"Jacob. He moved to Yakima the year before we were married."

"Uh huh. So what happened then?"

"Well, at that time, the place had a pretty large plot of land as well."

"It still does," Diane observed.

"For this day, yes, but in those days, it covered most of what's now the block on either side, and that had been whittled down from a much larger section they once owned. Some of it Priscilla sold to help Jacob and her folks buy a new place together in Yakima. That was a few years later. They tried to take Priscilla along, but she wouldn't leave. After that, the area was annexed to the city; they paved the street and started building a lot of houses right along here."

Diane nodded silently. She was cold, and began rubbing her hands as they walked. That failed to warm them, so she folded her arms and tucked her hands inside her jacket. She almost asked Warren if they could head home, but wanted to hear the rest of the story first—and as long as he was in the mood for telling it, she could endure a little numbness in her fingers.

"Then what?" she asked.

"Anyhow," Warren continued, "I had always asked to be cremated—left that instruction in my will."

"Why?"

"Because I've always hated graveyards," he said. "They always seemed like a waste of good land. So I was determined I wouldn't contribute to it."

"I see."

"Priscilla kept my ashes in her room, and they lived there very quietly for a year or so. Priscilla never married, but just after that,

Ludmilla got engaged—quite unexpectedly—and she left to live with her husband when they were married."

"Why do you say unexpectedly?"

"It's not fair to say so, I suppose," Warren said slowly, "but especially in contrast to Priscilla, Ludmilla was—well *homely* would be a polite term."

"So you didn't expect her to get married?"

"Nobody did. But old Doc Jarmsford—"

"What kind of name is that?"

"A corruption of something Scandinavian, I presume. It's spelled with a 'J' not a 'Y'."

"Oh."

"So Doc Jarmsford proposed to her. I think actually, they'd been lovers on the sly for a while. He was her physician you know, and I got the impression they had a few encounters in the office, maybe elsewhere. That's mostly inference on my part, though."

"Pretty wicked," Diane offered.

"I thought so—after all, the man was her *physician*. It might have gone like this, though. One day while examining her—probably with his cold forceps in her—uh—"

"Vagina."

"Or something like that, he simply cut loose. 'Ludmilla,' he probably said, 'I can't keep my hands off you, you lovely creature.'"

Diane giggled at Warren's gruff imitation of the Doctor's voice. "He sounds like an old goat."

"I'll get to that later," Warren said, laughing. "So he probably bellied right up to her—since she was on the examination table and couldn't go anywhere on account of her petticoats being hiked up and all bare down below—and he popped her cherry right there. She would have been so overwhelmed by any man taking an interest in her, let alone an older and quite successful man, she wouldn't have uttered a sound. I think they became lovers like that, and kept it up for a while. She did pay him an uncommon number of visits for a healthy young woman. I'd bet they were all pelvic examinations, too. Anyhow, he eventually proposed to her and they got married about six months later and moved over to Douglas County."

"Dullsville."

"It was, even then, but it was on the upswing, and he thought he could have a better practice there. Thought he could expand more than if he stayed here. I figured out a long time later how their relationship worked, though."

"How?"

"Ludmilla was always self-conscious about her looks—as well she should have been. But she did have a rather pleasant body."

"You've seen it I take it?"

"Of course." With a grin, he stopped to gesture with his hands. "She was about this tall," he said, holding one hand just above Diane's head. "And she had a rather ample chest, like this." Diane giggled when he demonstrated. "She tended a bit toward plumpness, but with an attractively narrow waist. And she had hips that old Doc could really get his hands around. I think she took after Grandma in that regard—their grandmother ended her days fat as an old sow, by the way, but that's another story. Ludmilla's proportions were very good, and her hips weren't all that big for her huge chest. She had very shapely legs, too."

"What did he see in her if she wasn't pretty though? Her tits?"

"Neither a pretty face nor a large bosom doth a man's attraction guarantee," he recited. "Doc probably wanted easy prey the first time he humped her. She was ripe young flesh, after all, and he was about forty or thereabouts. Oh, he was a widower, too, by the way, but he didn't have any children. And to be honest, Ludmilla had a few things going for her. Aside from being well-organized, she was a great cook, for one thing. I've eaten her cooking many times, and she could make anything better than anyone else in Priscilla's family. She was the younger—I think she was precisely twenty-one when they were married—but even from the time she could first reach the stove, they say, she cooked most of the meals."

"So Doc liked her cooking. What else?"

"This is the old goat part," Warren said, and headed leftward, walking across the rows of bare trees. A light snowfall had started, with big flakes settling softly on the branches. "They visited Priscilla occasionally in your house—well, our house—and I had the opportunity to watch them in bed."

Diane was not surprised, but she said, "Aha."

"They retired after dinner—this was the first time they stayed, so I remember it vividly. He put his arms around her and told her what a heavenly creature she was and how proud he was of her. She did have pretty good sense, and she had been quite entertaining to the whole dinner party that evening. So while he was telling her this, she was batting her eyes, rather soaking up all of his praise like a piece of plump cornbread. He started pawing her all over, putting his hands into her bodice and kissing her. She put up about two seconds of token feminine resistance before he had her petticoats up and they were engaging each other on the bed."

"She liked having him say sweet things to her?"

"Oh, she did, and even in public he praised her to the sky. She deserved it, too, poor thing, the way she bustled and toiled keeping house and cleaning up his office and taking care of their accounts and correspondence. She really was about the most dutiful wife I think anyone could have. And in return, he treated her like a little angel. The thing he got out of it, I think—besides having a wife that everyone agreed was a fine example of a hard-working spouse with no inclination at all to be anything else—was a lot of sexual activity."

"Which you followed closely, right?'

"Purely out of concern for their welfare," he added.

"Uh huh," Diane answered.

"Now, Priscilla used to visit them sometimes and she'd stay a few days in their guest room. I think Ludmilla liked to have her around because they had been pretty close, even though they were five years apart. And Priscilla never went anywhere overnight without taking my ashes along. That was the only opportunity I had during those years to get out of the house."

"Huh? So you knew all along it would work if I took you out?"

Had Warren been able to blush, he would have then. He probably should have told her before. "Well, yes, actually," he answered, adding quickly, "but I'd forgotten completely about it until you suggested it, so I'm just as grateful as I always was."

"Thanks," Diane said, smiling up at him.

"Anyhow, every time we went to Ludmilla's," he continued, seeing that she thought nothing of it, "I dropped into their bedroom to see how they were getting along in their married state. I think every night I ever spent there they went at it. For that time, she was rather uninhibited in bed, too. I've seen her suck him more than once, for example."

"Did she swallow?"

"Hah! That's a crude question . . ."

"Did she?"

"One time, they were playing and running around the bedroom. He kept after her and she was in her undergarments. He had only his nightshirt on, and his penis was bobbing around while he chased her. She kept ducking between his legs and running off, telling him to shush, or Priscilla would know what was going on. He quieted down and tip-toed after her, but finally caught up with her—she wasn't trying very hard to avoid him. She went onto her knees, and they played 'begging for mercy', and he shoved his member right into her mouth. She sucked and licked for a long time as if she really loved it, and then pulled it out just as he was about to finish off."

"Then what?"

"Then," Warren said, stopping under a tree near a barbed-wire fence, "she started pumping him with her hand, laughing and giggling while he spewed his stuff all over her face and down her chest. She rubbed it around and wiped it off and licked her fingers. Then he went at her with some kind of instrument and rubbed her insides until she had her little orgasm."

"How funny!" Diane exclaimed, and laughing, leaned up against a fence-post. "The doctor and his wife!"

"Other times," Warren went on, I've seen them do all kinds of things. Those two were almost as good in themselves as all of the sixties." He paused and straightened his bow-tie, regaining his composure. "I'll tell you about that some other time."

"How about now?" Diane asked, for she was feeling the excitement of the story and wanted to hear more about their antics.

"I thought we were originally talking about how I—"

"Right!" she exclaimed. "Hey, can we keep walking? I'm getting cold."

"Oh, sorry," he replied and let her start walking. "Yes, we'll leave Doc and Mrs. Jarmsford for another time."

"So how did you get buried?"

"Priscilla stayed in the house. She never married, and as far as I know, she remained chaste all of her days." He had always wondered whether that were true, though.

"How terrible," Diane said in sympathy.

"You say that, but you're still a virgin," Warren observed.

"Until I'm sixteen," Diane chimed, repeating her litany, though she really felt ready to fall for the first boy whom she halfway liked.

Warren smiled to see her aura flutter, then began to talk again. "She did play with herself, a little bit, but it only made her sad, even though I know she did reach orgasm—which was nice for her. So, Priscilla kept me around, and eventually she passed away. She never was happy after I was killed, though, and she only lasted about twelve years. I think she may have died of a broken heart, but she did it while she was away at Ludmilla's place. It was one of the only times she didn't take me along, strangely enough, and I only heard about it in a vague way from things they said later."

"That's really awful . . ."

"After that, Ludmilla and the Doc inherited the place, but since they had their own home across the river, they sold it almost instantly and only came a few times to make an inventory and supervise removal of the furnishings. I have no idea what happened to them later, and I don't know what became of Priscilla's body.

That fact," he said, looking away across the orchard, "has always bothered me."

"So who buried you?"

"Ludmilla did. She didn't want to keep the ashes I suppose, and knew she couldn't do much of anything else with them. She might have given them a decent burial, but didn't, and I'm not sure why." With a glance at Diane, he added, "Of course I'm thankful for it now that I've met you."

Diane looked at him tenderly, and exhaled to let her breath float away.

"She must have known my opinion of graveyards, I suppose," he continued. "Instead, she took a spade and buried them where you found them. She said a few prayers over them, and departed."

"What happened to Ludmilla after that?"

"I never saw her again. A few weeks later, I happened to see a reference to Doc Jarmsford's passing, without any details. The new people who moved in took the newspaper regularly, and I used to scan it over their shoulders once in a while—looking for news of people I'd known, of course. Ludmilla, I never heard anything about."

Thoughtfully, Diane looked at him. "Could she still be alive?"

"I suppose so," Warren said slowly. "She was younger than Priscilla. If she were still alive, she'd be . . . probably in her late seventies."

My grandmother's almost that old," Diane said, "and she's still healthy. If Ludmilla were alive, do you think she'd know what happened to Priscilla's body? Know where she was buried or whatever?"

Warren's face brightened as he looked at her. "She most certainly would. If she were alive, that is."

"Come on," Diane said, picking up her walking pace. "I'll bet we could at least we can find out if she's dead. Maybe there was an obituary for Priscilla too—we could find that."

She tried the phone book as soon as they got home, but was disappointed to find no Jarmsfords listed. "Did they have any children?" she asked Warren, who was looking over her shoulder.

"Not that I ever knew about," he said. "Either he or she must have been incapable of it. I think it was he, actually, because he didn't have any children by his first wife either. I was actually kind of sorry for Ludmilla in that way, because she did love little children, and she would have made a wonderful mother."

"Did she ever re-marry?"

"That I don't know," he said. "But given her looks, and being a widow, I'd expect she didn't. He was fairly wealthy, though, so someone might have married her for the money. Except I think by then she would have been sophisticated enough to see through that."

"What was old Doc's first name?"

"Harold," Warren replied instantly.

"I'll have to go to the library," Diane concluded. "Maybe I can find a lead that way. This is going to be fun. Just like a detective . . ."

Warren was nearly ecstatic, leaning forward eagerly in mid-air. "You're really going to try to find her, aren't you?"

"Of course," Diane replied. "Why shouldn't I?"

"It's just, well—it's not your problem."

She turned to him and softly said, "Warren, it *is* my problem, because you're the closest friend I've ever had." She looked at him silently for a minute.

"That's—that's terribly kind, Diane."

"It's more than that," she said, looking down while she closed the phone book. She almost told him she loved him, but instead she bit her lip and picked up the book, then put it back under the telephone. "Time for bed," she announced. "See you in the morning."

"Good-night."

She went to kiss her mother good-night, and when she left the room, Warren let her go. Her aura was big and beautiful, so she must have been thinking really wonderfully happy thoughts. He let her go to sleep, then went up and watched her for a while. If only he could have, he dearly wanted to lean over and kiss her. He did it anyway, ethereally, and though he could not touch her cheek, it made him feel satisfied to have at least put his lips as close as they could get to her cheek without going through the skin.

[14]

Warren suggested they try going to the cemetery for information, though Diane protested. On Halloween, she had forgotten completely about wanting to see the graveyard with him and simply stayed home, where they distributed candy to children all evening and read some Edgar Allen Poe before bed. The Poe had given her nightmares—she had always hated scary stories—and she swore off him in the future, along with all the other gorey Halloween movies her friends talked about.

"I've never even been near a cemetery," she told Warren. "Will you go with me?"

"Of course I'll go. It's a nice afternoon for a ride, too."

The snow was slushy, but the streets were clear and the weather was beautiful, so Diane took her pack and Warren's thermos, then rode out Western Avenue to the base of the hills. She turned into the wide lane that led through the cemetery, dotted with tombstones. There she stopped abruptly and jumped off her bicycle.

"No fucking way," she announced, and turned around. There were ghosts wandering all over the grounds.

"Oh, not very pleasant looking is it?" he said, continuing to look back across the snow-covered lawn.

"No way," she said. "I can't handle that."

"I don't blame you," he agreed as they rode past the ghost of a man who had been dreadfully mutilated.

Later, she phoned the cemetery office, but they told her she would have to come in, and could not seem to understand that she only wanted to find out if a particular person were buried there without appearing in person at their office. "Strike two," she said as she hung up the phone. "They must hire morons, too."

The public library yielded practically nothing detailed on local history—at least not the kind of history Diane needed. Their collection of newspapers only went sporadically back to the fifties, and other detailed records were of no particular value, being mostly about politics and land holdings and such. But the reference librarian, after listening to Diane explain a few very specific pieces of information she needed for a class project, suggested she go to the archives of the local newspaper—The Valley World. She put in a call herself to Quinn Forsythe who looked after the archives, saying she had a high school student who was a dear girl, and could she help. Everything was set for Diane to visit Miss Forsythe at the newspaper office on the following day.

When Diane called at the office, she was introduced to Miss Forsythe, a tall lady of gaunt build. She seemed somewhat past middle age, and wore a stern gray dress that came nearly to her ankles. A pair of reading glasses dangled on a chain around her neck. Her brown hair was obviously dyed and cut just below her ears, from each of which depended a massive green earring.

"Yes," she said crisply, looking over Diane and seeming to pause at her chest, and again at her face. She broke into a smile. "You're the girl Alice sent over."

"I'm Diane Kolansky. Pleased to meet you."

"The pleasure is mine," insisted Miss Forsythe.

"She could fell a tree with that nose," said Warren over Diane's shoulder. Diane cleared her throat to keep from laughing.

After shaking hands somewhat more warmly than necessary, Miss Forsythe escorted Diane along a hallway and down a flight of stairs while keeping up a continual monologue. Only occasionally could Diane interject a question. But Miss Forsythe seemed more delighted with each question, praising its astuteness, before launching into an overly detailed answer. While she talked, she made quick glances toward Diane's eyes.

Presently, they reached the archive room, and Miss Forsythe

pushed open the double glass doors. Diane could not believe the room when she saw it. It was simply a vast basement with rack after rack of yellowing papers between cement columns. She had imagined stacks of microfilm with a modern microfilm reader. But Miss Forsythe explained that they had only begun microfilming the collection, and were working their way backward from the previous year, because there was so little call for really old news. The room was in fact only a research room; the main collection was housed elsewhere in controlled atmosphere storage—which the town had plenty of, because of the apples, and the space had been donated by a local businessman. The paper was also lucky to have had a founder with a strong sense of how important local history always was to posterity; otherwise, they might not have had any archives to speak of. As it was, they had a vast trove, including rare copies of the Valley World's two predecessors which merged in 1915.

With apologies, Miss Forsythe pointed Diane to the stacks, and after instructing her quite carefully about the handling of delicate paper, let her look through them alone. There was not even an index for anything before 1960.

Priscilla's obituary was simple to find though, because Warren knew the approximate date of her death in 1923—and at least things were organized in chronological order. The obituary was concise and uninformative. It stated only that Priscilla Brannigan, widow of the late Warren Brannigan, had died and that her estate, consisting of a house on Orchard Street and miscellaneous other articles, was willed in its entirety to her sister Ludmilla Jarmsford.

"But listen to this," Diane said with a triumphant smile, and read aloud to Warren. "By her wishes, the deceased will be cremated—it gives the date, time, and funeral parlor too."

"That means we probably won't find her grave, either," Warren observed, greatly crestfallen. "I would have liked to visit her grave."

"I thought you didn't believe in wasting land."

"I don't," he said defensively, "but she was my wife, Diane."

"Sorry," Diane replied, her tone matching his. More softly, she added, "I didn't mean it that way."

"That's all right," he replied, again calming down. He sat back, and propped up his feet. "Let's see if we can find anything else."

On another day, Diane found an advertisement for the sale of the property on Orchard Street, but did not come up with any other information about it, nor could they find any advertisement or society column listing the name of a buyer, or any clue about it.

"This is ridiculous," Diane grumbled when she had spent four afternoons pawing through a year's worth of newspapers looking for anything further about Ludmilla. Miss Forsythe had come in at least twice each afternoon, asking if she had found what she was looking for. But since Diane herself was not sure what she was really looking for, she could only make a few vague stammerings. Nevertheless, Miss Forsythe praised her diligence, and said she was sure Diane would find her information sooner or later, since the entire archive was at her disposal—and that she hoped the teacher saw fit to give such a stalwart researcher an 'A' on her paper.

"I can't take this," Diane hissed at Warren when she left the newspaper building after her fourth afternoon rummaging in the archives. "I've never read so many obits and engagements and marriage announcements in my life." She unlocked her bicycle and began walking it down the street.

"There must be a faster way," Warren said.

"Miss Forsythe didn't think so," Diane replied. "And she ought to know."

"What about death certificates?"

"If we're looking for someone who died, that would be fine. You think they'd let me, a teenager, rifle the County Courthouse records? Fat chance."

"You could try."

"Forget it, Warren," she whined, turning to face him. He looked so distressed she could not be mad, though, and she told herself again that he had an emotional stake in finding information. "Look,

I don't mind this too much, 'cause it's for you. But if I'm going to go through all this trouble will you do me a favor?"

"What?"

Diane thought for a moment. "Oh, I don't know," she finally said. "I'll think of something. But will you owe me one?"

"All right," he agreed. "I'll owe you one, whenever you think of something that I can actually do."

Spending every afternoon in the Valley World archives became too much for Diane after another week, and she decided she needed to take her search in smaller doses. Her research was beginning to have an unwelcome impact on her social life, though that was meagre to begin with. By the time she got home at quarter to six, it was time to help with dinner and spend some time with the baby, then do her homework and go to bed.

She told Warren she would have to make it every other day at most. The search for Ludmilla was intriguing, but she was not very confident she would find anything. There were just too many papers—they had sixty-odd years of crinkled, yellowing paper to look through.

[15]

Well into March, Diane finally thought of something for Warren to help her with—the favor he owed her—and after mulling it over for a couple of days, she finally spoke to him about it one evening when she had finished her homework and stowed her books back in her pack.

"You're going to help me find the guy I'm going to give myself to," she announced.

"Oh my God," he said. "What makes you trust me? You're the one who's going to lose her virginity."

"You can see their auras," she said simply. "You've got a lot better idea what they're thinking than I do."

"Yes, but, I wouldn't take it as a very perfect indicator . . ."

"Come on," she said. "I'm looking through all this shit for you—the least you can do is a favor that I'm really desperately interested in. It's as important to me *who* pops my cherry as it is for *you* to find your wife."

Warren thought that was hardly the case—she had plenty of years to get over even a pretty nasty first experience. But he had already been pining for Priscilla for as long as Diane might live. He also had all of the foreseeable future to continue that pining. If only he could find Priscilla, he might finally be able to rest in peace—but he had told Diane nothing of that. It seemed sometimes as if she thought he would be there for her forever.

"You're right," he finally said. "It's important that you don't, heh, screw it up your first time."

Diane smiled at the limp pun. "Thanks, Warren—you're the greatest."

"Not really," he said. "You're like my little sister."

Diane's smile faded for a moment and she answered with great disappointment. "Yeah, I guess so, huh."

"What's the matter?"

"Nothing." She looked at him and felt her lip trembling. Biting hard, she sniffed and closed her eyes. "No, it's not nothing." Tears came welling up, and she lost control of them. "Shit," she said, letting her tears go and finally breaking into sobs. "Warren Brannigan, I love you dammit. And I want it to be *you*, but you're a fucking *ghost!*"

"Diane . . ." If he could have shed tears, he would have to see the way she broke down just then. It was pathetic to watch—and he knew that she meant what she said..

"It's true," she continued while tears dripped from her chin. "I've never been this close to anybody. So, if it can't be you, I want you to pick the guy for me."

It seemed to him an ominous responsibility, but one he must shoulder. "All right," he whispered, coming to sit beside her, holding his hands over hers. "I'll help you find him."

"Thanks," she sniffled.

"If it makes you feel any better," he said. "I love you, too, Diane. And if I weren't so—damnably indisposed at this time, without any flesh and all that—well, I certainly think I would take you up on that offer."

She looked up, and he made a movement to wipe her tears, but his hand went through her cheek. She laughed with a sniffle and reached for a tissue. "Didn't mean to cry on you . . ."

"Shh," he whispered. "It's all right. You're entitled once in a while."

He sat hovering nearby and sang while she changed into her nightgown and got ready for bed, then he came close after she got under the covers. She hugged a pillow to her chest, and he talked quietly to her for a while, sitting near her head. She put a hand into her panties, moving slowly, and he started singing a lullaby again. In a few moments she was asleep with a vague smile on her lips, and he slipped away to check on the baby.

[16]

The following evening Warren helped Diane with her homework, which he rarely did as it was against his principles to give her answers when she should have been expending her own effort. But after the previous evening, he wanted to be helpful to her and keep the mood jovial. Finally finished with the last page of her short-answer biology homework, Diane closed her Pee-Chee and stuffed it into her pack.

"I gotta go," she said jumping up.

"Where?"

"Bathroom," she called over her shoulder. "And don't follow me either—I'm on the rag again."

"Such crudity," he chided playfully.

"Got a better word?" she asked, pausing before opening the door to the stairwell.

"Indisposed?"

"Hardly," she answered, and wrenched open the door. "I shove in a tampon and forget about it."

"Did it start this morning?"

"Yes," she moaned. She had woken up with blood-stained panties.

"You are touchy, aren't you . . ." he teased. "Priscilla was the same way, you know . . ."

"What do you mean?"

"Irritable," he said. "I always knew when she was—ahem—menstruating. She would become quite short-tempered, and usually had headaches . . ."

"I'm not either irritable. Tell me when I get back," she said, and padded down the stairs, wondering if husbands were always so interested when their wives were on their periods. Warren might not know the answer to that one, but she decided to ask him about it. He probably had a good story. On her way out of the bathroom, she grabbed an extra couple of tampons and some pads to put in her purse, then stopped in front of the mirror.

"Husband," she said aloud, feeling quite warm. How beautiful it sounded to say that.

Instead of heading directly back to her room, she tiptoed to the kitchen and poured herself a glass of some French wine that her mother had sitting open on the counter.

"That's a good question," Warren told her when she posed her question later. "Since Priscilla and I never actually lived together, I can't speak from my own experience, but . . ."

"It reminds you of something, right?" she asked, and took a sip of wine. It was too dry, but she felt even warmer and sipped again.

"Yes," he said, settling back in the air with his hands behind his head, happy to see her feeling better. "It reminds me of someone who lived here once, for a short while. You might call him a dirty old man. The master and mistress—that's what the maid called them, by the way—lived in the front room, where your parents are now, and this man was a boarder who stayed in Rat's room."

"Robert," Diane corrected in her mother's exasperated tone.

"You call him Rat—I call him Rat," Warren shot back. "Or shall we both call him Bobby? Anyhow, I took some interest in this boarder, because on occasion I had the impression that he knew I was about, but I never got any direct confirmation."

"You didn't talk to him, in other words."

"Oh, I talked to him, and sometimes I thought he was aware of me, but he never answered."

"So what did he do that you were reminded of?"

"In the bathroom downstairs, which he sometimes used along with everyone else—guests, I mean—there was a receptacle for the disposal of—"

"Bloody rags!"

"Used sanitary napkins," Warren corrected with a smile. "Learn the word, Diane: 'Sanitary napkin'—it will stand you in good stead in polite company."

"Right . . ."

"So, this old geezer—"

"Watch your tongue, Mr. Brannigan . . ."

"—Used to peek into the receptacle on a regular basis to see if there were any such napkins inside. And when he found one, which was often, since there were quite a number of ladies who came regularly to a kind of English Tea with the mistress of the house, he would pluck it out—"

"Yuck."

"—and take it to his room."

"That's just gross."

"Isn't it though? But when you've seen as much as I have, it ceases to be merely disgusting and becomes interesting because of the light it sheds on the psychology of the fellow."

"What did he do with them?"

"Don't you have more homework today?"

"Nope," she said, and took another large sip of wine. "I'm ready to change for bed, though. But you have to finish the story, and I'm still drinking my wine."

"I'd be corrupting the mind of a young virgin," Warren said, and kept his lips tightly closed.

"OK, see you later. I'm going for a walk."

"Like I said earlier—touchy. Just like Priscilla. But if you insist, I'll tell you anyhow. This boarder collected napkins. He smelled them. He revelled in them. Sometimes he lined them up on his bed and looked at them. Whenever he could positively identify one, he attached a little tag to it and pencilled in the lady's name."

"He was a pervert, right?"

"Precisely—I don't think he was quite normal, as I've never seen anyone else do that. I think it wasn't so much the blood or anything, but the secret knowledge he thought he possessed about these women. When he chanced to have more than one or two belonging to the same lady he would sometimes take one of them, and—close your ears young lady—"

"Nope. The whole story, Mr. Brannigan."

"—he would relieve his sexual impulses with it, then sneak it out in the next trash to be burned."

"That is *really* gross," Diane groaned, rolling her eyes. "You mean he shot his wad in them?"

"Makes you wonder, doesn't it? If you keep these things around for long enough, they get rather stale, I'd suppose from the talk that happened later. So here's the end of the story. They used to employ a maid who came three or four times a week. One time, she happened herself to be on her period, and deposited her napkin there when she arrived in the morning. Being the maid, she came in later to collect the wastebaskets from all over the house. Imagine her surprise, when she discovered her treasure missing. She had never liked this boarder, and I think she kept a sharp eye out after that. Maybe she suspected he had been in the bathroom after her. To make a long story short—for this all took nearly a year to play itself out—one time when he was out, and after another napkin had disappeared from under her watchful eye, she took it upon herself to go into his room and search his belongings."

"Did she find them?" Diane's head was buzzing slightly, and quite pleasantly. She took another mouthful of wine, swirled it around, then took another.

"She certainly did find them, and you can hardly imagine the scene that ensued. She was all for calling the police and having him locked away. But—did I mention he was an uncle or something of the mistress?—well, the maid told the mistress, and brought a drawer filled with rank smelling evidence. The mistress threw up her hands and fainted at the stench. The mistress told the master, and he could hardly believe it. Had to see for himself, of course. But once he'd seen and smelled the evidence, he had a quiet talk with the old geezer about how he simply could not have such goings-on in his house, but seeing as he was a relative, he could not very well turn him over to the police. There'd surely be a scandal, or at least a heap of gossip about it afterwards. The man packed his bags that evening and left."

"That's a weird story," Diane said. She finished her wine thoughtfully while he told her more about the master and mistress, then as promised, she stood up to change her clothes, taking her time while Warren looked on admiringly. She stopped halfway through her change, in the nude, while she rummaged in a drawer for another pair of panties. She felt wonderful. Suddenly she let out a little laugh and went to her purse to get another tampon.

"What are you doing?"

"Teasing you," she said, and popped her used tampon out. Standing on a chair, she tied it by the string to a nail in one of the rafters, then set it swinging. "Not very bloody, sorry," she said.

"Disgusting," he replied, but he was smiling.

She unwrapped the new tampon, then looked at Warren while she bent her legs and inserted it slowly while biting the tip of her tongue. "Nasty, huh?" she asked, flashing her eyes when she finished.

"Thoroughly shameless," he agreed, in a jovial tone that suggested he thought otherwise.

Diane slipped on a pair of panties, merely for safety, and got into bed without putting on a nightgown. The sheets felt delightful against her skin, and she fell asleep quickly, with Warren singing a lullaby.

[17]

Two days each week during the following weeks, Diane took Warren down to the Valley World office to continue their search through the archives. They soon had a system worked out to make the search go more quickly. Diane would take the papers out two days at a time, and turn pages simultaneously. Then she would scan one while Warren scanned the other. They were up to 1952 already, but the search went slowly. Diane kept getting interested in details. She had begun their search by reading only the society pages, obituaries, and so forth. But at some point—during Prohibition, in fact—she began to be fascinated by the front pages, and later by leading articles. She began to follow the careers of certain journalists, and even began to backtrace their careers. The First World War. The Great Depression. Adolf Hitler. Carnage. The Atom Bomb. The United Nations. The Iron Curtain. The overwhelming flow of history had caught her up, and sometimes she stood breathing consciously, simply blurry-eyed, in awe that people had lived through it all, sipping one day at a time. She was receiving it in giant gulps by comparison, filling her cup from a raging waterfall.

"Bingo," she said one afternoon. "Listen to this: Deaths. May 12. Joshua B. McMonigle, 67. Et cetera—some stuff about him. Survived by his wife Ludmilla, et cetera. A private memorial service to be held at the couple's home tomorrow. And that's all it says."

Warren jumped up to look. "That's got to be her! Does it say where they lived?"

"Nope."

"There must have been a marriage before that," said Warren. "Look at the date—she must have been about sixty when he died.

Imagine that—her married to McMonigle. I'd never have thought she was his type."

"How can you be sure it was her?"

"Josh McMonigle was about our age—I mean about my age."

"You knew him?"

"Vaguely. He was an old friend of the family—I think Priscilla's parents had known his parents for a long time. He was at our wedding, even."

"There we go."

"McMonigle was living in Douglas County last time I heard," he said. "Let's check the telephone book."

"Great." Diane put back the papers and they stormed out of the archive room. "Bye Miss Forsythe!" she yelled on the way out.

"Did you find something?" asked Mrs Forsythe, looking up from her typewriter.

"One thing," Diane said. "I'll let you know!"

Warren defiantly let the revolving door swing halfway closed, then walked through the frame behind Diane. They walked her bicycle to the nearest phone booth where she leaned it against the door and yanked open the book. "Right here," she said after flipping pages for a moment. "J. McMonigle and M. McMonigle. Take your pick."

"Try them both. No, try J first."

Diane fished for a dime in her purse and dialed the number. "Hello?"

"Hello," said an older man's voice on the other end of the line.

"Is Ludmilla McMonigle in?"

"Ludmilla?" the man asked. "She doesn't live here. Who's calling?"

"My name's Diane Kolansky," she said as sweetly as she could. "I'm terribly sorry, I must have dialed the wrong number."

"Are you from the Masonic Lodge?" the man demanded.

"No, sir. I'm calling for a friend of mine."

"What do you want with Ludmilla?"

"Bingo," Diane whispered to Warren. "I just have to talk to

her," she said, in a girlish voice. "If you'd rather not tell me her phone number, perhaps you could tell me where she lives?"

The man paused, and Diane heard him take a few breaths. "Nope," he said, returning to the phone. "You got the wrong number."

"Shit!" Diane yelled, slamming down the phone.

"What?"

"He's some kind of asshole—I don't know. Sounds like he knows her, but we don't really know if it's the right Ludmilla."

"I'm sure it is," he said confidently. "Maybe we can find the marriage record."

"I don't know," Diane said, feeling ruffled. "Maybe we should try the courthouse after all."

"Let's go!"

"Warren—it's five fifteen. They're already closed."

"Oh. Well, tomorrow I guess."

Warren was excited all the way home, talking constantly about how they would find Ludmilla and that would lead them to Priscilla. "I'm certain of it," he said.

"We'll know tomorrow," Diane answered.

After she finished dinner, did the dishes, and slogged through her homework, Diane was exhausted. But even after she went to bed she found she could not sleep, and when she looked at her clock, saw it was past midnight. "Warren," she called in the darkness. He did not answer, so every few minutes, she called again.

"I'm here," he said finally, hovering nearby.

"You remember how you're always going to tell me about the sixties?"

"You want a bed-time story?" he said, smiling.

"Yeah," she said playfully. "Tell me all about the sixties?"

"Where should I begin?"

"How about 1960?"

"How about 1957?" he replied.

"When I was born. OK."

"1957," he began, "was a good year. The house was sold in the autumn of that year by the people who owned it at the time. They were a relatively nice family, and I liked the children. The parents had a terrible sex life, though. She was frigid as an arctic winter."

"Oh yeah?"

"It's the worst case I've ever seen," he said. "I can't figure how they ended up having four children."

"Didn't they ever have sex?"

"A few times. Generally it went like this, though. He had a pretty normal sex drive, I think."

"How do you know?"

"Well," Warren answered.

"Oh, come on," Diane said.

"He would, take care of himself a couple or three times a week."

"Beat off?"

"The word is 'masturbate'," Warren said.

Diane laughed. "Jerk off, beat his meat . . ."

"Are you going to listen?"

"I'm listening . . ."

"Yes, he used to do that fairly regularly. But about two months of that was all he could stand. She always dressed quite unflatteringly. Her skirts were always longer than whatever was fashionable at the time, and she always wore blouses that came right up to her neck. Terribly unattractive—for the times, I mean."

"So when did they do it?"

"I'm getting to that," said Warren. "He'd start off by pinching her bottom."

"Ooh."

"Usually he came home after work, and they all had dinner like one big happy family. While the kids ran off to play or do their homework, he'd carry his dessert plate to the kitchen. She would be doing dishes or baking something, usually. And if none of the children were looking, he'd pinch her bottom. She always slapped his hand away—'George, stop it.' He'd say, 'Come on, dear, it's been two months.' Of course, he'd always try to put his arm around her in bed. The funny thing was that they did sleep together in a double bed. She always wore long nightgowns, though, and he wore pajamas. After about a week of bottom pinching, he would get most irate, and they'd sometimes argue bitterly about it. She would call him a sex-crazed devil, and he'd always say it was perfectly normal—married folk all engaged in sex."

"She sounds like a real prude. Was she religious or something?"

"Well, she was. But as far as I've been able to tell, just having religion didn't interfere too often with married couples having a bit more fun than these two did. Finally, if he really pestered her and managed to pull her night-gown halfway up, she'd groan like and old milk-cow and say, 'Oh, all right. Hurry up.'"

Diane laughed at the way Warren imitated her voice. "Did she talk like that?"

"Worse," he said. "She had this grating kind of high-pitched voice. You should have heard her yell at the children, too. Anyhow, once she gave in, he would go right to it. In about thirty seconds, he'd have her nightgown up to her chest and her underwear down around her ankles. She wore the most awful underwear, too. She wasn't really bad looking, even though she was rather heavy.

"Fat? Or just heavy?"

"Just heavy. I think that's why he managed to pay any attention to her at all. If she'd have been really fat, I don't think he'd have bothered. But she always wore these underwear that made her look like a wrestler. And her brassieres looked like they could hold up a train. So he'd put on a rubber and go at her. Just stick himself right in without waiting for anything. She always complained that it hurt. And I imagine it felt about like being poked with a cactus, to her."

"No foreplay?"

"None at all. He'd pump a while and roll off. Then she'd go back to her book, or roll over and go to sleep. I don't think I ever saw that couple kiss each other."

"Never?"

"No. But, you know I think half of her problem was that he was incompetent. He never engaged in anything to warm her up, he'd just plug her hole cold. She would lay there like a ruminating milk-cow and roll her eyes at the indignity of it all. Then it would be over. The other half of her problem was that I don't think she knew it was supposed to be fun."

"Like those old 'wifely duty' types?"

"Exactly. I was actually happy to see that family move out."

"Who moved in after them?"

"They rented the place out for a long time, and finally sold it in about sixty-four. The first renters to move in were a younger couple with three small children. Their grandmother lived with them. I used to have some nice conversations with her, too."

"The grandma?"

"No," Warren said, "the wife. She was about thirty-three and pretty friendly. I think they'd been here about a week when I came to introduce myself. That was a kind of ritual I developed. I'd try to meet them one at a time when they were alone, and see if any of them could see me."

"And she could?"

"Before you," he said thoughtfully looking into Diane's eyes, "I think she was the only one I've really had a good time with."

She returned his smile, and they looked at each other for a few minutes. "So how did you introduce yourself?" she asked finally.

"I stood on the back porch, and she went out to get some potatoes or something. I stood on the steps and said hello. She just turned around and looked at me, then said, 'Oh, hello.' So I said, 'nice weather' or something like that, and she replied in kind. That convinced me right off that she could see me, so I said, 'it's a pleasure to meet you, ma'am' and she said likewise or something, and went back into the kitchen. I followed her in and said 'aren't you surprised to see me?' She said, 'No, should I be?' So I said to her that most people would be surprised, to say the least. 'Well,' she said and laughed a pretty little laugh, then said to me 'What's your name?' So I told her, and she put her hand on her hip—quite daintily—and said, 'I've been seeing ghosts all my life, Mr. Brannigan, and nothing they do surprises me in the least.'"

"Wow!" Diane exclaimed.

"Anyhow, we got along pretty well," continued Warren. "She introduced herself as Adrienne—I had already heard her name of course. It suited her to a tee. The first thing she did was make me promise that if I wanted her cooperation—and she knew all about how lonely it gets over the years—she said I'd have to leave her strictly in private except in the afternoons and only when she was alone. And if she ever caught me peeping, that would be the end of her friendliness. She swore she would cut me off cold."

"Did you peep, though?"

"Of course I did—she was quite pretty and had the nicest little bottom I think I've ever seen. I just made sure she never caught me watching her in the bath. Adrienne used to love the garden, too, and even though they were only renting, she spent a couple of hours at least in the garden, nearly every day unless there was snow on the ground. Her youngest son could see me, too. He wasn't too afraid of me after the first few times, and it got so that I would tell him bed-time stories once in a while—usually on Saturday night. It was supposed to be our little secret, but he did finally tell his mother about seeing a ghost. She always treated it like it was the most natural thing in the world that a little boy should see a ghost who told him bed-time stories. She never contradicted him, but made it clear that it should be *their* little secret because not everyone could really see them. She knew full well that he *did* see a ghost in the house, and wasn't about to disabuse him of that notion because it would do him irreparable psychological harm. She and her husband had a normal sort of relationship, too, nothing outlandish in the way of their sexual relations, but passionate. She was probably the most down-to-earth person who's ever lived here."

Diane looked at him poutingly, and he added, "Of course, that was before I met you."

She smiled and curled up closer to her pillow. "Then what happened?"

"Well, we went on for a year or so tending the garden together.

She was a very active woman—that's why she stayed so slim, even after three children. Then they moved out. I was really sorry to see them go, and the last time we had together was out in the garden. She went out specially to see me, and say a last good-bye to the roses."

"It sounds like they were a nice family. But what else happened in the sixties that you keep hinting at? It wasn't all Doris Day, right?"

"You just can't wait for the sexy parts, can you?" Warren laughed.

"Nope. And if you don't tell, I'm going to get mad. I'll leave you home on Friday night."

"It's late, though," Warren said. "It's almost one. Why don't you try to get some sleep. And I promise—"

"Tomorrow?"

Warren raised his hand and put on his best Long John Silver voice, "Aye, me lady, I'll swear on a stack of bloody tampons—that I'll tell you tomorrow night."

"It's a date, Mr. Brannigan," she said. "Good-night."

"Sweet dreams, Diane."

Warren tiptoed away, descending quietly through the floor to go check on the baby. There was a new little nest of mice, too, and he began to wonder if he could manage to introduce the baby to the mice, and whether they would take to each other. He would have to ask Diane to take little Victoria to see the cellar some time.

[18]

When Diane visited the County Courthouse and tried to see the records, there was a mean-looking middle-aged man behind the counter, and no amount of pleading could get her in to see anything. He told her she would have to fill out a form and pay a two-dollar fee for them to do a search. And then she'd have to pay for a photostatic copy, if she wanted one. The form was forbidding, so she folded it up.

"What's the problem?" Warren asked on their way out.

"I don't even know what we're looking for," she said. "If they just let me in, I could probably find it—eventually."

"What *are* you looking for?"

"Shit, Warren, I don't know. Ludmilla's marriage license or something. It must say where McMonigle lived."

"Maybe she has a Social Security number?"

"You want to deal with the feds?"

"I know what you mean," he answered. "Back to the archives?"

"I guess."

Miss Forsythe seemed pleased and surprised as usual to see Diane come back to search the archives again, and after a brief chat, let her into the archive room. Warren commented that she probably had not had so much excitement there for years. "Why don't you ask her if she knows anyone at the courthouse?"

"Great idea," Diane exclaimed, and left the room to talk with Miss Forsythe. She made her request as best she could without seeming to be asking for anything much. Miss Forsythe took off her reading glasses and looked at Diane thoughtfully for a moment, then began to smile.

"You're onto something fun," she said, pointing with her

glasses. "I can feel it in my bones. I think you have the makings of an investigative reporter—"

Diane blushed and murmured, "Not really."

"In any case—if I get you into the records room, and you find something terribly interesting—will you share it with me? Just—privately, of course?"

"Oh, yes," Diane said immediately. "Of course."

"Good," replied Miss Forsythe. "It's settled then. I'll let you know when to go."

When Diane returned to get her pack, she sat down flashing a big smile at Warren. "She's going to call someone she knows over there, and see if she can't get them to do a search for free." A while later Miss Forsythe returned, and handed Diane a white envelope, telling her to go over immediately and give it to the girl at the counter.

Diane dutifully appeared about twenty minutes later at the courthouse record counter. Behind the counter at a desk sat a homely woman with glasses in a formal gray skirt with matching jacket and plain white blouse.

"So you're the young lady," said the woman when Diane passed her the envelope from Miss Forsythe. She set the envelope aside and pushed her glasses down to the tip of her nose. "Honey, you must be something for Quinn to pull strings for you."

Diane looked puzzled. "Who's Quinn?"

"Bet you call her Miss Forsythe," the woman said, readjusting her glasses normally. "She's a real terror—used to be a middle-school teacher." The woman leaned over the counter and looked both ways. "Come on in," she said, buzzing the gate so Diane could slip behind the counter. "First door on your left, honey, and if anyone asks, tell 'em you jumped the counter. I don't know nothing."

Diane slunk down the length of the counter and went through the door the woman had indicated, closing it and flipping on the light-switch at the same time. The room was stacked floor to ceiling with file cabinets. "Oh, shit," she exclaimed.

"At least they're labelled," piped Warren.

Diane pulled a drawer open experimentally. "Oh, shit. No wonder they charge two bucks for a search." The drawers were arranged by record number. "How is anyone supposed to find anything this way?"

"I didn't arrange it," Warren reminded her.

"Thanks." Diane put down her pack and started hunting. The system was actually better than she had thought at first, because record numbers proceeded chronologically. After half an hour, however, while her paranoia increased by the minute, she had located nothing.

"This isn't going to work," she said.

"Keep trying," Warren urged. "There's nobody coming."

"No, it's useless," Diane exclaimed, slamming the drawer she had been looking through. They left the room, being careful to turn out the light and check the drawers. The woman behind the counter was reading a book when Diane walked up to her.

"Find what you need?" she asked, pushing down her glasses.

Diane plunked herself down in an empty chair and dropped her pack at her feet. "No way."

"What are you looking for, honey?"

"Why does she keep calling you 'honey'?" Warren asked over Diane's shoulder.

Ignoring Warren's comment, Diane replied, "These people," and held out a slip of paper on which she had written names and tentative dates with question marks. "Marriage licenses and death certificates."

"Just these?" the woman said, scrutinizing the list. "They wouldn't all be in that room anyway—too old." She looked up hopefully. "Maybe I can find them—I owe Quinn big-time. Will you put in a good word for me?"

"Sure," Diane answered, "no sweat."

"Listen, honey, could you come back tomorrow? Give me 'til almost five. Say quarter to?"

"That'll be fine," Diane said. "See you then, huh?"

"Go ahead and buzz yourself out," the woman answered, nodding toward the gate.

Diane and Warren left, to return eagerly at four forty-five on the following day.

"Hi," Diane said, approaching the counter.

"Honey, this took my whole lunch break and then some," the woman said bitterly, holding out a folder. "You'll have to look at them here, though—I can't let them go. They'd string me up."

"I understand," Diane replied, opening the folder.

While she looked through the documents, the woman regarded her, then leaned her elbows on the counter. Slowly she removed her glasses and put one earpiece in the corner of her mouth.

Warren frowned when he saw Ludmilla's marriage license to McMonigle. "No good," he said. "It lists his old address in Douglas County. And if Ludmilla's not in the telephone book, she certainly doesn't live there any more."

"Honey," the woman said suddenly, half in a whisper, "do people ever tell you what a sweet face you have?"

Diane looked up from the folder, startled by the woman's comment. "Me? No," she said. "Why?"

The woman laughed quietly, then removed the earpiece of her glasses from her mouth and put them back on. "Oh, just curious."

Diane swallowed and her face reddened as she went back to looking at the papers. After a moment she said aloud, "I'll just have to visit those McMonigles and ask them."

"Huh?" the woman asked dumbly, pulling her glasses down her nose again.

"Oh, nothing." Diane mumbled, and closed the folder. "Can I make photostats of these? Then I won't have to write this all down."

"All that stuff?" the woman asked, casting a furtive glance behind her. "Gee, honey, I don't know—"

"Listen," Diane said, "I'll give you a dollar for it."

The woman looked her in the eyes then sighed heavily and held out her hand. "Naw, that's OK. Here, I'll do it," she said, taking the folder. She went into a room behind the counter, and in a few minutes she returned with copies, haphazardly stapled together. "Here's your copies," she said handing them over.

"Thanks a zillion," answered Diane. She folded the papers on the counter, pausing to feel their slickness and sniff the chemical smell, then stuffed them into her pack. "Bye!"

"Hey, honey—make sure you tell Miss Forsythe you got those," the woman called behind her.

"I will," Diane answered as she walked away.

"Honey," Warren whispered. He paced beside Diane as she hurried down the hall. After a while he said, "you realize she liked you, don't you?"

"I don't even want to hear about it," she answered coldly.

"At least Quinn keeps her opinion of your sweet face to herself, even if her eyes do rove . . ."

"Come off it Warren . . ."

He chuckled and changed the subject. "Why don't we stop at the corner store for a little amusement on the way home?"

Diane was agreeable to that. "As long as you're good."

"I'll be good."

"OK then . . ."

Once outside, she glanced through the papers. At least they had something more than they had before. "Shall we visit Mr. McMonigle?" she asked while folding them again.

"That sounds like a good plan," Warren answered. "Maybe the gent will tell you something if you wiggle your boobs at him in person."

She grinned. "Not a bad idea. Want to try it?"

"Absolutely."

When she got home, Diane unfolded the papers and looked them over with more care while she munched on a candy bar. "Weird," she said with her mouth full. "Jarmsford's death certificate."

"What does it say?"

"Under his cause of death. Suicide. Poisoning."

Warren whistled. "Doesn't sound like Jarmsford to me. He wasn't the suicidal type."

"Maybe it wasn't suicide," Diane said. "Let's check the papers tomorrow."

The next afternoon, they found a brief article in the paper dated two days after Jarmsford's death.

"Listen to this," Diane said. "I'm paraphrasing. The sheriff's investigation concluded that he committed suicide by poisoning because of evidence found at the scene of death. No note was found with the body."

"That's interesting," Warren replied thoughtfully. "No note . . ."

[19]

"Now," Diane said after she finished her homework and daily chores. "What about the sixties?" She sat on her bed in a thin nightgown, but thought she would rather have been wearing nothing.

Warren took his seat in the air. "Just one story tonight, all right?"

"All right, just one."

"Once upon a time, just after Adrienne moved out in 1959, some students moved in—at least they called themselves students, but I don't think they went to college. They were forerunners of the people they called 'hippies' a few years later, but they were primarily interested in jazz and communist philosophy, and free love and that sort of thing. Two of them were men, and one was a woman, who was a painter. Her paintings were bad—mostly abstract kinds of things that looked like bird droppings to me, but she had a few friends who used to come over and look at them, expounding all kinds of hilarious mush about them. She always wore red, and nearly her whole wardrobe was red. She had very thin lips and rather sharp features. I only mention this because in a way she was quite striking. Her hair was very fine, and jet-black, and she cut it short, and trimmed very evenly. The two men had beards, and were nothing much to look at. They slept until noon practically every day, and played piano and double bass the rest of the day. One of them called himself a poet and he used to read quite awful poetry—a lot of which he wrote to go with her paintings. The woman also fancied herself a spirit-medium and that's how she made most of her money, but she was a complete fraud."

"You ought to know," Diane interjected.

"Well, she couldn't see me, which is a pretty good indication. And as far as I could tell, she never conjured any kind of spirit with her Ouija board and palm-readings either. But she held seances fairly regularly, and managed to earn a few dollars pretending she saw the ghosts of dead cats and that sort of thing."

"What was her name?"

"The woman was called Jocelyn. The two men were Horace and Teddy."

Diane giggled. "Like rough riders?"

"Hardly as respectable as Teddy Roosevelt," returned Warren. "Now, Horace and Teddy didn't work very regularly, but they seemed to play jazz at some place or another, and usually had enough to cover the rent. She kicked in her few dollars and acted like she could barely manage that."

"Was she a rich heiress or something?"

"No. She had another business on the side."

"She was a hooker!"

"Not exactly, but she did used to discreetly run what she called 'virility therapy' sessions for men—privately, of course—which consisted mostly, but not entirely, of sex. That's why I say she wasn't really a prostitute, because it was nominally therapeutic in nature. She did seminars for women too, along similar lines, but in groups."

"What did she do for women?"

"She spent lots of time with breathing exercises and massage, while spouting all kinds of laughable mysticism. For women who became regulars and attended her seminars in series, she also taught intimate massage, and made them practice on each other. They paid ridiculous sums for this stuff, too."

"Did it work?"

"Actually, for some, I think it did, to an extent. It was aimed ultimately at sexual fulfillment, you understand."

"Of course," Diane said.

"I knew you'd like that part. Jocelyn had women coming here who never, or hardly ever, had orgasms. And by the time she finished a full course on them, they did pretty well. It was highly stimulating, as you can imagine."

"I'm sure you watched every night, huh?"

"Absolutely—they were often held in the early afternoon as well. Most of her customers were women in their late thirties or forties who were trying to re-capture their youthful beauty."

"Ugly ones?"

"No," said Warren thoughtfully. "You mustn't think because she's thirty or forty or fifty that a woman is necessarily over the hill. Look at your mother, for instance, who is quite prettier to your father—and to me, for that matter—than she thinks she is. I frequently think that women's vanity is astonishingly over-developed. They think they're losing their beauty long before they really do, especially in the eyes of men who love them, which is where it matters most. A woman your mother's age, to a mature man, isn't ugly just by virtue of her age—in fact, I'd say that's about the age when a woman is really at her most erotically developed and sensually mature."

"As long as she likes it, right?"

"And if she maintains her body well, and if she has a competent husband or lover. Jocelyn did well with all of them, and I was surprised any number of times by her results with these ladies."

"What was her curriculum like?"

"She was moderately clever about it, I thought, and she spent quite a bit of time reading and preparing for her seminars. It would take her months of these six-week seminars to break down her pupils' inhibitions through breathing and massage exercises. The classes weren't large, you see—about five or six at the most, and they lasted a couple of hours twice a week, so she had adequate time with each pupil. She would start new pupils in her beginning level, and as they progressed, she would divide them into two or three groups. One group were those that she lured along at a slow pace, until they would eventually trickle away when they got tired of paying for it. The second group seemed to have strong inhibitions but more potential, and she would work on them diligently. But the third group were her select few. She would take only two or three of them aside, and when she had a chance alone with them, tell them about the advanced seminars she conducted for her 'most gifted pupils' in which they fully explored the erotic spirit through intimate massage."

"Sounds like a crock."

"Mostly it was, but it was interesting."

"And sexy?"

"Definitely."

"Was she a Lesbian, too?"

"Not at all—but that's beside the point. I'll get to her in a minute," answered Warren with a smile. "She managed to produce results in these women, aimed at bettering their responses, and I'm sure they had more fulfilling sexual relations with their husbands for it. I think it was the only thing she did that produced any results. Her painting was abominable, and I couldn't see that most of her seminars did anything except help people relax a little bit. Anyone could do that."

"But wasn't that worth it for them?"

"I suppose it was, because they kept coming to see her. Meanwhile, to Teddy and Horace, she claimed she was poor as a church-mouse. Actually she was making tremendous sums through these virility seminars, but she kept it all hidden in a can, way back in the pantry."

"On the back porch?"

"Yes, you know where the lowest shelf is, and there's that funny little nook?"

Diane nodded.

"At that time, they had a couple of barrels in there, and she would squeeze her arm through to get at her can."

"You were telling me about her massage classes."

"In a hurry?" teased Warren.

"No."

"Good. Eventually her 'master classes' of course required complete nakedness and privacy. She would usually have an even number of pupils—two or four. They always held these classes in the front bedroom—"

"Where my parents sleep?"

"Yes. The door would always be locked to make them feel at ease, and she would have them strip and lie on tarpaulins, with towels and pillows for their heads. Then—frequently with some soft music playing on the gramophone—"

"We call it a stereo," interjected Diane.

"Well, the phonograph, then. It was monaural at that time, you know. So, after they had relaxed and breathed, they would begin massage, first with the back and the neck. Then they would proceed to the legs, then the breasts, and finally—"

"The cunt!"

"Clitoral and vaginal massage," insisted Warren.

"Clit rubbing? Sounds lezzie to me," she giggled.

"It frequently produced truly amazing orgasms—you can imagine this kind of thoroughly relaxing massage, all over their bodies and genitals, and it went on for a couple of hours. She would be quite effusive with her praise for the way they mastered their lessons—of course her intent, I think was to produce consistent orgasm. It not only made the pupils feel good, but eager to continue."

"I'm going to make you teach me later, you know."

"We'll see," said Warren.

Diane laughed, and told herself that seriously she would make him show her what Jocelyn did. "All right, what else did she do?"

"She did not tend the garden at all. It began falling apart and everything was dying. Eventually, the kind old man next door came over and offered to take care of it for her. She agreed to let him work on it, and—the only time I've ever seen her be generous—she offered him three dollars a week to look after it. He refused at first, and said he would do it for nothing, but she eventually made him take the money. So the whole time they lived here, he came over four times per week and did gardening. He especially took care of the—" Warren stopped, seeing Diane's expression. She sat smiling with her eyes closed.

"You don't want to hear about the garden."

Diane opened her eyes. "It's not that—I was just getting interested in Jocelyn."

"Very well. I said I'd get to her, didn't I?" Warren said. "She actually carried on a polyandrous relationship with Horace and Teddy."

"What's that?"

"Like a marriage with two husbands."

"OK, so she was balling them both?"

"Not together, though," Warren said. "She had the front room, but she almost never slept there unless she'd had a fight with both of her husbands. Usually, she slept with one or the other of them—Horace had the baby's room, and Teddy had Rat's room."

"Was there anyone else in the other bedroom?"

"No, it was empty. It was a storage room filled with a lot of the owner's junk, but he almost never came over to check on things—and kept it locked with a padlock. At any rate, Jocelyn would sleep with one or the other of her husbands every night—I don't know if she was legally married to either of them, I just always thought of them as her husbands, because she treated them that way."

"Did they stay long?"

"They were here for about three years, I think. And their ending was quite explosive."

"How so?"

"Well, the owner came by one evening—I have no idea why. Perhaps he received a complaint about them. He came over and knocked at the door. Horace was home, but not Teddy. And Jocelyn was with one of her advanced classes. The owner demanded to be shown the entire house, and there was a bit of a scene because Jocelyn wouldn't open the bedroom door until her class had put their clothing back on. When they finally emerged, and the landlord saw the floor, with its rolled-up tarpaulins and oil, it took him about ten seconds to figure out that they were having what he called an orgy."

"Of course it wasn't."

"Well, it was the next thing to it, I suppose, since there had been seven naked women, including Jocelyn, deep in their meditative massage session. So it happened that the owner evicted them. They were given less than a week to gather their things, and then they left."

"Just like that?"

"After that the house sat empty for a month or so, and then some other people moved in."

"What about them?"

"They weren't very interesting," Warren said. "But—I think it's time for you to go to sleep."

"Not until you show me Jocelyn's techniques," said Diane, and began to remove her nightgown. She was already feeling wet and sexy, and would have played herself to sleep anyway.

"Let's do this tomorrow," suggested Warren.

"No, tonight," Diane said. "Do I need oil—you said she used oil."

"Do you have any?"

"In the bathroom," Diane said. "Baby oil." She jumped up, and tossed her nightgown back on, then went quietly downstairs, only to return in a few minutes with a bottle of baby oil and a glass of wine.

"I hope your mother doesn't mark her bottle," Warren said when he saw the wine.

"She doesn't," Diane answered confidently, then locked the door and threw off her nightgown again. While Warren told her a little more about Jocelyn's techniques, trying to remember all of the phrases and terms Jocelyn had used, she drank her wine somewhat quickly.

Warren apologized for not being able to actually demonstrate, but he sat near Diane's head while she lay prone on the bed, and he described in detail as much as he could remember of Jocelyn's advanced techniques. Diane attempted to massage herself, following his instructions. First she did her neck and legs, then her breasts and belly. She put a towel beneath her ass, in case she dripped oil, then squeezed a small amount into the hair at the peak of her pubic mound where the cleft began.

"You must take it very slowly," Warren said. "You can't rush it, or you won't get the same effect. If you rush, well, you might as well just rub yourself now and go to sleep."

"I'll do it slow," Diane answered. "Like this?" She began with her inner thighs, and lightly oiled fingers, progressing in tiny motions toward her labia, then up to the top of the cleft and downward again.

"Squeeze the lips very gently," he suggested, "and let your fingertips glide ever so lightly along their length. Yes, like that."

Diane proceeded, and he began to hum for her. "They always did it with music," he explained.

"How about if I put on a tape?"

"That might be good," said Warren.

Diane reached over to her night-stand and pushed the button on her portable cassette player with her least oily finger. A tape of Carole King started up in the middle of a song, and she turned the volume down, then lay back and adjusted the towel beneath her. After a while, she whispered, "How am I doing?"

Warren could see the great expanse of her aura, and he could tell she was getting close to giving herself an orgasm. "Very well," he said.

"It feels good."

"It's supposed to. Is it relaxing?"

"Yeah," she whispered. Her breathing had quickened, and forgetting herself began working mostly with her middle finger, circling her clitoris.

"Don't neglect the lips," he said, leaning over her face. "And you can use all of your fingers."

"OK," she said, then after a pause, "Warren?"

"Yes?"

"Will you do me a favor?"

"What?"

"Pretend you're making love to me?"

Warren came to sit beside her, and with a smile began slowly to take off his clothes. She let out a squeak when he pulled off his bow tie, surprised that he could remove it, but said nothing. He undid his buttons while they gazed at each other, and as he removed each piece of clothing, he simply hung it in the air beside the bed. When he had removed everything, he came to lie over the top of her, letting himself partially pass into her skin.

Seeing the small wound in his chest, Diane let out a soft exclamation and reached out with trembling fingers toward him. "Is this where the bullet—?"

"Yes."

"Did it hurt—very much?"

"Only briefly . . ." He smiled, his face close to hers. "Close your eyes," he whispered, and when she did, he filled her ears with faint words of love carried on wisps of ghostly breath. Delight and warmth settled around her, and she breathed slowly, touching herself.

"And press with your hands—harder," he said, finally.

Diane complied, increasing her pace and lifting her legs, bending her knees around him. Warren nestled between her thighs, sinking through her, and though she could not feel him actually, she tried to imagine that she could, that he was flesh against her. Her hands became his, decoupled from her body as if he controlled them, as if all her fingers, all the caresses emanated from him. He was everywhere, inside her, pressed against her warm cunt.

As she climbed, beautiful and serene, toward release, Warren lay over and within her, watching her face and her expanding aura through half-closed eyes, breathing and whispering close to her ears.

"You're a lovely woman, Diane. I really *want* to make love with you."

"You are," she said, beginning to undulate more quickly. "You're inside me, around me . . ."

"Yes," he whispered, wishing it were so. "I am, and you're beautiful, Diane. You're the best friend I've ever had."

"Oh, God," she gasped, desperately wanting to kiss him. "Warren . . ." She let herself arch back slightly, exposing her neck. "Warren . . ."

"I'm going to make you come now," he whispered in her ear. "Diane. Just a little more. You're ravishing. Diane . . ."

"Oh, please," she whimpered, and there were tears in her eyes. "Love me Warren . . ."

"Slide your finger in," he said, "and push harder. Now really hard, with your thumb and fingers . . . Push harder—it's me, there inside you, filling you. Moving forward and back . . ."

She closed her legs slowly around her hand, two fingers plunged into herself; then three. The sting of their immensity and the pleasure of their movement mingled into a clear wash, her eyes blurred with tears and ecstasy. Quietly after a few minutes, she turned on her side, curling up. Warren sat near her shoulders, merging himself into her body.

Opening her eyes, she managed a trembling, "Thank you."

"Get under the covers," he suggested. "You'll catch cold."

With sleepy eyes she smiled at him and slipped her feet under the covers, almost without enough strength in her arms to pull them over herself. "Thanks, Warren."

"Good-night, my dear one."

She closed her eyes, and until he was sure she slept, Warren sat beside her, stroking the air, and wishing he could touch her.

"You're going to be a sensation," he whispered, and tiptoed away. In the middle of the floor, he turned back to look at her again, sleeping so peacefully. The light was still on, and he regretted that he could not turn it off for her. He remembered to pluck his clothing from the air, and with a last smile, descended through the floor.

[20]

Diane's lovemaking with Warren, though satisfying in many ways, was not enough for her. She was sore the morning after their first experience together, and thereby knew that they had come as close as they could to actual coupling. But since he could never touch her, it left her yet with an unfulfilled feeling. She compensated, at first, by engaging in it frequently with him. It was always excessively pleasurable, and she had orgasms so intense they re-appeared in her dreams. She began to dream of his body against her and how powerfully he could take her into his arms, how deeply he could thrust into her; how his tongue would feel against her. Every night became a whirlwind of romantic and passionate encounters with him in her dreams.

But at last one evening after they had made incorporeal love, and after two weeks of frequent encounters, Warren sat with her on her bed and suggested that they should stop.

"We can't continue this," he said. "I don't think it's good for you. What are you going to do if I go away?"

"Go away?" It had never occurred to her that he might leave. "You can't go away. How can you?"

"I don't know," he answered. "But what if I did? Look, I know we love each other, but you have life ahead of you—I'm already dead, Diane. I just can't give you the kind of whole relationship you'll need. Besides you're so young—it would be ridiculous anyway."

"Why, because you're old enough to be my grandfather? Warren—I don't care about that. Can't we do something?"

"Like what?" he asked. "You said yourself I'm a fucking ghost—and now I really am a fucking ghost—"

Diane laughed. "You are, aren't you?" She frowned and twisted a strand of hair on her finger. "Warren—maybe you're right . . . I have to face it, huh? I ought to grow up, right?"

"Not too quickly—"

"It's just—I know we've been over this a hundred times."

"I'll help you find a new boyfriend," he said.

"But—it's not just that anymore. When he pops my cherry for real, I want you to be with me, OK?"

Warren smiled, thinking there could be little difference between the sexual relations they had been having and what she might have with a living man, if he considered the way she used her hands. "All right, we'll see," he conceded.

Diane slept fitfully, worrying, and with a little ache in her heart. But there might be just the right guy—Warren would find someone for her. And if Warren chose him, he would be perfect, and maybe she would not care, then, that it was not Warren himself. He would be there, too. And if he was, it would be even better.

She began taking Warren to school every day, but it was well into April before he made his first suggestion.

"Peter," he said to her one evening.

"Peter? You mean Peter Traverson?"

Warren nodded.

"Why him?" Diane asked.

"Don't you like him?"

"He's cute—yeah, I like him, but—isn't he a bit introverted?"

"He's shy, but that's not why I think he'd be good for you."

"Why do you think so?"

"He has the right name," Warren said flatly, enigmatically.

For a moment, Diane looked at him in puzzlement. "Huh? Like shit," she laughed. "Why really?"

"He absolutely adores you—idolizes you. In your creative writing class the other day for example, when Mr. Jackson read your sonnet, he was absolutely enraptured for the rest of the period. I'll bet he even thinks about you when he masturbates."

"Right, Warren . . ."

"Give him a try."

"I'll have to wait for a good chance, though. I can't just walk up to him and say, 'hey Peter, want to pop my cherry?'"

"I guess you can't, can you? Well, when you get ready—and after you turn sixteen."

"Which is in a couple of months remember—"

"Give him a try. I think you'll have a splendid relationship." Warren did not go on to expound on the short-lived nature of love at Diane's age, but when any chance arose after that, he talked to her about Peter to keep the possibility fresh in her mind. He also kept a sharp watch for other candidates, but nobody else captured his imagination right away.

[21]

With less enthusiasm than it began, Diane's pursuit of information pertinent to Warren continued. After she obtained her handful of records from the courthouse, she put them aside. She did not forget about them completely, but neither did she get around to calling either of the McMonigles again. Though she and Warren frequently went to the newspaper archives, she only half-heartedly looked for articles and announcements relevant to Priscilla and Ludmilla. She had some misgivings about the task—wondering whether she really needed to find out what happened to them; how that related to Warren—and while she mulled those problems over in the back of her mind, there was much else to occupy her in the papers, including the fascinating pageant of history. Warren, though he wanted to pursue things more diligently, was careful to first consider Diane's desires, and never suggested that she read anything particular. It was her life, after all, and being dead he had plenty of time. If he had learned one thing in death, he believed it was patience. Besides, he enjoyed watching Diane's blossoming fascination with local history, the way her eyes would light, and on the trail of some minor fact, she would flip through the pages in hot pursuit. It was a pity that at the moment her research was so aimless. But he believed that whatever she learned, even if disconnected, would give her a strong foundation for the next year's history course, when she would be required to do precisely the sort of ferreting research she was doing now, if more directed.

One afternoon, while perfunctorily going over newspapers from 1923, Diane's eyes stopped on a small article dated four days after the date on Priscilla's death certificate, and at once her heart leapt.

It seemed odd that she had missed the article, since she thought she had read through that year rather carefully. It was concerned with medical practice in the valley, rather than Priscilla, which may have been why she missed it, but it made passing mention of both her and the Jarmsfords. It was his name which stopped her eye. A couple of sentences so shocked her that she paused for a moment to absorb them before turning to Warren, who was reading another paper.

"What happened the day Priscilla left home?" she asked.

"Why?"

She pointed to the relevant part of the article, and he glanced over it.

"Fell out a window?" he exclaimed incredulously. "How could she fall out of a window?"

"Suspicious, isn't it?"

"I never heard anything of how she died. What was on her death certificate?"

"Didn't I show it to you? Internal hemorrhage."

A cold, distressed look came into Warren's eyes as he realized what must have happened. "Probably wounds suffered—she must have died in pain!"

Slowly he took a seat, hovering cross-legged over the table in front of Diane, and began to rub his temples methodically.

"She left suddenly that afternoon," he said, leaning back and propping his legs in the air. "A telephone call came, from Ludmilla, I presume, and they exchanged a few words—she mostly made affirmative noises, then hung up. She hurried upstairs where she packed a valise with an extra dress and some undergarments. The next thing I knew, she was walking out the front door. I remember it concerned me a bit at the time—the look on her face was troubled, and I worried about it for the rest of the day. I thought she must have rushed off because Ludmilla was taken ill or something. Of course much later, I felt devastated . . ."

"But if Ludmilla was ill," Diane asked, "how does that relate to Priscilla falling out a window?"

"They lived in a two storey house," he explained. "Maybe she was hanging laundry or something?"

"From where? Did they have a balcony?"

"Actually, they didn't."

Diane felt a rising indignation, as if someone had just taken advantage of her and been discovered. But it was not that; it seemed simply that Priscilla's death required a little more explanation. Her interest in the matter was rekindled. "I'm going to call McMonigle back," she concluded. "The guy I called before?"

"I remember," said Warren softly.

"Well, I think he knows Ludmilla. We've got to find her, now."

"Why?"

"Because Priscilla fell out a window, dammit—don't you want to know what happened?"

Inwardly Warren cheered that she had found something to latch onto, something to stir her, and was becoming interested again. He answered calmly, "Of course I want to know."

"Well, come on." She grabbed her pack and quickly put away the stack of papers she had taken out.

Nobody was home when she phoned McMonigle in the afternoon. She tried again later, and still got no answer. At eight-thirty in the evening, after she finished her homework, she tried again. After a few rings, the same man answered the phone.

Diane introduced herself and asked for Ludmilla.

"You the girl who called here a while ago?"

"Yes," she admitted.

"And what'd I tell you last time?"

"Find her myself."

"Well?" he asked, and waited for an answer.

Diane hung up. "I'm going go see that jerk," she said. She jotted the address listed in the phonebook onto a scrap of paper, then bolted up the stairs to her room where she stuffed Warren's thermos into her pack and checked a map of town to locate the street. She descended two steps at a time a few minutes later.

"Hey Mom!" she yelled into the living room. "I gotta pick up a book at Janet's place. I'll be back in an hour."

"What?" Nancy yelled back.

Diane sighed and stuck her head into the living room. "A book at Janet's. Yes, I'll be careful. And yes, my headlight works. Bye."

"If you're not back in an hour I'll call the police!" Nancy yelled after her.

"I'll be back, Mom!" she answered, rolling her eyes for Warren, who grinned and followed her out the door.

McMonigle lived far enough away that it took her over twenty minutes to ride there at top speed, including time for a wrong turn. The house was a small one-storey affair, typical for its neighborhood, with a living room that had a large picture window facing the yard. The lawn and garden, behind a white picket fence, were well-tended and a path of flagstones led to the door, situated atop a small concrete porch. She pushed the doorbell.

In a moment, the door was answered by a tall, middle aged man in wool slacks. He wore a dark, oversized sweater and looked to be in his mid-fifties, with deepset blue eyes. He had a full head of gray hair swept back neatly with Bryl Creem or something.

"Doesn't he know a little dab'll do ya?" Warren said when he saw the man.

Diane bit her lip to keep from laughing.

"Yes?" the man asked gruffly through the screen door.

"Mr. McMonigle?"

He recognized her voice immediately. "Now why the hell did you come here?" he asked, standing slack-jawed.

"I have to talk to you," Diane replied. "Can I come in?"

"Ah, hell," Mr. McMonigle said. "I guess."

He held open the screen door and Diane stepped into the entry hall. The living room had several large chairs with white doilies on the arms. A glass-topped coffee table sat in the center, and in two corners were tall floor lamps with yellowing shades. Diane stood looking about the room.

"What did you want?" he asked, closing the door behind her.

"I'm looking for Ludmilla McMonigle," she said. "I couldn't help but think you know who I mean."

"Tell him her first husband's name," Warren urged.

"You might also know her as Ludmilla Jarmsford—that was her first husband's name," she said, looking directly into Mr. McMonigle's eyes.

"Yeah," said Mr. McMonigle. "That's her. Why?"

"Have you ever heard of anyone named—Warren Brannigan?" she asked.

"Warren Brannigan," he said, so smoothly that Diane felt immediately that he had said the name before. "That's kind of familiar."

"How about Priscilla—what was her maiden name . . . ?"

"Canfield," Warren said in her ear.

"Priscilla Canfield? Priscilla Brannigan?" Diane intoned tentatively.

"Aunt Priscilla," said Mr. McMonigle simply, then with an air of defeat added, "Go on, have a seat." He pointed to the nearest of the large chairs, and when she sat, he took the chair opposite her. "What do you want to know about 'em?"

"Ludmilla's still alive?" she asked.

"She is."

"Can you tell me where she lives?"

"I could."

"But you don't want to?"

Mr. McMonigle seemed to be thinking, and withheld an answer. Warren sat on the arm of the chair near Diane's elbow. "Ask him about Priscilla's death."

Diane frowned at Warren by way of saying that she would get around to that, then turned back to Mr. McMonigle. "Warren Brannigan is—was—a relative of mine," she said. "I'm tracing the family, and I just wanted to ask a few questions if Ludmilla is still alive."

"Is that all?"

"Ask him about—"

"And what happened to Priscilla," she said, then paused before adding, "I heard that Priscilla fell out of a window."

Mr. McMonigle blanched and looked at the floor.

"I think that's suspicious," Diane continued in a whisper.

"You're dredging up a lot of old muck," he said sourly.

"Just—please, Mr. McMonigle—tell me where Ludmilla is and I'll leave you alone."

"Ask him if he's Josh McMonigle's boy," urged Warren.

"Are you the son of Josh McMonigle?"

Mr. McMonigle stared at her. "I am."

Warren spoke to Diane again, and she relayed his message. "You must have been ten or twelve when Ludmilla married your father." That was purely Warren's guess.

"I was eight," Mr. McMonigle corrected.

"What happened to Doc Jarmsford?" she asked.

"My God, little lady, you know an awful lot already, don't you?"

"I try," Diane answered. "Who poisoned him?"

As if punched, Mr. McMonigle let out his breath all at once. "What are you going to do when you find Ludmilla?"

"I'm going to ask her about Warren Brannigan, my relative," she said sincerely. "Then I'm going to leave you both in peace."

He looked at her closely, and made a couple of noises over the course of a minute or more. "Ah hell, you'd find out if you dug hard enough anyway," he finally said. "Want some tea?"

"I have to be home in half an hour," she said, stressing the time, "no thanks."

"All right, I'll tell you what I know. Where shall I start?"

"How about at the beginning?" Warren suggested to Diane, who relayed the sentence verbatim.

"As near as I can tell," Mr. McMonigle began, "there was never any proof of anything, but there was talk around. It died away pretty gradually, but it kind of followed the family, if you know what I mean."

"Uh huh." Diane wished she had taken his cup of tea, and interrupted him. "Maybe I will have some tea, after all."

"Good," he replied, making an attempt to smile graciously. "I could do with some too. Come on into the kitchen."

"I think he's all right," Warren said as she stood up. "He's not going to rape you or anything."

"Thanks," she murmured over her shoulder. "I'm glad I brought you along!"

"What?" called Mr. McMonigle as he flipped on the kitchen light.

"I was just asking if you live here alone," she said.

"Just me," he replied, putting on the kettle. "My wife passed away a couple years ago." He turned on the stove just as Diane arrived at the kitchen door. "This won't take long; water's already warm. Sit down." He pulled out a chair from under the table and Diane sat in it, with her hands in her lap.

"My mother died when we were pretty young," Mr. McMonigle said, still standing to keep watch over the kettle.

"How old were you?"

"About seven. Mrs. Jarmsford—that's what we called her then— used to be pretty friendly with us. She knew my mother pretty well, and they got on nicely, from what I heard. It was after that she came more often. We'd just lost our mother and all, so she used to come over sometimes and bring us a cake or an apple pie or something like that. We always looked forward to those, too, 'cause she was a fine cook."

"I told you, didn't I," Warren interjected. He had taken a seat in the middle of the kitchen table, purposely putting his boots upon the sugar bowl.

"What we didn't know then, and later we found out, was that Ludmilla and my father—that's Joshua McMonigle—had kind of a fling even before they were married. I guess it would have been more of a scandal then than nowadays, the way those hippies run around. But anyway, we didn't know anything about it, that was all later talk."

The kettle began to gurgle, and he put his hand down on top

of it to speed it along. "Anyway, what I heard was this. Jarmsford found out that she'd been, well, fornicating with my father."

"It's called adultery," Diane said automatically. "She was married."

"Smart girl," he laughed. "Adultery, then. The rumor was that Doc Jarmsford didn't poison himself, but it was really my father who did the deed. I guess the sheriff would know, if anyone did, because he and Pop were pretty close. They used to play cards once in a while, and they went to school together when they were boys. In any case, I don't think there was much of an investigation, and their secret died with 'em."

"What happened later?"

"Well, after that, Ludmilla and Pop got married, and it wasn't six months later they had a little one. That caused another big stir I imagine, but I was too young to know it takes nine months to cook up a baby, and I never heard about it 'til later."

Diane asked a few more questions while the water came to a boil, and thanked Mr. McMonigle when he finally poured her tea into a pink floral cup.

"That's one of Ludmilla's tea-cups, too," he said pushing it in front of her. "She gave a whole set to the Missus."

Diane smiled and thanked him for the tea.

"Anyway, you asked about Priscilla, too, didn't you?" he went on. "This part is all just what I heard, 'cause she died before Ludmilla came into my life. The story goes that Ludmilla and her husband—Doc Jarmsford—had a blissful marriage for ten years or so, but it kind of fell to pieces. And the bone of contention between them was that they couldn't have babies. She wanted to adopt one, and he was dead set against it. He wanted his own son and heir, and used to rail against her 'cause she never had any children. He used to scold her for being barren."

"I think it was him, don't you?"

"Of course it was, if it was anyone," Mr. McMonigle agreed. "Seeing as how Ludmilla—we never called her mother, by the way, always Ludmilla, so you'll excuse me if it sounds disrespectful."

"Not at all," Diane said.

"Anyway, the story goes that Ludmilla called her sister on the telephone in the middle of one of their fights, and when she came over, she tried to break 'em up and make 'em see some sense. Jarmsford had been drinking something awful that night—a thing he never did much of when they were younger, they say. And somehow, in all this, Priscilla fell out the window. Some folks said even then that he pushed her—murdered her for coming between him and his wife. Ludmilla always swore up and down that he never pushed Priscilla, and that's the story she gave to the sheriff. There weren't any other witnesses, and everything kind of dropped after that."

"That's enough," Diane said. She sipped a little of her tea, but felt she should get home as soon as she could without seeming too impolite. "Mr. McMonigle, I'm terribly sorry, but I really have to get home," she said. "Can I come to see you again sometime?"

"Why not," he said. "Hell, I feel better talking about it anyway. Ludmilla's a cranky old thing, and we haven't gotten on together for years. I'm the only one left around here, and she's getting so old she just can't take care of herself anymore. But it's a chore, because—well, just say we don't get along."

Warren grunted, but said nothing.

"Would you mind if I went to speak with Ludmilla?" Diane asked.

"I don't guess so." He went to rummage in a drawer for a pencil and paper. "She's in Cashmere, now." He jotted a phone number and an address on a slip of note paper, then handed it to Diane, who read it and looked up suddenly.

"Ludmilla's in a nursing home?"

"Like I said," Mr. McMonigle replied. "She can't really take care of herself these days. Mostly she's not too senile, though. If you catch her on a good day, she can usually remember who you are."

"Thank you," Diane said, feeling suddenly that she did not, after all, want to see Ludmilla. Especially not if Ludmilla were senile. She apologized for leaving her tea, and Mr. McMonigle showed her out.

"That's that," Warren said as they went out the front door. "She's going to be incoherent and we'll never find out anything."

"Maybe not," Diane said, trying to sound more hopeful than she felt.

It was ten-fifteen when they arrived home, and Diane listened half-heartedly to her mother tell her that she should have called if she was going to be that late, and then give her a lecture on how dangerous it is for young girls to be out alone at night.

"Next time I'll call, OK Mom?" she said.

"All right," Nancy said, letting out a laugh and tousling Diane's hair. "Hey—I know you're a big girl, but even big girls can get into trouble at night."

"I'll be more careful."

"Good-night." Nancy kissed her daughter on the cheek and let her go upstairs to bed.

[22]

"The house stood empty half the winter," Warren was saying. Diane had finished changing into a nightgown and pulled the covers over herself while he settled down next to the bed. "There was a good snowfall that year, and nobody bothered to come and shovel snow from the roof. I was beginning to worry about it a little, because at night I could hear the roof creaking more than usual."

"OK," Diane answered. Thinking of winter, she pulled the blanket up around her closer and smiled at Warren. "Can we get to the good part?"

"This is the good part," he said. "Just wait. Anyway, it was March, I remember, and things were beginning to thaw. It started to snow early in the morning, but by the time the sun came up, it got warmer and began to rain. The street turned to slush, and a lot of the snow started to slide from the edges of the roof. About evening there was a rattle in the keyhole of the front door, and I went down to take a look. What do you think I saw?"

"I don't know," said Diane. "Robbers?"

"Even better," Warren replied. "There was a young couple at the front door. The woman was a tiny oriental thing, but she had huge gorgeous eyes. Between them they had one raincoat, and the man—who had the longest hair I had ever seen on a man until that day—had his arm around her. He wore the raincoat while she huddled inside beneath his arm. 'Isn't it great?' the woman was saying when I got there. 'It would be if I could get the door open,' he said. Something like that. In another minute, they had the door open, and they both tumbled through, dripping water all over the entry hall."

"What were their names?"

"You always want to know their names first thing, don't you?" teased Warren.

"It makes it easier to listen."

"Very well. But I didn't know their names until later. Everyone called her Orchid—that was her nickname. The man's name was Dan."

"Dan and Orchid."

"Yes. So they came in, and she just stood there looking back into the dark house, with a very large smile on her face. It was heartening to watch, because her aura was huge, and I could tell she really loved it—she had a wide mouth, too, and big teeth to fill it, so you really knew when she was smiling. He closed the door and then fumbled around for the light switch."

"It isn't in a very obvious place," Diane commented.

"Right. So it took him a minute, but when he turned on the light, she burst out with an exclamation of pure joy. 'I'll take it!' Dan laughed, and came up behind her to put his arms around her. He said 'don't you want to see the whole thing first?' and she said, 'Oh, yeah, but . . .' Then she turned around and kissed him. He was much taller than she, and even when she stood on tiptoes, he had to practically bend down to kiss her she was so tiny. That warmed my heart, as I'm sure you can imagine."

"After such a long, boring, winter, right?"

"Yes. I knew that evening spring had finally arrived," Warren said. "Now, they didn't just kiss and then go look at the house. They had a long kissing session—I could tell they were new lovers, and I guessed they had decided to move in together—which was being done rather frequently at that time. Later on, I found that the landlord had given them the key to come and see it that evening, because they had answered an advertisement in the paper. Eventually, Dan had to pull himself away, and unwrap her arms from around his neck. 'Hey,' he said, in a very lover-like way, 'let's take a look around.' She nodded just like a little girl, and together— holding hands the whole time like babes in the woods—they went to look at everything. The only place they didn't really look was the attic. She adored the bathroom, because of the bathtub. It seemed that she had never seen such a deep tub, and she jumped right into it."

"Huh?" Diane asked. "Our bathtub isn't big."

"The whole place was renovated in '71," said Warren. "Before that, there was a big, old, cast-iron bathtub. You've probably seen them—with claws on the feet, holding little balls?"

"Oh yeah," she said, smiling and putting her hands under her cheek. "We used to have one of those when I was really little."

"So you know what I mean. Anyway, she said, 'Won't it be fun?' Dan stepped into the bathtub right behind her, and they sat there for a while, sighing. He had his arms around her, sitting behind her, and started to feel her breasts with his hands under her shirt. I think they could hardly wait to get the place."

"Did they?"

"Well, of course they did, or I wouldn't have started this story," Warren replied. "Would you want to hear about it if I only saw them once?"

"No," she admitted.

"I rest my case. Anyway, a few days later, they came with their Studebaker—they had an old Studebaker that was painted with big pink and yellow flowers, with peace-signs on the front doors. On top, they had a green light—sometimes I've seen them drive off with the green light flashing."

"Kind of like a cop car?"

"They called themselves the Peace Patrol. Anyway, they moved in and brought all their things in a U-Haul trailer—I think that was the first time I'd ever seen a U-Haul trailer, come to think of it. A couple of friends came over to help them move in. They all unloaded boxes, and then their friends left after a big Chinese dinner that they ordered. Well, no sooner had they left, than Orchid piped up and said 'Let's take a bath.'"

"They screwed in the bathtub!" Diane exclaimed.

"Do you want to tell the story?"

"OK," she said, then impatiently, "It just takes too long."

"All right, I'll hurry. Before they took a bath, though, they did something I had never seen before."

"What?"

"They sat down on the floor in the living room, right in the middle of all the boxes. From one box, Dan took out a bag filled with green clumpy weeds, and then they stuffed it into a hookah—I'd seen hookahs before, but this was quite a nice one. So he put some of this weed—"

"Marijuana, right?"

"Yes, it was. At that time, I had no idea what it was, because I'd never seen it before, but I guessed after while."

"So they smoked some dope, and then what?"

"Impatient aren't you? Later they moved out. The End," Warren said flatly. "Good night."

"Hey, wait a minute!" Diane jumped out of bed to follow him across the floor.

Turning, Warren laughed and sat back down in the air. "Are you going to let me tell it my way?"

"All right," she said, getting back into bed.

"They sat and smoked the hookah together, and started talking. In a few minutes, they were giggling and saying completely nonsensical things to each other. They sat right across from each other, spouting the most ridiculous nonsense and staring into each other's eyes with huge grins on their faces. Then Dan touched her face, and said, 'bath time!' So they giggled up the stairs and started drawing the bath water. They undressed each other quite slowly, kissing and fondling. He stood her up and kissed all down her shoulders and breasts, taking off her shirt—she never wore a brassiere that I saw. I think she had a couple in all of her stuff, but she never wore one. Then he got to her skirt, and slid it down. She had no undergarments beneath, and the most delightfully little hairless delta."

Diane laughed at his term for it. "Completely hairless?"

"Well, not completely," Warren confessed, "but the hair was very thin and straight, and only along the crack. He started kissing her belly, and running his hands along her legs, and of course—"

"Finger-banging her."

"Yes. He still had half of his clothes on, but they had taken so long, that the bathtub was full. They noticed something was wrong when their feet started to get wet. Their clothes on the floor were sopping wet, too. But they giggled their way into the bathtub and sat down. Of course water went everywhere, but they weren't too concerned about that."

"What about the floor? Didn't they care if it leaked?"

"I think that was the furthest thing from their minds," Warren said. "They weren't so much taking a bath as making love in the bath. They had put two big towels on top of the toilet, so those were safe. They knelt in the tub, rubbing each other and kissing. He had quite a large organ, too."

"How big?"

"About like this," Warren said, measuring the air with his fingers. "She began to suck him, but the water was so deep, she made him sit up on the side of the bathtub. I was afraid they would slip and crack their skulls. After a while, he stood her up against the wall, and fingered her from behind, rubbing soap into her breasts with the other hand. She loved it, and squirmed her bottom around. He pressed his organ up against the crack of her ass from behind, and rubbed it there, then spread her legs a little and let himself slide up in between, and—what are you doing?"

"Hmm," Diane answered, smiling at him with bright eyes. "Sounds like fun."

Warren smiled when her aura leapt outward, and he came to lie beside her on the bed. Her hand moved slowly beneath the sheets.

"So of course he went into her from behind while she leaned against the wall," he continued. "Then I really did think they would slip, because they were gyrating like a couple of animals. After a while he pulled out, and turned her around. She had soap all over her front, and he massaged her breasts. She wanted more, and put her hands down, fingering herself."

"Like me, huh?"

"Yes," he whispered. "Just like you . . ." Resuming his normal voice, he continued. "They rubbed themselves up with soap, and then he rinsed just his penis and went back into her again. I think they made love in that bathtub for two or three hours, and he came twice in that time."

"Twice? He must have been dying, huh?"

"I think it was the uh, the 'dope' they smoked. I've seen it a lot since then, too. Anyway, back to the story. They were quite a nice couple, but no sooner had they moved in, than things began to be quite lively around the house. Of course, I was thrilled, since the house had been empty, and I'd never had so many people living in the place at once."

"How many were there?"

"All told, there were about twelve people who actually more-or-less lived in the house. They had constant parties, and at first I wasn't too sure I really wanted all of those people. But after a while I got quite used to their ways, and even began to enjoy hearing Jefferson Airplane—"

"White Rabbit?"

"Yes, that album. Of course, I'd not heard anything of the sort before at all, and I think had I been alive I never could have been open-minded enough to listen to more than five seconds of it."

Diane laughed. "Like screeching noise, huh?"

"I would have described it that way, I think, but you know—it's quite interesting that I came to have much greater tolerance after I was dead. You could say I've had sixty years to see behind the domestic scenes, and learn the differences between what people really do in private and what they say in public. With some people there's quite a gulf."

Diane nodded thoughtfully. "But that's a digression. This is supposed to be a bed-time story."

"All right," he laughed. "Anyway, Orchid loved that record with such a passion. She would put it on so it repeated, and let it play half the night sometimes while they all smoked their hookahs and talked and made love in the corners."

"What about the other people in the house? Tell me about them."

"There was an Indian fellow they called Half-Moon who slept in the back bedroom. He had long hair that he braided, like an Indian brave, and he wore a lot of beaded things. He had a girlfriend, too, named Tamara—a white girl. The poor thing was in a terrible mess, too. She had long brown hair, and she dressed like an Indian squaw, and they had a few Indian friends. But she seemed to do nothing but drink and smoke marijuana. Half the day, Tamara would just sit around drawing. She drew with a black pen and would sit for hours making beautiful intricate designs. She had a great interest in Indian art, and she would draw little animals all chasing each other in borders around the paper. But when it came to getting her to stop smoking or drinking, she'd fly off the handle. Half-Moon was very kind to her, though, and I think it almost broke his heart to see her sadness. She was running from something—there was something wrong with her. Maybe she had a husband somewhere else, but it wasn't clear, because she never talked about it. Their lovemaking was sad to watch, too. I don't think she enjoyed it, but did it to please him. But most of the time, it didn't please him at all, because she wasn't lively."

"She just laid there, huh?"

"Positively passive as a lump of clay. They'd have fights when he tried to take her drugs away and try to get her to go out. He constantly wanted to take her places, but she just wanted to sit and brood. They'd fight about her drugs, and then she'd go stay somewhere else for a day or two, but she'd be back, eventually, crying at his feet. It was too sad, so I tried not to take too much interest in them."

"What about the others?"

"There was a negro—"

"Black," Diane interjected automatically.

"All right," he laughed, "a black woman named Elly, who was a dear. Her real name was Heloise, by the way, but they called her Elly. It was interesting to see the contrast between her and Tamara, living in the same house. Elly was a large woman—not heavy, but very tall, like a Watusi, and somewhat flat-chested. She wore African dresses and let her hair grow into a big ball like this." He briefly put his hands around his head in a circle. An afro you call it?"

Diane nodded.

"The wonderful thing about Elly was how incredibly happy she was. She smoked their marijuana with them, but it seemed the effect on her was to make her want to work in the garden. She spent a lot of time, there, hoeing and picking up rocks while she sang African songs. She was a marvelous singer, and she used to get people to help her outside sometimes, and she would teach them work songs. And later in the spring she grew vegetables. Most of the vegetables they ate in the summer were grown by Elly."

"Did she have a boyfriend?"

"She didn't, but . . ." He stopped reflectively for a moment.

"What?"

"She had a great fondness for Half-Moon, and they used to talk quite a bit. She was always trying to help him out with Tamara. Well, one thing led to another between them, and one time when Tamara had left and been gone for two nights, they ended up in bed together."

"How was she?"

"Elly? Well—I don't think she had slept with anyone for quite a long time, and she was magnificent to watch. They had been talking all evening, and Half-Moon was almost in tears. He was a sensitive man, and he'd cry every time Tamara left. Elly was comforting him, embracing him, and then he quieted down, and she kissed him. He returned her kiss, and almost instantly, she let herself loose. She was all over him like a boa constrictor, and it didn't take him long to return her affections. Finally he grabbed her hand, and she followed him quietly up the stairwell to the room he shared with Tamara. As soon as they closed the door, Half-Moon turned on the radio, and they fell upon each other. Elly rather took the lead, too, and stripped herself. She laid him down on the bed, kissing him all over, and rubbed her body against him. They started playing, and wrestling while they laughed. I think it's the most real fun I'd seen a couple have since Ludmilla and her husband. Well, Half-Moon finally wrestled her onto the bed—it was just a mattress on the floor, you understand—and covered her body with kisses and touches. She reached up to grab her own ankles, spreading herself open for him while he ate her and afterwards used both hands to rub herself."

Diane still had her hand in her panties, and had been quietly masturbating while Warren talked. "Like this," she said laughing, and threw off the covers to spread herself. "It's hard to grab your ankles like that though, isn't it?"

"Elly had no trouble," said Warren.

"Wait a minute." Diane spread her legs comfortably and slowly rubbed herself until she reached a faintly glowing orgasm, then curled up again with her pillow. Warren was smiling at her.

"I'm OK," she said.

"Can I continue then?"

"Yes," she peeped. She felt terribly sleepy and lay still with her pillow in her arms.

"So they had their wild night like that. The next day, Tamara didn't come back either, and Elly just stayed with Half-Moon. The day after that, though, early in the morning, Tamara came back and found them in bed together."

"What did she do then?"

"She opened the door and went in. It was dark yet, since they had heavy curtains on the windows. She sat on the mattress and started to get into bed, but she took a good look, and saw that Elly was lying in Half-Moon's arms, on the other side of the bed. I think she shrivelled into a little ball and just burst into tears. Without a glance back, she ran from the room, leaving the door open, and fled the house again. A couple of days later, everyone, including myself, was shocked to hear that Tamara had jumped from the Columbia bridge."

"She killed herself?"

He nodded slowly, rhythmically. "Yes, she did. Only she didn't drown—she landed on the rocks and—"

"Don't tell me about it."

"All right. Anyway, it threw a pallor over the entire house. Elly had her hands full trying to comfort Half-Moon, and saying that maybe Tamara was happy now as she hadn't been in life. It didn't do much good, though, and for weeks he was despondent. Elly worked the garden and encouraged him to help her out. By autumn I think he got over it—and then they were really quite happy together."

"Meanwhile, what was everyone else doing?"

"Them? They did the same as they'd been doing. Dan and Orchid couldn't stop having sex whenever they had a free moment, it seemed. They had huge parties—really, I once counted over two hundred people in the house. Sometimes they would do what they called 'dropping acid'. The first time I heard that, I was quite concerned, you know. What did they mean by dropping acid? They made a huge vat of stuff called Kool-Aid. I soon learned it was harmless enough for the house, because it was—"

"LSD, right?"

"Precisely. I thought at first they were going to intentionally damage the floors or something with all the stuff they concocted. Well, this first acid-dropping party was one of the most amazing spectacles I have ever seen to this day. It was like suddenly finding oneself in a camp of primitive barbarians or worse. They painted each other, and painted the walls and I thought their record-player was going to burst from the noise—and other people played their guitars at the same time. Some of them found their way into the kitchen and began making God-knows-what, but having a tremendously good time and using everything they could think of. It was a cake, I suppose, if it was anything. They put it all in the oven, and when it was done, they ate it. Another bunch of them drew pictures and pulled flowers apart in the living room until it was strewn with flower petals. One of the people who came to the party worked at a florist shop or something and brought huge armfuls of flowers."

Diane's eyes had closed somewhere during the story, and she left them closed, speaking dreamily. "It sounds like fun."

"It was, I can assure you," said Warren. "Even I was having fun simply watching the event. Oh, yes, and there was a young man named Hasty—at least that's what everyone called him. I think it was because he did everything quickly. Now Hasty could sometimes see me."

"He had the gift, huh?"

"He had, well, half a gift anyway. When he had smoked enough 'pot', he had no trouble at all seeing me, and we had an occasionally interesting conversation."

"What kind of a guy was he?" Diane asked.

"He was terribly skinny, but good-natured. He had curly hair, which he wore long of course, as everyone did. And he wore bell-bottoms and beads and the usual sort of things everyone was wearing. He had four or five pairs of glasses with different colored lenses, and he used to wear one or the other depending on his mood. Some of them had a different colored lens for each eye. Hasty had quite large teeth—buck teeth, to be precise—and the thing you noticed most about him when he smiled was his long teeth. The saving grace was that they were intact and white—at least he did brush his teeth often enough to keep them from decaying. A man with such prominent teeth must always be careful, since they could be hideous things if they were yellow and silver. I often commended him on taking such good care of them."

"But what did he do?"

"As near as I could tell, nothing. I think he sold a few bags of marijuana and probably lived off the proceeds of that. But he didn't pay any rent to Dan and Orchid—they were in control of the house, if anyone was, you see."

"Did Hasty have a girlfriend?"

"No, never. But, when Tamara was living in the house, he sometimes slept with her."

"With Tamara? I thought she was with Half-Moon?"

"Well, she was, but—Tamara would sleep with practically anyone, as long as Half-Moon wasn't around to see her. Everybody knew that, but Half-Moon refused to believe it, no matter what anyone said. I think that was part of her problem. She had such little esteem for herself it was just crushed away when she found him in bed with Elly. And yet she needed other people to want her. She committed suicide when *he* was unfaithful to her, but at the same time, *she* seemed to think nothing of spreading her legs and getting screwed by anyone who happened to take the lead with her."

"I see," Diane said. "Poor thing."

"Worst of all, she did it for drugs, too. There were a couple of high-school boys who came over from time to time and bought drugs from Hasty. Sometimes they'd sit and have a smoke there in his room, to test the stuff they were supposed to buy. Hasty never tried to steal anything from them—he was good in that way, and of course I often spoke to him about it when it seemed to me he was in danger of dishonest dealings. Quite funnily, he began to think of me as an embodiment of his conscience. So when these boys would come over, they'd sometimes go to see Tamara, too. I think they were both virgins when they first came here, but Hasty made a deal with them. For about ten dollars each, he approached Tamara for them, and managed to soften her up. Eventually, she agreed to sleep with them. She shrugged her shoulders, as if she were saying 'hell, all right, I'll sleep with anyone'. She didn't care either way; but she got her drugs, too."

"She sounds even sadder than before."

"Yes," Warren agreed quietly, and pondered for a moment. "Perhaps I shouldn't have told you about Tamara. In all the years I've been here, she's the only one I really know died while she lived here. Everyone else I lost track of, when they left of course. But Tamara—well, I kind of wished there was something I could have done for her."

"It might not have made any difference," Diane said, then feeling suddenly very lonely, "Tell me something happier."

"There was a lot of happiness while those people were here," he continued. "Especially Dan and Orchid. You know, the thing about Orchid that made her so delightful was *her* delight with positively everything. I think Dan was trying hard to be a good husband—I found out later they were actually married, though I'd suspected they weren't. In one of their drawers in a locked box they had their marriage license.

"A locked box?"

"Neither of them trusted any of the people they lived with very much. They were trying to be on their way up—half the people who lived here were on their way down. I don't think they'd have had anyone share with them if they didn't need to pay the rent. It was much too expensive for them alone, you see. Later on, Orchid got pregnant. No, I guess that was about the time Tamara died, now that I think about it. She must have been four or five months along, and they'd been living here a little over a year." Warren stopped for a moment to think things through.

"Yes," he said. "That would have been right. "Anyway, there's another thing that happened related to Tamara, too."

"What?"

"Her brother."

"She had a brother?"

"I suppose she had parents, too, but I never saw them. No, Tamara's brother wasn't anything to be proud of either. He was one of those 'biker' types, and quite an unkind fellow. It's not that I have anything against people who ride motorcycles, and even the worst of them are usually kind to children and dogs. But Tamara's brother—his name was Oakley, by the way—was about the most horrible person ever to walk through that door. Sometimes he came over, and when he did, practically everyone in the house except Tamara suddenly had something else to do. So they usually had the living room to themselves. Oakley also had this woman who hung around him like a stray dog. She was an awful sight, too. Oh, I mean she was pretty enough—under a thick pasty layer of foundation and eye-shadow and bright-pink lipstick—precisely the sort of thing your mother and I both warn you against."

"All right," Diane whispered, "I get it."

"She had blonde hair, trimmed short and always wore blue jeans with a black leather vest—the same thing Oakley wore, too. The only time I ever saw her in anything else was when she took a bath. Sometimes she and Oakley would stop in just to take a bath. A couple of times, he got so drunk he forgot what he'd come for, then he would pass out and she'd end up in the bath alone. I'd say she was pretty well built. And when she took off her hideous make-up, she wasn't bad looking either."

"Did she and Oakley do it in the bathtub too?"

"Of course," Warren replied. "Every couple who ever took a bath in there did—I think there was something about that room that incited people's amorous natures. Oakley was like an ape-man with her, too, poor thing. It's not hard to see where Darwin was right. I don't know how she could stand that—she had bruises all over her poor bottom, and between her thighs, from him. He'd always grab onto her and dig in his fists. Mostly took her from behind, too, rarely from the front. And he spanked her a lot. He'd get her in the bathroom, and as soon as she had her clothes off, he'd turn her over and wallop her ass a few times, just to redden it up. She liked it though."

"She did?"

"Some women do," Warren said reflectively. "A little of it, I mean. But I think a lot of times he went too far with her. It's one thing to tease up her juices with a few slaps in the ass, followed by some finger exercises—but it's quite another to wallop her until she's really crying."

"Sounds like a jerk," Diane observed.

"I just wanted you to know what kind of man he was. Anyway, after Tamara died, he blamed Half-Moon for it. One night just after she died—I guess when he first found out about it, he came over with a shotgun and blasted out the two front windows."

"You mean the ones in the living room?"

"Yes," said Warren. "Those aren't the original windows. Originally, there were two beautiful stained glasses there. The center panels were regular plate glass, lined on either side with about fourteen inches of stained glass depicting vines and flowers."

"I wish I could have seen them."

"They were nice, and they used to make the living room feel like a cathedral. Anyway, after that, he stood out in the yard swearing and yelling like a drunken sailor. One of the neighbors called the police right after he fired the shots, but when he heard the sirens, he got onto his bike and rode away. I don't know whether they ever caught him. But he never did come for Tamara's things."

"What happened to those? Did Half-Moon take them?"

"No, he didn't. He left about five or six months later, and just took his own things. Everything that was Tamara's, he left exactly as it was. He and Elly moved in together, actually, and I heard they took an apartment across town somewhere."

"That's a happy ending, isn't it?"

"That's one of them," agreed Warren. "They were both fine people and I think they were quite good for each other. Of course, I never found out what happened to them later. That was just about the time Orchid's baby was born, too. They stayed here another year or so with the baby while everyone else drifted away. Dan got promoted on his job, and then they eventually moved out, too. By then, it was just turning 1970. The next year, the landlord decided to sell the place again—maybe I've never mentioned it got sold several times, but everyone who bought it after 1955 rented it out. Anyway, he had the house remodelled. They fixed some wiring and put in a new heater, and fixed the roof and patched holes—there were especially a lot of holes along the front facade and in the living room, left over from Oakley's shotgun blast. Then they painted the whole place. That's the time they put in the new bathtub with the built-in shower. I really hate that hideous pre-fabricated thing, you know."

"It's serviceable," Diane commented. "If you've never lived with a shower, you can't imagine how great it is, not to have to wash your hair and leave soap all over yourself."

"Well, I don't like the look of it. They should have left the old bathtub there, and put in one of those hoses to shower with. Anyway, right after the remodelling, he sold it pretty quickly. Then the couple who bought it turned around and sold it to you folks and made a regular killing on the place."

"They did?"

"I think your father could have offered them about three quarters of what they were asking, and they'd have taken it."

"Shit, Warren—thanks for telling me now, huh."

"It's not my fault," Warren protested. "If I had told you that you could buy it for less when you first came to see it, would you have believed me? Are you going to believe some ghost who comes up to you the first time you walk into the place, and tells you something like that?"

"I believed you were who you were when I met you didn't I?"

"Yes, that's true," admitted Warren, "but—you were scared, too. Don't you remember that? And it took you a long while to really believe."

"Maybe," Diane whispered. It seemed so long ago that she barely remembered not having known Warren. Had it really been that long? She had not even lived in the house a year, and already she felt that way—like they had always been together.

"Sigh to you, too," said Warren, who had been watching her stare into space.

"Sorry," she said. "Where were we?"

"We were too tired to keep listening," he said. "Go to sleep."

"Good night, Warren."

"Good night, sweet dreams."

[23]

"Tom," Nancy said, setting her book face down on the bedspread. She turned to her husband, who looked up from his book to answer.

"Yes?"

"Do you think Diane's a normal girl?"

"Normal? Of course she is—well, I think she is. Why?"

"I was talking to Stella today—you know, Janet's mother?"

"Uh huh."

"Well," Nancy continued, closing her book firmly and laying it aside. "She made some comment about rebellious teenagers, and it kind of surprised me. So I said something like 'Oh, Diane isn't like that'. Of course we got to talking, and—"

"Diane isn't like that," he said. "Why? Is Janet rebellious?"

"Tom—you'd hardly believe the things Stella had to say. The way she talked, it's like Janet hasn't a decent word to say about anything."

"Like what?"

"Well," Nancy said, sitting up and turning to face him directly. "I guess Janet had the stereo on full blast, and Stella was on the phone—so she knocked on Janet's door—to tell her to turn it down, of course—and when Janet didn't answer—it was no wonder, with the volume so loud it was apparently shaking the house down—Stella opened the door. Janet jumped up red-faced apparently—Stella didn't elaborate, so I don't know what she interrupted, but anyway—when Stella finally got it through to her to turn down the music, she made some remark about what an old biddy Stella was."

"Old biddy, huh," Tom said smiling.

"See, even you don't think so, right?"

"I've only met her a couple times, but—"

"It cut her to the quick, Tom. You know, she turned to me—I could almost see the tears in her eyes—she said, 'My God, Nancy—am I an old biddy already?' and I said of course she wasn't."

"I was going to say, even I'd agree she's hardly an old biddy."

"Oh, checking out other women, huh?"

He grinned. "Just a fact, ma'am."

Nancy ignored his comment and continued, "Well, I got to thinking about it on the way home—and you know, Diane *isn't* like that."

"She doesn't have to be," Warren said from his seat at the foot of the bed, though they could neither see nor hear him. "She has lenient parents and her own ghost to talk to about anything she pleases. The combined effect is relative tranquillity."

"I started to get worried," Nancy continued.

"About what—should she be rebellious and rude?"

"No, it's not that, but—have you noticed how much of a loner she's become? She hardly ever invites anyone over."

"It's probably just a phase," Tom said.

"It's been six months since she's dated anyone."

"Has it been that long?"

"See—you didn't even notice, did you?"

"OK, last year she had lots of boyfriends. We just moved here, she's bound to take some time to take her bearings and fit in. Wait 'til next year—she'll bounce right back."

"I think she should have bounced back already. Sometimes I think we shouldn't have moved."

"Let's please not start that one again—"

"I'm not," Nancy said defensively. "Not at all. Just—I hope she's all right."

"Have you talked to her about it?"

"What would I say—tell her to make more friends? Tell her to find a boyfriend?"

"No, just ask her how she's feeling and tell her if she needs someone to talk to—"

"She talks to me," Warren assured, "so there's nothing to worry about."

"Maybe I will," said Nancy. As Tom picked up his book again, she thought of something else. "Oh, and another funny thing . . ."

"Yes?" Tom smiled serenely and laid his book down.

"Her odd taste in music—you know when Stella talked about the stereo full blast, it reminded me that Diane's taste in music is—well, frankly bizarre for her age."

"Like what? I thought she liked Carole King and Roberta Flack."

"Really, Tom. That was months ago."

"What's she listening to now?"

"Now it's—well, awful."

"What do you mean by awful? Steppenwolf?"

"Try Sidewalks of New York? By the Light of the Silvery Moon?"

"Hmm. Nance, it's probably just a nostalgic phase or something . . ."

"For turn of the century pop music? Come on, Tom. She's listening to crap my grandmother used to sing."

"Ha!" Warren snorted, "it's far better than the mush you listen to when you're alone."

"Is she shaking the house down?" Tom inquired.

"No, but—"

"Well, then? What's the problem?"

"Maybe you're right . . ." Nancy let her words dangle. Apparently he could not see her point, or maybe Diane was going through a strange type of nostalgic phase.

Tom picked up his book again, and gave her a quizzical look.

"Yes, honey, I'm finished," she concluded, and kissed his cheek. With a smile, she went back to her own book.

[24]

On Friday after school, Diane asked Janet to cover for her on Saturday by pretending that she was going to her house.

"Yeah, sure," Janet agreed. "If your Mom calls, I'll say you're in the bathroom or something. Where are going really, though?"

"Cashmere," Diane said.

"Cashmere," Janet repeated, then her face lit up. "Who's the guy?"

"It's not a guy," Diane said.

"Right, sweetie. You want me to cover for you and it's not a guy—"

"It's not," Diane insisted. "I'm going to see somebody—"

"A guy. So who the fuck is he?"

"It's an old lady named Ludmilla," Diane said. "I'm going to visit an old lady in a nursing home."

"Uh huh, sure," Janet said, adjusting her purse over her shoulder. "Fuck you, then."

"Wait a minute . . ."

"Just kidding," Janet said. "But—"

"Lie to her!" Warren shouted in Diane's ear. "Otherwise she's going to back out."

"Oh shit," Diane said. "Yeah, it's a guy named Jason Hardwick—I met him, uh, at the dentist's office."

Janet burst into laughter, shaking her head. "God you are weird Diane—that's what I like about you. So fucking off-beat . . ."

"I did meet him at the dentist, honest. He's got great teeth, too."

"Right," laughed Janet. "Just what you notice first about a guy, huh? Did he kiss you? Or just carry your toothbrush?"

"Tell her he ripped off your clothes and laid you in the dentist chair," Warren offered. "She should try it sometime. Go ahead . . ."

"Neither," Diane said, laughing. "He just—well, shit, he's really cute, and we got to talking and he asked me for my phone number, and he called, and I said I'd go see him."

"OK," Janet said. "What time are you leaving?"

"About nine—and I'll be back by five. Look, I'll drop by your place on the way back, OK? Then I can call my Mom like nothing's going on, and tell her I'm coming home, OK?"

"Sounds cool to me."

"Later, huh?" Diane said. "And thanks a zillion."

"Later."

"Oh, hey," Diane said, as she turned her bicycle around. "What are you up to tonight?"

"Wouldn't you like to know?"

"Dave, huh?"

Janet grinned widely. "Yup. Skyline drive after the dance."

"Give him a kiss for me, huh." Diane pedalled out of the parking lot and headed for home.

"Beautiful lie," Warren said when she got onto Miller Street.

"You liked that, huh?"

"Oh, yes. Jason HARD-wick!" He laughed. "What do *you* have on the brain?"

"S-E-X!" chanted Diane, leaning back on her bicycle seat to ride down Miller Street with her hands flapping the air.

The ride to Cashmere on Saturday morning was grueling. Diane forgot her water bottle in the garage, and had to stop on the way to drink out of an irrigation spigot. After quenching her thirst she sat back for a rest.

"Jeez, I hope I don't get dysentery," she said.

"It used to be all right in my day," said Warren.

"I hope it still is. Ready to go?"

"You're the one who's resting," he answered. "I'm always ready."

Most of the remainder of the ride was downhill, and took less time than Diane had expected. Warren pointed out that the way back would be harder, but she shrugged it off saying she would have plenty of time. When they arrived at the first gas station in Cashmere—practically a village that straddled the river—she stopped to ask directions. The nursing home was another mile and a half away. The station attendant's directions were not very clear, and she had to stop once again after she crossed the river to ask further directions. At last she arrived, and after parking her bike next to the building and locking it, she made her way through the front doors. The lobby was a whitewashed room with a few hard chairs, a table, and a reception counter at the far end next to a hallway. On each wall hung a single insipid oil painting of flowers and fruit.

"The place looks like a morgue," she whispered to Warren while she walked directly to the front counter.

"May I help you?" inquired a heavyset, elderly receptionist who sat behind the counter, apparently trying to look busy at her typewriter.

"Is she an inmate, or what?" quipped Warren.

Diane put one hand on the counter-top and adjusted her pack over her shoulder. "I'm here to see Ludmilla McMonigle."

"Really?" the receptionist ejaculated with some surprise, and took off her glasses to let them drop to the front of her enormous bosom.

"Yes, really," said Diane, and deciding her tone was a bit too flippant, added with more care, "Is there some problem? Is she sick?"

"Heavens no," the lady boomed. "It's simply unprecedented—nobody but young Mr. McMonigle has ever called for her." She began to smile, only slightly. "You must be his grand-daughter, is that right?"

"No," Diane answered. "I'm—uh—I'm just a friend—of the family, that's all."

The lady looked at her for a moment as if she were puzzled that Ludmilla would have any friends, then put on her glasses.

"Your name?"

"Diane Kolansky."

"I'll call the nurse to show you in," she said, then dialed a couple of numbers on her phone and spoke briefly with whomever answered. "She'll be right out. Have a seat, please."

"Thank you." Diane sat and looked over the few magazines that littered one square table in the lobby. All of them were old, some dating back two or three years. "This is a motherlode," she whispered sarcastically.

"No Playboy," said Warren. "I've already looked."

"How about Playgirl?" Diane whispered.

"I'm sorry?" came the receptionist's voice drifting up from behind the counter.

"Oh, nothing," Diane called back. "I was just thinking of having my hair curled."

"It looks beautiful to me," called the receptionist. "When did you have it done?"

"She is an inmate," said Warren.

At that moment, the nurse appeared. She was a tiny wisp of a woman in her forties, who looked to Diane as if she had put her wig on backwards. Her hair was brown, streaked with gray at the temples, and piled up over her head. "Follow me," she said in a nasal voice.

Diane followed into the back corridor, taking a couple of turns. "She's right here," the nurse said, pointing into a room. "Last bed on the left." With that, she turned abruptly and left Diane standing in the hallway.

With some hesitation, she entered the room. There were six beds lining the walls with a corridor in the center. Four of the beds had curtains pulled partway around them. The last bed on the left was bent at an angle so its occupant could sit up, and the curtains had been drawn back fully.

"Oh, my God," Warren whispered the instant he could see Ludmilla.

"Is that her?" Diane asked in a whisper.

"Yes," he said. "Listen—I'm going to wait outside, Diane. This is simply too much for me. I'm sorry." He strode quickly out the door behind her.

"Mrs. McMonigle?" Diane called softly as she approached the bed.

The emaciated old woman appeared startled by her voice and looked toward her feebly. "Henrietta? What are you doing here?"

"Are you Ludmilla McMonigle?" Diane asked.

The woman's face, wrinkled into a little heap of leather-covered bones, seemed to brighten momentarily, but then she stared blankly with tilted head. Her hair was so thin Diane could see her spotted, pinkish scalp.

"Who are you?"

"I'm Diane Kolansky." Seeing the way Ludmilla's thin mouth and hands continually jittered, Diane was reminded of her last visit to her maternal Grandmother, and she had to turn away briefly. She almost fled, but instead sat down carefully on the edge of the bed. "Can I ask you a few questions?"

Ludmilla sat looking at her as if trying to remember something, then said, "You're not Jake's daughter—who are you?"

Diane repeated her name, adding, "I came to visit you."

"A visitor," Ludmilla said seriously, appearing flustered. "Gracious, I'll have to put on tea. Joshua didn't tell me we had a guest."

"I just came to ask a few questions," Diane said. "Can I ask you some questions?"

"Questions?"

"What happened to Priscilla's ashes?" Diane asked.

"Oh!" Ludmilla exclaimed, lifting one hand suddenly. "Did Priscilla come too? Land sakes. What did you say your name was?"

Diane tried to smile, and repeated herself. She got little further no matter how many times she asked after Priscilla's ashes, or any other thing. After a while it seemed hopeless to even continue— and Mr. McMonigle had said she was lucid. She seemed to know who Priscilla was, but all Diane could get from her was the incantation that Priscilla was dead.

"Yes, I know," Diane said, answering for what seemed the tenth time, then paused to sigh and think for a moment. "Did Harold Jarmsford push her out the window?"

"Who? Priscilla? Is she coming, too?"

"What happened to the body?" Diane asked. "Where is Priscilla buried? Her burial."

"Priscilla? Oh, land sakes, no. She was cremated, just like her husband, the dear." Ludmilla continued her incoherent ramblings, sometimes running out of steam, and then sat waiting for another question.

In frustration, Diane finally stood up. "Ludmilla, it's been— so pleasant to meet you, finally. Good-bye," she said, and gently took Ludmilla's frail hand, to pat it.

"Good-bye!" Ludmilla called happily after her. "Thank you ever so much. Good-bye!"

Outside Warren was waiting. "What did you find out?"

"Nothing," Diane said flatly. "God, I hope I never live to look like that . . . Why didn't you come in?" she asked, and began to walk toward the lobby.

"I prefer to remember her as she was," he said, pacing her.

"I can understand that." He looked mildly downcast, so she added, "Hey, it's no problem. I understand exactly what you mean."

In the lobby, she thanked the receptionist, and chatted for a moment, saying how well Mrs. McMonigle looked. After she exited the building, she turned to Warren, wailing. "But I didn't find out anything—so this whole damn trip was a waste!"

"Wasn't it an exhilarating ride?"

"Oh, yeah," she said rolling her eyes. "Now we have a nice, long, hot ride back."

Warren let her sulk, which lasted for almost five minutes. During the ride back, she told him about her entire conversation with Ludmilla. It was easy, since she had repeated herself so many times. "I guess we've hit the end of the road, haven't we?" she said finally.

"Maybe not," countered Warren, trying to sound positive. "What about McMonigle? Come on, as a last resort, maybe he knows something."

"Maybe," Diane said. "I guess it's worth a try, isn't it?"

"Let's stop and see him on the way back."

"OK. If he's home, that is."

[25]

"Well, hello again, Miss—uh Miss—Ko—"

"I thought you preferred 'Ms.'" Warren said jovially over her shoulder.

"Diane Kolansky," Diane said with a smile, and took a tiny step backward into Warren's chest. "'Ms.'—May I come in?" She opened the screen door herself.

"I suppose so," Mr. McMonigle replied, standing away from the door to let her through. "Did you visit Ludmilla?"

Diane nodded and entered while he closed the door quietly behind her.

"What can I do for you, then?"

"She's completely incoherent," Diane said, bluntly. "How long has it been since you've seen her?"

"Almost a year," he admitted, and turned toward the kitchen. "Have a seat. Would you like some tea?"

"Yes, thanks," she answered.

He ambled into the kitchen, and rather than sit down, she followed him and stood in the kitchen doorway, leaning against the door jamb with her arms folded.

"I guess she's gotten worse," he said over the sound of water pouring into the tea kettle. "Completely incoherent, you say?"

"I couldn't get a straight sentence out of her," Diane answered.

"Here, sit down," he said, pulling out a chair. "How about a cookie or something?"

"Sure, thanks." She sat slowly, taking off her pack and stowing it between her feet. "Can I ask you another question?"

"Fire away."

"Do you know happened to Priscilla Brannigan's ashes?"

"What do you mean?" he asked, taking a seat across from her.

"I mean, does Ludmilla still have them?"

"Probably in storage, if they're anywhere. I don't know what she'd have done with 'em. Why do you ask?"

She didn't answer for a long moment, but looked down at her knees and picked at a thread in her jeans. "It's important that I find them."

"Oh?" said Mr. McMonigle. "Why's that?"

"Tell him," Warren urged.

Diane kept silent. "I just—I just want to see them."

"Well, you must have a reason."

"Are all of Ludmilla's things in storage? Doesn't she have a house?"

"We sold her house almost ten years ago," Mr. McMonigle replied. "What little wasn't sold, we put in storage."

"Where?"

"Why do you want to know?"

"Tell him," Warren said. "He might believe you."

"Look," she said quietly, still studying her jeans. "I'd do anything to find those ashes. It means a lot to me—and—well, it just does."

The kettle began to whistle faintly, and Mr. McMonigle got up with a frown to fill the teapot. He brought two cups and set them down on the table, followed by the steaming teapot.

"Sugar?" he asked.

"Two lumps," Diane answered, and when he held the sugar bowl toward her, she took them. "Cream if you have it?"

"Sure," he said, and went to pull a small pitcher of cream from the refrigerator. "Now young lady," he said when he had sat down and poured out two cups of tea, "I don't know who the hell you are, but if you want something, we're going to have to up the ante."

"OK," she said, looking into his eyes. "Tell me where the ashes are, and I'll show you my tits."

Warren burst into laughter. "Stop it!" he yelled. "You're just asking for trouble."

Mr. McMonigle dropped his spoon and chuckled. "I don't know what civilization's coming to!" he exclaimed. "Look here young lady—if I was an old lecher, I've had plenty of opportunity to try something like that." He picked up his spoon again and shook it at her. "But I'm not, and I don't want to see your bosom. I meant we'll have to be straight with each other. You want something, and I just want to know why you care. That's all."

"OK. Sorry." Diane picked up her cup and took a sip of tea, then set it down with a jittery hand. "Warren Brannigan is a friend of mine, and I'm trying to help him find his wife's ashes."

"What's that? Warren Brannigan's been dead for—"

"Sixty two years," Diane shot back. "His ghost lives in my house."

Mr. McMonigle chuckled again. "You'll have to do better than that."

"It's true," she said, blushing deeply. "I guess you can't believe me, can you?"

"Nope. Not for a second. I don't believe in ghosts."

"Most people don't," Diane said. "Except people like me who can see them. Not everyone has the gift."

Mr. McMonigle sat sucking his lip quietly, and tapped his finger a few times on the rim of his teacup.

"I'm sorry I bothered you," Diane said, and stood up quickly. "I have to go, now. Thanks for the tea."

Mr. McMonigle continued to sit, still tapping on his cup, while she let herself out the front door.

"Now what?" she said to Warren while she unlocked her bicycle.

"We can find out where he keeps the things in storage, maybe?"

"Maybe. Do you know how many storage places there are in town?"

"No."

"I don't either, but there must be a dozen."

"Check the telephone book."

"Hello, operator," Diane said sweetly. "I'm looking for a storage locker rented by a Mr. McMonigle . . ."

"Then we can break in and steal them," Warren said happily.

"No," Diane insisted, as she got onto her bike. "We're not going to break into anyplace. We'll have to think of something else."

On the way home, Diane stopped at Janet's house and rang the doorbell. Janet herself answered the door. "Shit!" she exclaimed and slammed the door behind herself to stand with Diane on the porch. "You better get home, fast."

"What's up?"

"Your mother called about ten o'clock to say she was taking your kid brother and sister to the park. I told her you were in the bathroom—then she fucking called again at noon."

"Oh, shit," Diane said.

"That's not all," Janet continued in a whisper. "Later on *my* mother saw *your* mother at the corner store. Then the shit really hit the fan. She came home bitching like crazy. I'm grounded for a week—and I'll bet you are too."

"Later," Diane said, and ran down the steps. "I'll call you."

"No," Janet called behind her. "I'll see you at school. No phone calls either."

"OK. Bye!"

When Diane walked in the front door, the house was quiet, so she peeked into the kitchen. In the back yard she could hear Rat's voice, and then her mother's voice. "I better tell her I'm here," she said to Warren. After tossing her pack on a chair she went out the back door onto the porch. Warren floated to the back window, and watched Diane trudge across the lawn. Victoria was out in a playpen, and Bobby was helping Nancy dig something up in the back yard.

"Hi Mom," Diane said casually.

"Where the hell have you been!" Nancy yelled. "Bobby, here, take this and dig a little hole right here," she said, handing him a spade. "I'll be right back." With a cross look at Diane, she curled a finger. "Come here."

Diane followed her mother as she stalked angrily into the house, and sat in the chair she pointed out.

"Where have you been?"

"Janet's."

"Like holy pig-shit, you little liar."

"Jesus, Mom, do you have to swear?"

"It feels good," Nancy shot back in a sudden rush of anger. "Shit fuck piss goddam pussy cunt cock!" she yelled in Diane's face, then paused, breathing heavily for a moment. "I thought I had the finest goddam daughter in the world. Diane never lies. Diane never cheats. She's so goddam good about her chores I feel guilty asking her to do anything. She writes like a fucking college graduate. She gets on the frigging honor roll every quarter . . ." Nancy was in a frenzy, and Diane could see tears welling up in her eyes. "God, I must be gullible. Where the *hell* have you *been* all day?"

"Mom, calm down," Diane whispered, with a lump in her throat.

"No, I won't calm down. Where have you been?"

"I went to Cashmere and visited an old lady in a nursing home."

"Oh, shit," Nancy said, unable to hold back tears, which burst in a stream down her cheeks. "You expect me to believe that bullshit?" She yanked a chair out from under the table, turned it around, and sat down backwards with her face two inches from Diane's nose. "Don't you dare lie to me, Diane."

"Mom," Diane said quietly. "It's the absolute truth." She reached across the table and dragged her pack toward herself. "Here's the phone number and the address. I visited a Mrs. Ludmilla McMonigle. The receptionist will remember me. Call them."

"All right," Nancy said, standing up. Ignoring the paper Diane held out, she walked to the telephone table and pulled out the phone book. "What's the name of the place?"

"Columbia Valley Nursing Home."

Nancy called and spoke to the receptionist. "What was the lady's name?" she asked, covering the receiver.

"Mrs. Ludmilla McMonigle."

Nancy repeated the name into the phone, then said, "Can you

describe her?" She waited a moment, and answered, her anger clearly dissipating. "Thank you very much, sorry to have bothered you." She hung up, then took her seat in front of Diane again and began to blush. "OK," she laughed and let out a rushing sigh. "God, I'm sorry. But why the hell didn't you just tell me you were going there?"

"'Cause it's too far to ride alone," Diane answered. "I knew you'd be worried."

Nancy laughed and sniffled, wiping away her tears. "You think I was less worried when I found out you weren't at Janet's house?"

"I'm sorry, Mom. I screwed up. It won't happen again."

"OK," Nancy answered. "I'll believe that. Now—why did you go all the way to Cashmere to visit some old lady that I've never heard of?"

"Mom," Diane said quietly, blinking her eyes. "Have you ever done anything incomprehensible that your parents never would have understood or believed had you told them?"

"You sound just like your father," Nancy said, tight lipped. "Something incomprehensible? Like carrying around a thermos full of ashes everywhere I went? No, Diane, I never did anything quite that incomprehensible. Oh, and the other great one is the newspaper archives. For months you've been hanging around down there doing some kind of research, but you haven't got any reason that I can see. You haven't written a term paper—at least not one you've shown to us. I never brought it up before because it seemed educational at any rate."

Diane glanced at Warren, who was hovering cross-legged over the other end of the kitchen table.

"I'm sorry," he said with a shrug, "I can't help you out of this one."

She frowned and looked back at her mother. "OK, Mom. I'll level with you," she said. "I might have a few neuroses, but I'm perfectly sane. I'm not having sex with anyone yet. I'm not smoking pot, or cutting classes, or shoplifting."

"All right," Nancy replied, trying to keep herself calm, though her hands were still shaking mildly. She put her palms on her knees. "Then what's going on?"

"You wouldn't believe me, but just—just trust me, Mom. I'm not in any trouble, I just can't tell you yet."

"That's levelling with me?" Nancy asked incredulously. "Look—I try to have a close relationship with you, but I'm not a goddam saint. Shit. I've never had a teenage daughter before, so give me a break, huh? I know you're not half the problem I was at your age, so I should count my blessings. I'm just so damned curious about why you have this—this bizarre aberration. What is so important about this damned thermos that you carry it all over the place?"

"Tell her," Warren urged. "It can't hurt at this point. She won't believe you, but I don't think it matters."

Diane sat quietly staring at her knees while Nancy looked at her. She dramatized an answer in her mind: "Mom, the thermos contains the ashes of a man named Warren Brannigan who was killed sixty-two years ago on his wedding day and cremated. I'm looking for the ashes of his wife, Priscilla Brannigan." It sounded absurd. Instead she said, "You wouldn't believe me."

"I might," Nancy said. "So far, I think I do believe you."

Diane felt herself beginning to cry, and picked at her jeans again. "Mom, this is one of those times where, if I told you, it would be a lie. So—so I'd rather you didn't ask."

Nancy rubbed her hand down her face, then sat with her chin in her palm, her elbow resting on the back of the chair. "Hmm." She looked at the ceiling and let her eyes wander, then focussed on Diane's face again. If she were honest enough to admit she would have lied, then it would be impossible to get the truth out of her. Maybe, as Tom thought, it was nothing important. And Diane had frankly admitted everything she was *not* doing.

Diane swallowed thickly. "Can I get some water?"

"Huh? Sure." Nancy said. "You want some juice?"

"No," Diane answered, getting up to find a glass. She filled it with water from the tap and took a long drink, then sat down again holding the glass. She had not really thought as far as what she would do when she found Priscilla's ashes, but supposed she would follow things to their romantic conclusion and re-unite Warren with Priscilla. Then what would happen? She blanched suddenly and set down her water glass. Was that what he meant about leaving? He had said that at least once. Would he go away once he had Priscilla back? "It's just something I have to do," she said. "And Mom," she pleaded, looking up, "please don't tell Dad?"

"OK, I won't," Nancy promised.

After a thoughtful pause, Diane asked, "Aren't you going to punish me?"

"I hadn't thought about it," said Nancy. "Should I?"

"Janet got grounded for a week."

"OK. You're grounded for a week, too. How's that? Fair?"

"Uh huh," Diane nodded. "Can I go now? I have to take a shower."

"Sure, go ahead. I'll give Stella a call and let her know you're all right."

As Diane stood up, Nancy smiled and pointed to her own cheek. After an embrace and a kiss, she let her daughter go.

Warren joined Diane in the shower, a habit they had evolved over the months, having begun soon after they first made love. He simply followed her up the stairs and into the bathroom, but she had not spoken to him at all. They took off their clothes in silence, turned on the shower in silence. Every time he joined her, she said she wished he could scrub her back, and they always had a good laugh about it. But now she washed her hair in silence while Warren stood looking at the delicious curves of her youthful body.

"What are you thinking?" he asked.

She began to lather her hair a second time. "Warren—what's going to happen if I get Priscilla's ashes?"

"I don't know," he said.

"Don't lie to me, OK?"

"I'm not," he said, coming closer to her. "I've never, ever lied to you and I won't start now. I have no idea. I suppose that depends on whether Priscilla is still around or not."

"What do you mean?"

"I mean, whether she's a ghost or not."

"Oh. You mean you're not sure of that either?"

"Of course not. Not at all."

"Ah," she said and rinsed her hair again. "What if she is?"

"Then I'll be the happiest ghost in town," he said. "Shall I scrub your back?"

"Sure," she said smiling at him. "You can rub anything else you want, too."

"How about here?" he teased, and put his hand through her pubic triangle.

"Feels great," she said, though she felt nothing, and slid her hand between her thighs, and rubbed forward with her middle finger. "Really great." Suddenly serious, she turned off the shower. "I couldn't handle it without you," she said. "You're the best friend I've got."

"I know," he replied, matching her sudden turn to seriousness. "And you're the best friend I've got. Sometimes I think I know you better than I ever knew Priscilla. Better than I've known anyone."

"But you still love her, right?" She dried her face and looked at him inquiringly while she dried her legs, putting up first one, then the other onto the edge of the tub.

"Diane—the whole reason I'm here at all is because I love her. It's unfulfilled love—or something like that—that keeps me here."

"And when it's fulfilled?" She dabbed her crotch dry, then tossed the towel over her shoulders to try her back.

"Then I hope I'll go somewhere—I don't know 'where' any more than you do, but I can feel the outward pull. I've always felt the pull. It's like a little string behind me, trying to yank me along, away from Earth, but I can't leave because the pull of loving Priscilla is greater, so I'm caught."

Diane thoughtfully wound the towel around her hair like a turban and slipped on her panties. "You know," she said, "I'm starting to believe this old saying I heard once, and in a way, it's scary."

"What old saying?"

She opened the bathroom door and turned on the fan, setting the timer to shut off in ten minutes. "I'm jealous," she said, as the timer knob began to purr. Warren followed her down the hall and up the stairs to her room while she continued. "I'm fucking crazy in love jealous, and when I look at this honestly—I don't want you to leave, I don't want to be alone—and I don't want to give you to another woman. They say: 'a woman will give up a man for anything—except another woman' and that's scary, because I think it might be true. I'm supposed to be too young to think about things like that. But that's how I feel."

"I've never heard the saying," Warren said.

"Now that you have—what do you think?"

"I think you're an adult, and you'll do what's right."

Diane sat on her bed, not bothering to put on any clothes. "What if I told you I'm not going to look for Priscilla's ashes any more?"

"I'd be sad," he said, "but I wouldn't storm out and leave you or anything. I guess it would mean I'd have to wait for someone else to come along. And—try this from my perspective for a minute. I've been here sixty years already and there's all the time in the *universe* to wait for someone else. How long would I wait? A thousand years? Ten thousand? Maybe I never would meet anyone like you again. Eternity is infinitely lonely without friends." He paused to look into her eyes, but she kept them downcast. "I care for you, Diane, and I wouldn't let anything spoil our friendship."

"Huh," Diane grunted. "I think it'd be really cold if I let you down, wouldn't it?"

Warren did not move or say anything.

"But I think I love you—I mean *really* love you Warren, not just puppy-love you. I need some time to think about it. But at this moment, I think—I'm not sure I could live with myself if I just dumped you, let you down. I'm jealous, maybe confused—

but I want to make you happy, too. I can't just say forget it, good-bye. Isn't that what real love is all about?"

He smiled, and watched her aura wax in smooth, yellow waves.

"I mean," she continued, "true love is what you feel when the happiness of the loved one is essential to your own, isn't it?"

"Yes," he agreed.

"That's how I feel. Is fifteen too young for that?"

"I don't think so," he said, then grinned. "You're almost sixteen."

Diane bit her lip, and returned him a tearful half smile. "Can I be alone for a while?"

"Any time," he answered. "I'll see you tomorrow?"

"Yeah. Wake me at seven?"

"Yes, ma'am." He faded gracefully, sinking through the floor.

Diane felt so tender and happy and sad all at once, she could never have described it. Of course, she must continue to look for Priscilla's ashes—for Warren, because she loved him so much. For a while she simply lay on her bed *feeling* everything at once until she tingled. Then she turned over and cried herself gently to sleep.

[26]

"I don't want to believe she's crazy," Nancy said to Tom, having finally cornered him while he brushed his teeth.

"You haven't even told me what she said to you," he answered lightly. "So I don't have an opinion yet."

"I promised I wouldn't," replied Nancy.

"Then why bring it up at all?"

"It's—well its *weird*, Tom. She seems perfectly sane in every respect—does she seem that way to you?"

"Of course. I don't think there's anything wrong with her."

"How would you know, though? You hardly see her."

"If I weren't so busy, I would," he said. "Are we going to go through this again?"

"No—I know. I don't want to needle you about it."

"Thanks," he said, reaching out to pat her cheek.

"She's got some kind of secret that she won't share. I just wish I knew what it was, that's all."

"Do you want me to talk to her about it?"

"Oh no," Nancy replied hastily, "then she'd know I talked to you for sure. That reminds me—do you know what she said to me today?"

"What?"

"It was so eerie, it made my flesh crawl. She was trying to decide whether to tell me—this thing which I promised not to tell you—"

"I wouldn't ask you to break that promise—you know that, right?" he said, looking at her closely. "If it's a secret, then that's it. Fine." He spit out his toothpaste and rinsed his brush.

"Anyway, she asked me if I hadn't ever done anything so incomprehensible my parents would never have understood."

"And?"

"Those are almost the exact words you used to me, Tom."

"That's what was eerie?"

"Uh huh. And this is the *second* time she's done that. Doesn't it give you pause to think?"

"About what?"

"Why she'd use the same words you did."

"Are you implying I've been talking to her?" he asked, suddenly taking a defensive tone.

"No, I'm not—it just gave me the creeps for a second."

"I don't think there's anything to worry about." Tom had no intention of continuing a conversation that would end in an argument. "Look," he said, "let's just drop this? You're making me curious, but if you blurt out Diane's big secret, you'd be breaking your word to her. If you assure me she's not in any trouble, I'll take it at that. Otherwise, secret or no secret, I want to know what's going on. So—is she in trouble?"

"No," Nancy replied, dearly hoping that she was right—and that Diane's word was as good as her earnestness had made it sound.

"Good," he said firmly. "Let's go to bed before the baby wakes up."

Nancy smiled and held out her cheek to receive his kiss, but he turned her face with his fingers and kissed her on the lips. "Tired?" he said.

"Just a little," she replied.

"Want to snuggle?"

"Maybe," she answered, and took his hand.

He led her toward the bed, and on the way, she flipped out the bathroom light.

[27]

Peter Traverson took Diane out once in April at Janet's instigation. It was a double date with Janet and her latest boyfriend. They all went to dinner at Pizza Inn, then to a school dance, where Diane had a great time dancing and talking with Peter all evening. She hardly spoke to Janet.

She and Peter had a great deal in common, she found out, especially their tastes in poetry and history. He wrote wonderful essays, too, and when the band took a break and they went outside for some air, she told him how much she had admired his essay on Vincent Van Gogh. He seemed too embarrassed to talk about it, and she thought he was self-conscious the rest of the evening. Diane hoped desperately that she had not ruined things. She had not, though she lived in dread of it for a week. Janet finally asked Peter how the date went, and he admitted to her in confidence that he really liked Diane. Yet he was too shy to ask her out again on his own until May. Warren encouraged her to ask him out sometime, but she thought it better to let him take the relationship at his own pace, because he was so sensitive—he had not even tried to kiss her, even though she practically presented herself to be kissed.

His sensitivity was what she really liked about him—he never talked about football or basketball, but more about serious topics. After she made it plain that she liked him, by seeking him out sometimes at school, he got his nerve up and asked her out twice toward the end of May to see movies. She once tried the trick of asking if he could still smell her perfume, and turned her neck toward him. When he bent to inhale, she turned and let her lips brush against her cheek; yet he still did not kiss her. Afterward, he walked her home and left her shyly standing on the porch. It was on their third date that, standing on the porch after walking her home, that he finally kissed her good-night.

He leaned forward so hesitantly that Diane—who had waited patiently, and when the moment came felt her heart racing—wondered if he would ever make it to her lips, but when his arm went around her slowly, she thrilled so much that a tiny shiver went through her and she let herself slowly relax into his arms. He was slightly taller than she—only enough to seem a little strong and comforting when she looked up into his face. Gazing quietly into his tea-brown eyes, she smiled, parting her lips and closing her eyes with a tiny exhalation. He kissed her lightly on the lips, then again.

"Oh, God," she sighed, hugging him tightly around the chest. Then easing her pressure looked at him again, and slowly let her head fall backward, exposing her neck. He kissed it softly beneath her ear, then in front, and let his lips brush back up her chin to kiss her again on the mouth.

"Good night," he said against her cheek. "Parting is such sweet sorrow—"

"That I shall say good-night till it be morrow," she whispered, burying her face against his collar to inhale the faint scent of patchouli.

Peter pulled away, stroking her face with his fingers. "Can uh—can I see you tomorrow?"

"Yeah," she whispered. "What time?"

"You want to go bike riding?"

"Sure."

"How about eleven? Too early?"

"Any time."

"I'll call before I come over, OK?"

"OK."

He kissed her lightly again, holding her chin in his hand, then jumped the porch stairs two at a time and walked off across the lawn. He looked back once, waving boldly. She waved back and stood on the porch until he was halfway down the block.

"Bravo," Warren said, appearing beside her.

"It was great!" she whispered loudly. "God, it was wonderful."

"How long has it been since you've been kissed?" he asked.

"I don't know," she said. "A long time . . . Let's go in." She opened the door and stood back to let Warren through. He walked through her, then together they went upstairs, where she told him all about her evening with Peter.

[28]

Diane was doing her homework one evening after the middle of May. It had been a hot day, and she had all the windows open to let the night breeze in. Warren sat across the desk with a paper-back book spread out, weighted with a thin iron bar. At intervals, he would nod or wave his hand and Diane would turn the page for him. Their system had been so perfected over the months that she scarcely noticed the momentary intrusion, and her homework never suffered for it. But that evening, her full concentration was not on her history, even though it had become her favorite subject. She was normally enthusiastic not only to do her assignments, but to do projects for extra credit.

It had been more than three weeks since she had gone to see Ludmilla, but Ludmilla and Priscilla had never been far from her mind, and she had even called Mr. McMonigle once to see if he had visited Ludmilla. There simply was no way for her to tell what would happen if she ever really did find Priscilla's ashes and bring them home. If Warren were being as honest as she wanted to believe he was, then he had no more idea than she. Logically though, if she could apply logic to a situation so seemingly incompatible, if he was really only remaining on Earth to finish the unfulfilled aspects of his life, then re-uniting him with Priscilla could only have the effect she most dreaded: she would whisk him away with her—to where? Heaven? Diane had studied enough science and philosophy both to wonder whether any religion had any idea what happened after death. But she was thankfully certain about one thing—there was *something* beyond life, and beautiful Warren Brannigan had proved it to her. Not just him either—she had begun to see other ghosts since meeting him, having attuned her perceptions to their presence, but she had never ventured to talk with any of them. In passing, on rare occasions, she would glimpse them, and her heart would suddenly race. One glance from her—not through them but *at* them—might be enough for them to know that she could see. And that might be the end of her peace, every time she passed by their haunts. A part of her wanted to believe there might be other ghosts perhaps not quite as interesting as Warren, but a little interesting, yet so many of them were mutilated that she had to look away and avoid them assiduously. She knew from Warren that very much of their post-life appearance and personality depended on how they died. Warren himself was different, of course; his wounds were almost invisible—in his breast pocket was a tiny hole that he had once pointed out, and beneath his shirt, the small ragged wound that she had come to know so well. It was the only unbeautiful thing about him, really; his only flaw. In every other way, he was adorable, even down to his out-moded clothing.

"History," she sighed, and recalling herself from the reverie ran her finger down the page of her textbook.

"What?" Warren asked.

While reading he was so quiet that she had almost forgotten his immediacy, across the table. "Want me to turn the page?" she asked.

"Not yet," he answered, having only read half of it. He had been watching her frown and stare at her paper, doodling in the corner with her pen when she should have been writing short answers to the chapter questions. "I thought you might have something on your mind."

"I have to concentrate," she said.

"You want me to walk around for a while, leave you alone?"

"It might help," she said, tossing down her pencil. She looked at him, and he sat there with his head cocked, staring at her. "Do you really love me, Warren?"

"Yes," he said.

"How do you love me?"

It was a question he had never wanted to answer fully, even to himself, for all that an honest answer might imply. "It's hard to say," he murmured. "I suppose that I love you in a womanly way. In the way a man loves a woman and wants to be with her always. But also, in a friendly way, because you're certainly—how to put it delicately?" he wondered aloud, then grinned cheekily. "You're looser than anyone I've ever known."

"Thanks a lot!" she laughed. "So I'm a wanton, shameless girl?"

"I don't mean that in such a negative way," he said quickly. "I only meant that it's easy to be friendly with you, and say what's on my mind, like with a good pal—for example, knowing that you'll have a positive reaction to my jokes. Even if they're—not very decent." He leaned back slightly, adjusting himself more comfortably in the air. "Now, why do you ask?"

"I don't know," she said.

At that instant, Nancy's voice rose loudly from the bottom of the stairs. "Diane!"

"What!" Diane yelled back, then stood up and went to open her door. She stuck her head out.

"Telephone," Nancy said in a quieter voice.

"Who is it? Janet?"

"I didn't ask. It's a boy, I think," Nancy said.

"Oh," Diane said. "I'll be right there." She turned back toward Warren and whispered. "I'll be right back, OK?"

Warren nodded, and she quickly closed the door and went downstairs.

"Maybe we should get you your own phone," Nancy suggested, walking down the hall ahead of her.

"I don't get that many calls, do I?" Diane asked.

"No, you don't honey," Nancy replied with a quiet laugh. "I was just thinking it could save us both a bit of running around."

"But if most of the calls are for you or Dad," Diane observed, "then I'd end up doing half of the running."

"You're probably right."

When Diane reached the phone in the kitchen, she pulled her

hair away from her neck, and putting the receiver to her ear spoke in her sweetest girlish voice. "Hello," she said. "This is Diane."

"Miss Kolansky," said a voice on the other end. Diane was surprised to hear Mr. McMonigle's voice—at least, she thought it was his.

"Mr. McMonigle?" she asked quietly.

"Yes," he said. "Listen—I hope I'm not calling too late?"

"No, it's still early." It was only eight-twenty, she saw glancing up at the kitchen clock. "How did you get my phone number?"

"There's only one Kolansky in the book," he answered.

"Oh."

"After you left the other day," he went on, seeming to forget that it had been three weeks, "I got to thinking a little."

"Uh huh," Diane whispered.

"Hello?" he said.

"I'm here," she answered in a louder voice.

"Ah," he said. "Well, I got to thinking a little, and—I don't know exactly what put me onto it."

"Yes?"

"I was thinking—you have a pretty deep interest in Ludmilla and the family. I can't figure exactly where you got it, but— something about you, I just—"

He paused while Diane hung on, twisting the phone cord in her fingers.

"Sometimes," he continued, "I'm not sure why I keep some of Ludmilla's things. Maybe I had some hope she'd recover or something, but—she's not going to." There was a long pause. "In fact, Ludmilla died last week. The day before, I went to see her for the first time in a long while—well, you know how long it's been."

"Uh huh."

"Anyway, she turned to me and asked about Henrietta. And she said how nice it was that Henrietta had come to see her."

"She said that to me, too," Diane offered.

"Henrietta's been in Australia with her husband for years, and she's not likely to be back. So I thought of you." Mr. McMonigle paused again, but Diane said nothing. "I don't know exactly how to say this, so I'm sorry if it sounds a tad abrupt."

"That's OK," she answered.

"I took a trip down to the storage locker yesterday. Stayed a good long time, too, and it sure brought back memories. There's a lot of things I haven't seen for years and I spent the whole afternoon there, looking in boxes. Well, she won't be needing any of it now. I know you're interested in Priscilla's stuff, too."

"Uh huh," Diane answered quietly, to let him know she was listening.

"If you have a few minutes, say tomorrow or the next day, I thought maybe—" He paused again, for a long time. "Well, I'd like to give you something. Do you think you could stop by some afternoon?"

"Sure," she said, then added, "I'll have to think about it. I don't know when. Can I give you a call?"

"Of course," he said. "I know you must be busy with school and all."

"Just in case," she said, "what's your phone number again?" He recited it for her, and she repeated it back. "I'll let you know."

"I'll be expecting your call," he said politely. "I hope I didn't disturb you."

"No problem," she answered. "Good-bye."

"Good-bye," he said, and slowly hung up.

Diane swallowed, and went back up to her room, deep in thought. Warren was sitting in front of the desk and looked up when she came in.

"Who was it?"

She sat down and pulled her history book forward. "Just a guy." She shrugged and flipped her hair over her shoulder. "Asked me if I wanted to see a movie on Friday."

Warren didn't answer. Diane started reading, concentrating on trying to see the words, though her mind was racing as quickly as her heart.

"That hurts," Warren said quietly, standing up.

"What?" she said defensively.

"That you'd lie to me like that."

They stared at each other in silence, and Diane felt herself blushing deeply. "Sorry," she said. "It isn't fair, is it?"

He closed his eyes and shook his head.

"OK," she said. "It was McMonigle. He wants to talk to me and I'm supposed to call him back when I can come over."

"What did he want to talk about?"

"I'm not sure," she said. "He was kind of vague. Ludmilla died."

"Died? When?" asked Warren. "Are you going to see him?"

"I don't know," Diane said, and went back to concentrating on not thinking about or looking at Warren.

"I understand," Warren answered quietly.

The next time Diane looked up, a moment later, he was gone. There was no use trying to study. She was in the wrong mood for it, and had far too many conflicting emotions swirling in her brain to even try. With a sigh, she dumped her books back into her pack, then got up to change into her nightgown. It was too early to go to bed, but she got into bed anyway, and flipped out the lights to think. Long after midnight, having lain in bed restlessly all evening, she finally fell asleep.

In the morning, Warren was not with her. She took her pack, and removed his thermos from it. Setting it on top of her desk, she went down to breakfast, leaving Warren at home.

He stood in her room dejectedly and watched her walk her bicycle down the front path, then get on it and ride away. It had been the first time since meeting her that he had not said good night or good morning—at least one of those greetings, and almost always both.

Diane skipped her last class before lunch and sat by herself in a corner of the library between the stacks. What did Mr. McMonigle want to talk about? If he wanted to give her something, what was it? Priscilla's ashes? Did she really even want Priscilla's ashes? It would only mean that Warren would leave, and much as she wanted him to fulfill his life and go to—well, heaven or where ever it was—she was becoming more frightened that she could not face the emptiness of life without him. They had been together every day, sometimes almost every hour for months and months. He was like a husband—and in a way, she thought they had more intimacy than any marriage. He was like part of her own mind. And if she really loved him in the way she thought, then her reasons for not wanting to re-unite them were childish; not only childish, but incompatible with the noble kind of love she felt for him. By the time the lunch bell rang, Diane had begun to have a good, quiet cry.

Lunch break was almost over when she went to the lavatory to wash her face, then to the cafeteria where she called Mr. McMonigle on the pay-phone.

"Hello?" he answered.

"Mr. McMonigle? This is Diane Kolansky."

"Ah, Miss Kolansky," he said brightly. "Would you like to stop by?"

"Can I see you after three today?"

"Of course," he said. "I'll be waiting."

"See you then," she said. "Good-bye."

"Good-bye."

The two afternoon classes went by in a blur, and Diane got absolutely nothing out of the lectures. As she left the school building, she realized she had forgotten to write down the homework assignments, and went back to see her history teacher in the teacher's lounge. It was a few minutes wasted, however, because there was no assignment that evening.

Mr. McMonigle answered the door when she arrived, and bowed her in. "I'm glad to see you again," he said.

"I'm kind of in a rush, though," she lied. "I've got a test coming up tomorrow, and—"

"I won't keep you long, then," he said. "Have a seat?"

She sat in the living room with her pack between her feet. "You said you wanted to talk about something—give me something?"

"This," he said, and dangled a key in front of her.

She took it from his hand. "What's it to?"

"Ludmilla's storage locker. Locker fifteen at Ace Storage down on Jefferson Street. You know where that is?"

"I can find it," she answered. "But—why are you giving me this?"

"Like I was saying," he said, "Ludmilla won't be needing anything she had there. She's dead. And I'm not a young whipper-snapper anymore either, in case you haven't noticed."

"Oh, you're young," she said.

"Ha," he laughed. "Thanks for the compliment—I wish it was true."

"But why are you giving me this?" she asked, holding up the key.

"'Cause I think you're interested. You know a lot about those people, and—hell, sometimes I get a wild hair, and even think you might be telling the truth about Brannigan's ghost. You wouldn't be the first person to believe they've seen a ghost."

"It's true," she stated. "I'm not lying."

"I almost believe you," he said, "but not quite. Either way, though—whatever's left down there might probably mean more to you than it would to me."

"Oh. So you want me to go look at it?"

"I want you to *have* it," he corrected. "All of it. Whatever's there is yours for the taking. Rent's paid up two months in advance and I've already told 'em who you are. Signed it over to the first person who comes in claiming to be Diane Kolansky."

"What if I didn't show up?" she asked.

"Well, then I wouldn't have to worry about it, because they'd sell it off eventually if I didn't claim it."

"Why are you doing this?" she asked.

"Already told you that," he said. "Just take it. Go have a look anyway. I know you want to, don't you?"

"Yes," she said. "I do, but—"

"But what—go on, girl! Hell, if you like antiques, there's plenty of 'em there. Even if you don't want any of it, I'll bet you could find someone to buy most of it. A lot of good things, and you know how people love antiques."

"Thanks," she said.

"Now, I don't want to keep you too long—you have a lot of homework and all that."

"It's OK," she said. "I lied about that. I don't have much homework."

He smiled. "Would you like some tea?"

"Sure," she answered. "That sounds good."

They went to the kitchen and spent another hour talking. By the time she left, she had a pretty good idea what kinds of things she would find in the storage locker, but even Mr. McMonigle had not looked at everything. There were boxes and boxes of things, because Ludmilla had been a real collector of knick-knacks; pictures and music; letters from all of her friends and relatives. He could not even tell her for certain whether or not she would find Priscilla's ashes. She left his house in an uncertain mood and pedalled slowly home. A couple of times she stopped at street corners, lost in thought, and forgot to go across when the light turned.

Even if Priscilla's ashes were not in the storage locker—it must be full of all *kinds* of things. It might be so much she would have to spend two months just looking at all of it to figure out what she wanted to keep. And maybe she could simply not tell Warren she had the key, until she knew something more definite. In a way, she still did not want to find Priscilla, who would come between them—surely she would come between them. After all, she was Warren's real wife. Again she stopped on a corner, telling herself that he was married. Dead and married—to someone else. He was not hers to have and to hold, no matter how much she loved him. And if she loved him as much as she believed she did, she should do anything to make him happy. And whatever she did for him, even if she lost him, should only make her happier. That was the measure of true love.

[29]

Warren did not appear to Diane that night—and she did not call to him. Ordinarily, he would have dropped in as he always did, but she seemed suddenly unapproachable. When he thought she would not be aware of his presence, he watched her, with growing sadness. She was hiding something from him. Her aura fluttered constantly, always tiny and withdrawn, and very dark. Sometimes there were instants when it would flare and seem to almost blaze again, but she would quench it. She was not herself at all, and he could not help wondering what had happened at McMonigle's place. Had she learned something dreadful? He thought not, but until she told him, he believed he had no real right to intrude on her. That had been his promise, as early as the first day they met. She had not called his name, so he waited, contenting himself with the company of little Victoria.

Sometimes the baby woke up at night, as all babies do. Normally they scream in the darkness for Mother, who comes hurrying. But Victoria had a playmate in Warren—a smiling face she trusted and loved. To Diane and her mother, she seemed like only the happiest little infant they had ever seen. She almost never cried, and from the very first, woke only rarely at night. Warren knew better, though. Truly, Victoria was a happy baby, and he thought her very intelligent. At night she woke often, and always—nearly always—found Warren there by her crib. She would coo and smile, watching his face and playing fingers. He told her stories and sang songs— she especially adored 'Silent Night' and 'Frere Jacques'. She would wiggle delightedly with wide eyes and open mouth when he would begin to sing, then quiet down and stare into his face, enraptured until he finished.

Sometimes he felt terrible that he had not lived long enough to have a baby of his own, but little Victoria was so adorable, she was almost consolation for that. Priscilla would have been enthralled with her too, he was sure. Often he sat outside under the stars after playing with Victoria, simply thinking about how it might have been to raise a family with Priscilla. She would have made a lovely mother.

Diane's silence continued for two days, and on the evening of the second day, she said his name. When she arrived home, she ate dinner moodily, hardly speaking to her parents, and when that was over she washed the dishes while still thinking, then did her homework.

"Warren?" she called softly. On the edge of her bed she sat and called his name over and over. She had been calling for half an hour before he appeared.

"Hello," he said from the doorway. "May I come in?"

"Come here," she said. He did not move, and she smiled. "Come on, I'm not mad. Look, I'm sorry, OK?"

"All right," he said advancing across the room. He took a seat next to her on the bed in silence.

"I have a question," she said.

"I'm listening."

"Warren—will you promise me something?"

"If it's something I can do, yes. Of course I'll promise."

"If I bring Priscilla's ashes here—if I find them, I mean—will you promise not to leave? At least—at least say you won't leave right away."

"Diane," he said softly, looking into her moist eyes. "If there's any way I can stay, yes. I'll stay here as long as I can—or as long as you want me to stay, which ever comes first."

"That's what I want," she said. "I need you. I want you to stay forever and ever."

"If I can," he replied.

She sat for a moment longer, then went to get the key from her pack. "I got this from Mr. McMonigle the other day."

"What is it?"

"It's the key to Ludmilla's storage locker."

Warren jumped up smiling. "You mean—Priscilla's there? Did you see her?"

"No," she said. "I don't know what's there. Neither did Mr. McMonigle. But I can go look any time."

"Tonight?"

"It's too late tonight," she said, sitting again on the bed. "I'll go by tomorrow, though. But—I'll go by myself, OK?"

Warren nodded. "If that's what you want."

"I'd like to go by myself, the first time anyway."

"I understand," he said. He could sense that her emotional state was so delicate he dared not make any request to go along. "Go ahead."

"Thanks," she said.

Later in the evening, she got ready for bed, taking her time about changing her nightgown. Warren approached her delicately, sweetly, wishing he could kiss her and hold her. Diane wanted him. Desperately she wanted his arms and his body to hold her. Her own hands could almost do nothing to soothe her desire, and she finally lay down with him, whispering love-words. She began to rub her moist vagina slowly, listening to the sound of his voice. He could tell that she needed his closeness, but at the same time, knew she wanted to be pursued and made love to. The frustration welled in him, unable to really be with her.

With the light out, she tucked a pillow between her legs, and embraced another, wanting to feel something in her arms, and to be in his arms—pretending he was with her physically, making love to her and filling her with his strength. She attained a tiny, comforting release at last, and fell asleep to the sound of his voice singing softly nearby.

For most of the night, Warren sat out on the roof looking at the stars and watching the neighborhood. He checked on Victoria every so often. Near dawn, he slipped back into Diane's room and lay down beside her, to be with her when she woke up at seven.

[30]

Nancy was happily cleaning up the breakfast dishes. Tom had long since taken Rat to school. She scraped pancakes into the wastebasket absent-mindedly, still thinking of the previous, wonderful evening. She and Tom had not made love like that for months it seemed, and maybe it had been a year. Anyway, it had been lovely and romantic enough to last all night and right through breakfast. She hoped her feeling would last all day. The baby was asleep, and Diane was getting ready to leave. Nancy heard her come down the stairs, then pause in the front hallway.

"Mom," Diane said at the kitchen doorway.

"Yes, dear?"

"Can I ask you a really serious question?"

"Of course." She turned to look at Diane, who stood hunched in the doorway. "Yes," she said wiping her hands on a towel. "Are you all right?"

"I'm fine."

"Sit down," Nancy suggested. She took out a cup and poured herself some coffee from the percolator, then walked toward the kitchen table. Diane sat across from her.

"Mom, have you ever been *really* in love?"

"What do you mean *really*," she rolled her eyes, "in love?"

"I mean—heart and soul and I'll die if I can't be with you sort of stuff." She tried to keep herself speaking as lightly as she thought her mother would think she thought about love.

"You mean the Romeo and Juliet kind of stuff?"

"Yeah, like that. Well, sort of."

"Are you in love with someone?"

Diane nodded.

"That's wonderful," Nancy said sipping her coffee. "God, I do remember that feeling." She smiled at her daughter, but then looked quizzically, because Diane did not seem elated. "Isn't it wonderful?"

"Have you ever been in love like that and then—and then known that there's no possible way—nothing in the universe can keep you together, because it's just not possible? Nobody would understand, and nobody would condone it?"

"What are you trying to say?" Nancy asked.

"Well, I have someone like that," Diane said. "Really," she added abruptly, "it's not puppy love. It's serious."

Nancy smiled, remembering all the gorgeous wonderful feelings—how adult and serious she had felt. Dizzy for a week and broken hearted the week after—and, "Oh My God," she thought suddenly—Diane must be trying to say she had lost her virginity. "What's the boy's name? Do I know him?"

"Not a *boy*, Mom."

"Oh dear," Nancy intoned, and put her cup down carefully. She paused a moment with pursed lips, looking into her coffee, then swallowed. "What's *her* name then?"

"Her?" Diane squealed, beginning to laugh and cover her mouth. "Oh, Jesus, Mom! He's not a she—I'm not a *Lesbian!*"

"Huh? Then what do you mean?"

Diane suddenly saw that there was no possibility her mother would understand about Warren, and the potential conversation ran through her mind with great lucidity: He's married, Mom— oh shit, you're way too goddam young for that—who is he?—are you pregnant?—what's his name?—I'll kill him—he's already dead, Mom. Then Nancy would drop dead at her feet.

"It's Peter," she lied instead.

Nancy tilted her head, smiling and biting her lip sentimentally—so her daughter was in love with Peter. At least he was a nice boy, and they seemed to—apparently they did—get along well. "I'm happy for you," she said. "But it's breaking up, huh?"

"Yeah," Diane said. "It won't work."

"And you wanted some advice?"

Diane nodded. "Yeah."

"You'd tell me if you were—in trouble, wouldn't you?"

"Yes, Mom."

"My advice . . . If it's not working, let him go," Nancy said. "It seems really painful, I know, but—oh shit . . ." She snapped her eyes open. "Look out! Here comes the same damn lecture Grandma gave me!"

"It's OK," Diane laughed.

"When you're fifteen or sixteen," Nancy said, reaching out to pull a strand of Diane's hair, "and you start being in love and having sex—life seems really long, and every love is the beginning and end of the world. It's a wonderful, delicious time, and there will never be anyone like your first lover. But love like that doesn't last at your age, and it's not supposed to last. It's preparation, exploration—preparing your heart for the realities of adult love and sometimes pain. While it does last, it's absolutely beautiful. But you also learn how to let it go sometimes. Hopefully, you learn to handle your feelings—and your *body*," she emphasized the body, "with respect and responsibility. You'll still be alive when it's over, and you'll meet someone else. For a while—hey, I'll be here for you, Diane."

"Did that happen with you?"

"It sure did," she said. "I had lots of boyfriends. A couple of them I slept with. And eventually, I met your father and found out my Mom was right, too. Everything before him was part of the dress rehearsal."

"Thanks, Mom." Diane stood and went to kiss her mother on the cheek.

"Feel better?"

"A little."

"If you want to talk later, we can. Better hurry though," Nancy said glancing at the clock. "You're late already."

"Bye Mom!"

[31]

When Diane entered the office of Ace Storage after school, she found a young man whose hair seemed as greasy as his coverall. He was leaning back in a rickety office chair and reading a dilapidated hard-cover book. His feet were on the desk, and he was so completely absorbed in what he was reading that his mouth hung open. The book was a fifth-grade reader—Diane had used the same one and recognized it.

"Hello," she said from the doorway, standing with one hand on the door jamb.

Immediately, the man's feet dropped to the floor and he set the book carefully aside in the middle of the desk. "Hello," he said slowly, then smiled and continued as if he had practiced intently, "Welcome to Ace Storage, Ma'am. May I help you?"

"I'm Diane Kolansky," she said. "Is the manager here?"

"Oh," the man said, his face suddenly sinking into a frown. His forehead wrinkled and he looked at his feet. "Guess I can't help you, huh?"

"Maybe you can," she said. "Does my name ring a bell?" She bit her lip quickly, thinking 'Pavlov'—but no, she told herself, he could not help it.

"Yes, Ma'am," he said, nodding vigorously.

"Oh, good," she said, entering the room to stand before the desk. "Did he tell you about me?"

"Yes, Ma'am. You're the lady who's getting Number Fifteen from Mr. McMunginell. I remember that."

"Do I need to sign anything? Or can I just go open my locker?"

"I guess it's all right," he said, looking confused again, as if trying to remember why she was there, then his face brightened as he came to a decision. "We're expecting *you*, so I think you can go right in."

"Thank you," she said, and turned to go. "I'll stop again on the way out—will the manager be back soon?"

"He said, uh—yes, real soon. Back in a few minutes."

"Thanks," she said, and waved. "Bye!"

"Good-bye, Ma'am. Thank you for choosing Ace."

Ace Storage was a compound of long brick buildings lined with roll-up metal doors, all surrounded by a stone fence capped with tangled strands of barbed-wire. Locker fifteen was at the end of the first row, so Diane had no great distance to walk. It was locked with probably the most expensive padlock Mr. McMonigle could have found, and she opened it with a click, then threaded it back through the opened latch. The door seemed well-oiled, and she had no trouble sliding it up a few inches. It was also heavy, so she had to crouch down and push, then stand again and shove with all her strength to push it up over her head. Light streamed into the tiny room-like locker. On the right wall was a light-switch, but she had no need of light to see what she wanted to see.

There were two rows of boxes, one on either side of the locker, with a narrow walkway between them. In the back was a table with four chairs piled on it, and to the right of that, an upright piano beneath a drop-cloth, with several boxes and a lamp on top of it. In one chair, on top of the table, sat a woman in a black skirt hemmed at mid-calf, and over it a pressed white blouse, long-sleeved and modest. On her shoulders was an open-knit shawl, also black, and her golden-blonde hair was pinned up above her collar and wound into a bun behind. Diane's first thought was that the one thing Warren had never mentioned was that Priscilla Brannigan, nee Canfield, was a stunningly beautiful woman. She could do nothing but stand in the doorway and stare at an apparition of loveliness, still as a statue, and feel quite ill with butterflies raging in her stomach.

"Priscilla Brannigan?"

"My God, child," Priscilla said as she stood up, and in one step floated slowly to the ground. "Can you see me?"

Diane nodded twice, gravely, without a smile. "I can hear you too."

"I think I'll be faint," Priscilla said, and leaned against a tall box.

"How long have you been here?"

"Been here?" Priscilla asked, her voice rising. "You mean in this horrible room?"

"It's called a storage locker."

"I've been here for—it must be ten years," she said, then rushing toward Diane, fell to her knees, pleading. "My God, please, Miss, please don't leave me here!"

"Where are you? I mean—where is your urn or your ashes or whatever?"

"There," Priscilla said, practically crawling on the ground. "Oh, my God, will you take me? Are you going to take me with you?"

"I'm still thinking about it."

"No," Priscilla said vehemently. "Please, please—I'll do anything for you, but please take me with you? Won't you?"

Diane felt suddenly horrible, as guilt-ridden as if she had been spiteful and nasty. Perhaps she had been, to Warren. And Priscilla was so pathetic—and gorgeous. She went forward a few steps and sat down with her back against one of the boxes. "I want to talk to you first," she said.

"Will you take me then?"

"I might—but first, can we just talk?"

"Of course," Priscilla said sweetly. She pulled her shawl more tightly around her shoulders and sat down on the floor close to Diane with both feet tucked under herself, then arranged her skirt carefully. "What shall we talk about? What's your name? Shall we start with that? You already know my name."

"I'm Diane Kolansky," Diane said.

"Do you like games, Miss Kolansky?"

Diane smiled. "That's not what I had in mind," she said, trying not to sound condescending. "I'm fifteen—almost sixteen—so I'm not a little girl."

"Yes, I can see that," Priscilla said, taking on a more adult tone with her. "Well. Shall we talk about your schoolwork then?"

"No," Diane said. "Let's talk about you."

"Me?" Priscilla blurted. "You want to talk about me? How funny!"

"Is it?"

"Oh, God, yes," she said, throwing her whole body sideways in mirth. "I've been dead so long I think I'm looking at Moon People or something every time I venture out on the roof. And that's all there is to know about me!"

Diane felt amused by her sudden change and laughed aloud. "How long have you been dead?"

"I'm only guessing, of course," Priscilla said. "It's been ages since I've spoken to anyone, you see. Ludmilla was the last, I think—but then, she couldn't see me once I died, so she wasn't any sort of fun after that. It's been, oh more than fifty years I suppose." She smiled at Diane. "You've no idea what a relief it is just to use one's voice again. Why, I feel almost giddy!"

Though Diane had wanted to hate the Priscilla she imagined finding—the Other Woman, the witch, who would step between her and Warren—she discovered instead after talking to her for only a few minutes that she really liked Priscilla. The quaint way she prattled on about herself and Moon People; how much she missed a real home; how Ludmilla and she had played the violin as girls; how she and her fiance—meaning Warren—had sung and played together at the piano.

Generally Priscilla played the piano, but her fiance had the better voice—a lovely baritone that she claimed sent her into absolute rapture. Sometimes she would be so overcome with emotion when she listened to him that she had to stop playing. The piano was the one sitting in the corner, and she pointed it out. Nobody had touched it for years. Diane went to push a few keys and Priscilla gasped at how out of tune it was. But that reminded her of something else, and she was off instantly. With growing admiration, Diane listened and followed Priscilla around the room as if enchanted while she pointed out furnishings and told Diane how she had imagined re-decorating the place, if she really had to live there. The piles of things and boxes were intolerable to anyone with a sense of order, yet she laughed at it all. Nothing seemed to quench Priscilla's voluble gaiety, and she continued to tell Diane all sorts of things, despite having originally claimed that there was nothing to know about herself.

"It's no wonder Warren married you," Diane said finally.

"Warren?" inquired Priscilla. "What do you mean?"

"He talks about you all the time," replied Diane. "But he never told me how—how really *wonderful* you are . . ." Her eyes began to blur. "I wanted to hate you, I really did—but . . . Oh God!" she said, letting herself go into tears.

"There now," Priscilla whispered comfortingly, and taking her shawl tried to cover Diane's shoulders. The shawl fell slowly through Diane as if she were not there, and for a second Priscilla was puzzled. "How silly," she said suddenly, laughing at herself. "Oh, please don't cry—I can't dry your tears even if I do have a kerchief," and pulling a kerchief from her sleeve, she held it up. "It's not much good, but I can't seem to get rid of it."

"I'm not crying." Diane wiped away her tears with one hand and tried to smile.

"All right," Priscilla said, evidently trying to maintain her detachment. "You know Warren it seems, so he must be still here as well. Did he send you to get me?"

"No," Diane said. "I mean, no he didn't send me, but yes, I know him. I know him very well."

"Oh," Priscilla answered. "You've no trouble seeing ghosts, I take it?" Diane nodded, and Priscilla continued, "I never could—when I was alive, that is. It's rather funny, really, I never believed in ghosts. Neither did Warren, frankly—we were neither of us superstitious, you know."

"I didn't either," Diane admitted, "until I met Warren."

"Tell me about him. Is he well?" Priscilla asked.

"He's fine," Diane replied. "He misses you terribly."

"Will you take me to him?"

"I wanted to talk first," Diane replied. "Maybe we can get to know each other first. Is that all right?"

"All right? I should say it is. It's a pleasure simply to meet someone again. And we've a good start already, haven't we?"

"I've known Warren almost a year," Diane said. Priscilla was listening intently, suddenly quiet as if eager to hear whatever Diane would say. "We've known each other—very intimately."

"Oh?"

"Yes," Diane continued. "Quite *intimately*, but—but it's not as if he's been unfaithful or anything."

"Unfaithful?" Priscilla laughed. "My dear, you've no idea how funny that is!"

"What?"

Priscilla poked her face forward and opened her eyes widely. "'Til *death* do us part, Miss Kolansky!"

Diane smiled, and began to laugh. Together they laughed, until Priscilla finally stopped and sighed, a hand to her breast.

"Do you know," she said, "that's terribly funny. I suppose it's true though. We're both dead, if not buried. God's pulled us asunder if ever he did anyone—and," she began to laugh uncontrollably, "and we hadn't even been married a day!" Suddenly she stopped, taking a deep breath and holding a palm to her chest. "Oh dear, that's not funny at all, is it?"

"Warren's waited sixty years to consummate your marriage."

Priscilla's blue eyes flashed brightly. "Has he really?" she said. "Oh, he *is* a dear! How thoughtful of him. I've been waiting for him, too."

"Did you die a virgin?" Diane asked.

"Me?" Priscilla cocked her head with a smile. "Just between us *ladies*?" Diane nodded affirmation and Priscilla whispered, "of course not—hadn't been a virgin since I was seventeen." Earnestly she asked, "Did he think he'd got a virgin bride?"

"I think he still does," Diane confessed.

"I suppose we should have talked about that more directly. Well, it's all water under the bridge now, isn't it?" She placed her hands in her lap. "I never slept with him, you understand, though I truly did *want* to. But, well, any girl knows—at least we did, and I don't know about you Moon People these days—any girl knows it's impossible to catch him if he's satisfied that way."

"Is it?" Diane asked.

Priscilla looked at her thoughtfully. "Well, perhaps not these days—but I thought so then. At seventeen, when I'll admit I was a bit flighty, I found that out."

"The man didn't marry you?"

"Heavens no," she said, then began to laugh. "He married my sister!"

"Not Doc Jarmsford?"

With some surprise Priscilla inquired, "You know about him then?"

"Yes," Diane said. "He married Ludmilla."

"I almost died when he proposed to her, but never—I mean never—did I let her know he'd had *me*." Priscilla paused, then said as if to herself, "It's a pity she found out."

"Speaking of Doc Jarmsford," Diane said a moment later, "there's a question I have."

"Yes?"

"Did he push you out the window?"

"Harold? Of course not. He wasn't that kind of man."

"Who did then? Or did you really fall?"

Priscilla blinked and said clearly, "Ludmilla pushed me."

"Ludmilla?"

"My own sister. Right out the window. Shoosh!" Priscilla said with a shake of her head and a wave of her hand. "There I was, picking myself up off the ground. You can't imagine the shock it was to see them hovering over my dead body, and me there screaming that I wasn't dead."

"That must have been a shock," Diane agreed.

"Indeed, it was—I could have died."

"What happened after that?"

"Well, Ludmilla had me cremated, of course—I'd made it clear I wanted that, at least, just as Warren always had. After that, I lived in her house for years and years. I suppose you must know, if you know anything about her, that she married a man named McMonigle after that. Say—was it Jake who gave you the key to this room here?"

"Yes," Diane said. "He's Joshua McMonigle's son, right?"

"The eldest, yes. He looked after Ludmilla in her dotage."

"You never re-married, did you?"

"No, I didn't," said Priscilla. "I had a proposal or two, but I wasn't interested. It was just too much of a shock, you know, losing Warren as I did, and I had this feeling in the back of my mind that I was jinxed for marrying. That's not to say I was celibate or anything, though. I wasn't a tramp, either, but I had a few flings."

"Did you?"

"Yes, and I'm not ashamed of them, either. They were nice men, and—I felt it was justified. Warren would have understood."

"Do you think he would?"

"Of course I do—I loved him and he loved me. He was dead, and I was alive to enjoy what I could. He would have cheered me on, I'm sure. Through those years, you know, I kept Warren close beside me. Never when I slept with another man—that wouldn't have been quite proper—and now, knowing you know him, and he was watching me!—heavens, I'm glad I was prudent enough to leave him at home . . ."

"He might have enjoyed watching you," Diane said, then stood and picked up her pack.

"Really?" Priscilla asked, sounding concerned. "He might have enjoyed it? Should I have taken him along do you think?"

"Ask him when you see him," answered Diane. "I have to go now. It's been really fun meeting you." She paused for an instant, wishing that she could press Priscilla's hand in her own, then turned to leave.

"Oh, dear." Priscilla stood up to follow Diane asking, "You aren't going to leave me here?"

"No—well, yeah. I am now. But tomorrow," she said, half feeling it might be a lie, "I promise I'll take you somewhere. Can you last until tomorrow?"

"Of course," Priscilla said, leaning forward to touch her arm but plunging her hand completely through Diane. She laughed at her own awkwardness and caught her balance. "Well, it's only one night, and I've lasted all this time."

"I'll see you tomorrow, all right?"

"Do hurry back," Priscilla said as Diane slid down the door and locked it. "Please, dear God, let her come back," she murmured to herself, then sat in a chair to wait.

[32]

How unexpected and odd, Diane thought as she pedalled home, that she should like Priscilla. She had no question at all of why Warren loved her. She put her bicycle in the garage and hurried into the house. For her mother, who poked her head out of the kitchen, she had only a brief greeting before running upstairs and flinging her pack across the room.

"Warren!" she cried when she had slammed the door behind her.

"Hello," he said, strolling down through the roof.

"Come here," she entreated, holding out her arms, and he came forward to embrace the air in what passed between them for a kiss.

"You seem happy," he said, feeling immensely relieved to see her in high spirits. "How was school?"

"The same," she said. "It's what happened after!" She flopped onto her bed and kicked off her shoes, speaking animatedly. "I went to Ace Storage, of course, like I said. You know what I found?" She wiggled her toes.

"What?"

"Priscilla Brannigan."

"Thank God!" he exclaimed leaping into the air. He pulled a somersault that took him through several rafters, before landing on his knees at Diane's feet. "Did you bring her home?"

"No," she said, smiling wickedly at him.

"But you will, of course?" he said, half questioning and hoping.

"Tomorrow."

"Why wait?"

"Practicality," she said. "I wouldn't bring her home until I'd talked with her, and if I talked with her, I couldn't very well dig through all that stuff—you should see it Warren! McMonigle's a nut—he's got to be. There must be a thousand dollars worth of stuff in there!"

"But how is Priscilla," he asked, coming forward on his knees to sit admiringly before her, resting his chin just above her knee.

"Warren!"

"What?"

"She's fine of course—come on. She's as dead as you are, so it's not like she can have an accident or anything."

"I mean psychologically," he said. "Does she seem stable?"

"I *really* liked her," Diane answered. After an instant, she opened her heart completely. "She's a doll—I could tell right off why you married her. She's perfect for you."

"What did you talk about?"

"All kinds of stuff," she said. "A bit about you. A bit about us."

"Us?"

"You and me and fucking and all that."

"You told her that?"

"No," she laughed. "Just teasing. I said we knew each other quite intimately."

"Meaning we 'do it' as you say."

"No," Diane answered in a quiet voice, feeling a tiny burst of tenderness. "I meant we're really intimate with each other—it's not just sex, right?"

"You're right." He gave her a warm smile, nodding his head. "You'd be surprised how many people don't know the difference."

"Well, I hinted, too," she admitted playfully, "and I think she figured we're doing it, but she didn't mind."

"Is that so?" Warren said, sounding most surprised. "She didn't mind?"

"You know what she said to me?"

"No, what?"

"'Til death do us part, she told me, and laughed about it too."

"How odd."

"I thought it was funny—isn't it funny?"

"I suppose it is," Warren conceded. "She does still consider us married, though?"

"You'll have to ask her about that," Diane teased.

"When you bring her tomorrow."

"Uh huh. Meanwhile—can I ask a little favor?"

"Anything," he said sweetly. "Ask me anything at all."

"This is still hard for me, even if I joke about it. But I want it to all be wonderful. So can we have this one last night just between the two of us? I want it to be romantic. No regrets or mushy stuff—just—let's take a walk in the moonlight and have some tea here and talk, OK? We can play chess later, too, OK?"

"Sounds wonderful," he said.

"And we can start right after dinner. Meanwhile, I have homework," she said, picking up her pack. "So while I do that, why don't you read this." She pulled from her pack the latest issue of Playboy. "Ta da!"

"You're wonderful!" he said, clapping his hands. "My libido is never far from your mind."

Diane laughed and laid the magazine out on her table, then flipped pages for him every so often while she worked on her geometry and history assignments. She also had a poem to write for English—the assignment was one of those 'out of the hat' poetry topics, and she had to write about something white and soft, but not snow. She spent an hour musing and saying lines aloud to see what Warren thought of them. In the end she had carved out seventeen lines of free verse:

> White pearls at the collar,
> open and low
> await her pale throat
> to fill them.
> Veiled sleeves
> await her limbs
> to give them movement.

Cascading lace,
spume of a frozen waterfall,
caught in mid-leap over satin
rippling toward a train
bedecked with roses.
Gathered in anticipation:
old lace,
blue garter,
borrowed broach,
and virgin bride.

Warren smiled when she had read it over. "Reminds me of my own wedding," he said.

"Does it? I'll call it 'Warren's Bride'—how's that?"

"Won't make any sense to the reader," he said critically. "You should make it more abstract."

"It'll mean something to me," she said, "and that's all that matters."

"No," he countered. "Your grade is what matters."

"It's an 'A' poem," she said.

"And you'll get a minus attached for its incomprehensible title," he insisted. "How much shall we bet on that?"

"Want to bet—" she bit her lip and smiled, "you don't have anything to win or lose."

"Too bad," he teased in a serious tone. "That's what you get for keeping company with ghosts."

The remainder of the evening was as romantic as Warren knew how to make it. He walked out with Diane to look at the horses in a nearby field. They were the only horses within a mile or more, and lived in a shack in a corral next to a cherry orchard. They climbed the fence and gave each horse a sugar lump and a pat on the nose. Warren recited what few things he could remember of Coleridge and Keats as they strolled between the rows. The quarter-moon was in the sky, and they sat for a while watching it behind the branches. And when they returned home, Diane was feeling

exhilarated by the fresh air of the late spring evening. She brewed
a pot of tea with lots of honey, then took two cups from the kitchen
and went upstairs. Her desk was clean, and she laid out a table
cloth, then set out their cups. In the center she put the chessboard,
and they sat down to a game by candlelight.

Warren offered to let Diane have white. He was a far better
chess player than she, and gave her that advantage, though he
would never stoop to letting her win. She saw through that too
easily and argued with him the few times he had done it. He soon
found she liked it better, even if she lost, when she played a hard
game. Most of the time she did lose, and then asked him to give
her a few pointers. Warren was gratified that she learned rapidly
and rarely made the same mistake twice.

They had just begun their second game, when Diane heard a
step upon the stairs and a knock at her door.

"Yes?" she called.

"It's me," said Nancy. "Can I come in?"

"Just a second." Quickly, she put Warren's cup beside hers,
then turned the chessboard sideways in front of her, as if she were
playing both sides. "Come on in, Mom."

Nancy entered sheepishly. "Hi. Just wondered what you're up
to."

"Just studying some chess," she said.

"Playing by yourself?" Nancy came over to stand near the table,
leaning over on her elbows. "How can you play by yourself?"

"I'm not," Diane said quickly. "I was playing a game out of a
book. Bobby Fischer."

"Oh. Anyway—how's Peter?"

"Umm." Diane blushed hotly and swallowed. "We're doing
OK now."

"Well, that's good," Nancy said, then brushed a hair from
Diane's face and patted her cheek, resting her hand for an instant.
"If you want to talk about it, I'm free any time, OK?"

"Thanks, Mom. It's going great, really," Diane said cheerfully,
covering her mother's hand with her own. "I think you were right."

"About what?"

"It's only a rehearsal, right? I think I was taking it too seriously."

Nancy laughed. "I didn't mean for you to take that literally," she said. "But I'm glad to see you're happy."

"I'm doing fine, Mom."

"Are you going to let us actually meet him sometime? He never comes in."

"Yeah," Diane said, still blushing, feeling it was half a lie. "I'll make him come in to say hi next time."

"OK. Anyway, just thought I'd ask." Nancy walked to the door and turned back while she opened it. "See you in the morning, huh?"

Diane waved, and Nancy closed the door.

"What was that?" Warren asked when Nancy had gone.

"Oh," Diane said quietly. "I asked her advice about Peter."

"About what?" he asked.

She looked at him. "That's a lie. I asked her about us, but acted like it was Peter." She slid the chessboard back into the middle of the table and placed Warren's tea in front of him. After a second, she swapped their cups, since he never drank his and hers was nearly empty. "I hadn't decided whether to bring Priscilla here or not, so I asked her about breaking up—just to kind of get my bearings."

"I see," he said. Her aura had shrunk, so he knew the subject was somewhat uncomfortable for her. "Shall we finish the game?"

"Sure," she said. "Whose move was it?"

"Wasn't it yours?"

"I don't remember. Want to start over?"

They started a new game, and played two more before Diane felt tired enough to sleep. Warren talked to her while she changed clothes, whispering romantic things and telling her how sweet and beautiful her body was.

As if it were the last time—knowing it would be their last time—Diane let herself be swept into delirious oblivion by their lovemaking. Though she accomplished her orgasm on her own, she could almost feel Warren's hands upon her, feel his breath soft upon her neck when he spoke. And when she climaxed, the shudder in her entire body, the buzzing of every nerve was so intense that she lay in complete rapture, smiling, eyes closed for nearly an hour.

"Warren, I love you," she whispered finally, pulling the covers over her naked body.

Warren lay beside her on his side. "I love you, too."

"I know you do," she whispered. "Or we wouldn't have such incredible sex . . ."

He smiled and stroked the air near her cheek.

The pauses between sentences in their lover's conversation grew longer, and finally she slept. Warren skipped his normal rounds of the house. About two o'clock, however, the baby woke up screaming. He let Nancy comfort little Victoria, and stayed unmoving by Diane's side. "You're going to be a wonderful woman," he said to her as she slept, curled up with her hands beneath her cheek. "I envy your future husband . . ."

[33]

Diane put on a flowery midi skirt in the morning, with a freshly pressed white blouse. She even put her hair up, as well as she could, in two braids which she pinned behind her head. Then she took Warren to school. He was too restless to sit and listen to lectures. He gadded about the room playfully, sometimes imitating the teacher until she finally stopped and stared at Diane, who kept chewing on her lip to keep from laughing.

"Is there some problem, Miss Kolansky?"

"No, Ma'am," Diane said, sitting up straight in her chair. "I'm just—I'm having my period," she lied, "and I have terrible cramps today."

The class burst into laughter.

"Maybe you should go see the nurse?" inquired the teacher.

Wearing a stoic expression Diane answered, "I'll be fine."

For the rest of the class period Warren calmed down, but Diane scolded him afterward. "Another outburst like that," she said as they walked down the hallway, "and you won't see Priscilla."

"Right. Of course," he said marching beside her. "I'm sorry if I got you in trouble."

She curled up her lips in her wicked smile. "I bit my tongue I was laughing so hard."

"Does it hurt?"

"It's OK—but really, just cut it out, OK?"

"Maybe I'll walk around for a while," he offered.

"Why don't you do that," she said. He could, and often did at school, walk far enough from her to look in on four or five other classrooms.

The manager was in when Diane and Warren arrived at Ace

Storage after school, and she had to stop to sign a rental agreement. She almost asked him if she could legally sign, being a minor, but since he seemed unaware of just how young she was, Warren advised her to sign the thing and worry about any problems later. She signed.

"Now," she said to Warren as they approached locker fifteen. "Wait behind me, and I'll give you the signal to step out and let Priscilla see you, OK?"

Warren agreed, and stood well to the side while she opened the door.

"Oh, thank God!" Priscilla exclaimed, floating down from her chair. "You did come back—I was so afraid!"

"I said I'd be here, didn't I?"

"You never can tell about people though," Priscilla said. She came forward to give Diane a little embrace. "Still—I'm so glad to see you, dear."

"I brought something for you," Diane said.

"For me?" Priscilla cried. "How thoughtful of you!"

Warren stepped forward. "Hello Priscilla."

"Warren!" she exclaimed, and running straight through Diane flung herself into his arms. "Oh, Warren! My God—I'm so happy, I just . . ." She burst into tears and Warren hugged her, whirled her around and picked her up completely in his arms. To each other they were as corporeal as flesh, solid and real. They stood simply touching one another's faces, then hugged again and whirled in the air.

"You've gotten lighter!" he exclaimed at last.

"The best part of being dead, I suppose," she said, laughing. "Oh, Warren!"

Diane stood back with tears rolling down her cheeks to see them stop, and looking at each other, slowly draw together in a passionate kiss. Their faint luminosity seemed to increase tenfold with their passion—he caressed her, kissed her neck. She threw back her head, laughing while he kissed her again and again, then took her hands and kissed her wrists.

When they finally had done with their greeting, they stood with their arms interlocked to tell Diane how perfectly happy she had made them, to finally be with each other after so many years.

"It's the happiest moment of my life," Priscilla said, throwing one hand to her bosom. "I thought my wedding day happy—but compared to this—this absolute giddiness—it was nothing!"

It was nearly an hour before their bubbly thankfulness and tears subsided enough for Diane to ask Priscilla to guide her to the urn containing her ashes. Of course, it was near the bottom in the back, and took Diane nearly another hour to retrieve. Finally, after sliding things around and lifting boxes out of the way, she had in her hand the wooden box containing Priscilla's urn.

"I brought something else for you," Diane said, opening her pack. She pulled out a large-size thermos. "This is your wedding present."

"Heavens," Priscilla said looking it over. "Whatever will you do with that?"

"Watch," Diane said. "Observe—nothing up my sleeve." She unscrewed the cap and made a cone of notebook paper, then holding Priscilla's blue and white urn carefully over the mouth of the thermos, emptied the ashes into it. "Does that feel any different?" she asked

"Not a bit," Priscilla admitted.

"And now, for my next trick," Diane continued. She took Warren's thermos from her pack—it was smaller by half—and emptied it into the thermos containing Priscilla's ashes. "How's that?" she asked when she began to pour.

"Oh my!" Priscilla exclaimed, wiggling her body. "Oh, dear," she said again. "Warren . . . hold me . . . It does feel more cozy, doesn't it?"

Warren glanced at Diane as he took Priscilla into his arms. "Can we be alone?" he whispered.

"I get to watch," Diane said. "That's all I want—just to watch."

"Can you at least close the door?"

Diane flipped on the light and pulled the door down almost all the way.

She had thought lovemaking beautiful when Warren was beside her. She had thought kisses delightful. But the love that Warren and Priscilla showed her surpassed them all. They removed their clothes slowly, admiringly, one garment at a time and hung them in the air. Priscilla's bosom was gorgeous, and when he had opened her blouse, he stopped to praise and kiss her full breasts, playing his tongue across their taut nipples.

Diane sat down on the floor to watch them explore each other, quietly talking and each observing every detail of the other's body. Priscilla's fingers went slowly to Warren's wound.

"Was it here?" she asked, and kissed it. "Was it painful when you died?"

"The only pain was the pain of leaving you," he said. "Nothing else mattered but that I was losing you."

"You poor dear," she said. "Did you know how I cried? How I did cry—it was a descent into darkness."

"But you, too," he said, touching her lips. "You're unblemished—but inside it must have been horribly painful for you."

"No," she said, "it wasn't at all. I broke my neck in the fall, you see, and then there I was—the most painful part was watching them treat me as if I were dead!"

"But it's all over," he said, and kissed her again. "We're together again at last."

"I've been waiting for you," she whispered. "Waiting for so long."

"And I for you," he replied.

Setting her carefully in the air, he kissed her body from toe to head, then dwelt between her thighs, his fingers playing in the air and brushing lightly over her breasts. And when she begged him to hold her, to love her, he climbed into the air and slowly began to press his love forward.

"It's beautiful," she said, reaching out to touch his penis when he set its head against the ripe and swollen lips of her vagina. "It's more than I imagined."

"Here," he said, "won't you taste?" and pushed forward until the head of his organ resided inside her.

"Delicious," she whispered, urging herself forward with undulations. "I must have it all."

"You shall have it all," he said. "You shall."

Welded into a single rhythmically pulsating organism, they moved together in the air. Diane sat cross-legged on the floor and watched them in complete silence. When they began to move together, she put her legs up and raised her skirt, then let her hand wander into her panties. She was damp and soft. The sudden pressure of her finger was so welcome that she pulled her panties off entirely and used both hands.

The three of them, after building to a peak of passion they could no longer sustain, climaxed almost simultaneously. Diane came first with a tiny moan, and as if this were a trigger for their own ecstatic explosion, Priscilla followed with a long, drawn out sigh, clutching wildly at Warren. He thrust harder and faster, then clamping his arms around her waist, let out a shuddering whimper of delight.

[34]

After Diane took Warren and Priscilla home, they spent the evening catching up on their lonely years apart. Priscilla had surprisingly less to say than Warren—and much of the evening was taken up with their endearing comments to one another, interspersed with a great many kisses. They made love, too, while Diane watched again, and when they finished, sat on the bed together talking.

"You said yesterday that Ludmilla pushed you out the window," Diane said, turning suddenly to Priscilla.

"Ludmilla!" exclaimed Warren.

"She did," Priscilla confirmed.

"I'd have thought it was Jarmsford," offered Warren.

"I gather a lot of people thought that," said Priscilla. "It isn't true—but there was nothing I could do then to clear his name."

"Nobody would have believed it was her," said Warren. "Given what I know about him."

Priscilla smiled and said, "What did you know about him?"

"His lecherous tendencies—"

"How did it happen?" Diane asked.

"It started a long time before that," said Priscilla.

"Then start at the beginning."

"All right." Reaching out to pluck her shawl from from the air and adjust it over her naked shoulders, she said, "It began I believe with Harold's advances—"

"When he popped her cherry, you mean?" Diane asked.

"Yes," Priscilla laughed. "Ludmilla told me about having sexual relations with him almost as soon as it happened. Now, you must know that the same thing had happened to me *years* before that—but I never told anyone."

"You weren't a virgin?" asked Warren with some distress.

"Of course not," she said lightly, patting his thigh. "But—we'll go into that some other time."

"Nice hobby for a doctor—" Warren mumbled.

"Popping young virgins in his office . . ." Diane said, then turning to Priscilla, "How was it?"

"Hurt like the devil," Priscilla replied with a laugh. "I thought he'd run a hot poker into me! I was so petrified I couldn't scream, of course, and it wasn't funny at all. After that—having been spoiled by my own doctor—I decided it was all for naught. What was the use of being prim and proper? So I was a bit easy for a year or two. I gave myself to a couple of young men. The thing that surprised me was that they were incredibly different than Harold—at least, the one experience I had with Harold. And I found after a time, that I really quite enjoyed sexual relations."

Warren smiled. "You seem to still."

"It was something my mother certainly had never taught me." Turning to Diane, she said seriously, "Of course—it's so much nicer with a man you love, dear. But it was rather apparent after a while that once a man had taken you that way, he didn't often ask you to marry him."

Warren tilted his head questioningly.

"Yes, love," Priscilla said aside to him, "that's why I eluded you until we'd tied the knot. I had ever such great plans for our wedding night, too. Now," she said turning to Diane, "that's enough about me. Well, after I heard that from Ludmilla, of course I didn't say a word to her that wasn't kind. She was so absolutely happy that a man had made that kind of advance to her, she wouldn't hear anything unkind about him even if I had said anything. But I knew better." She looked at Warren with a twinge of sadness. "Since he was my first, too," she said.

"He deserved what he got," added Warren.

Priscilla did not speak up to agree with him, but after a moment continued her story. "So I made an appointment with him the next day—after Ludmilla told me what had happened, that is—

and threatened to expose him. When I walked into his office, he said hello as if nothing at all were the matter. I took off my gloves, I remember, and holding them out told him, 'you know, my sister was a virgin until after her last appointment'. You can imagine how flustered he was. Of course he denied it, but by the end of our little interview, I think my threats gave him pause to think. I reminded him of our little encounter, too, I assure you."

"He did well by her, though, I thought," Warren said.

"Yes—in the end," Priscilla said, "He did. Anyway, he proposed almost immediately—and what a shock that was to the family."

"I'm sure it was," Warren interjected.

"But their happiness only lasted a few years. I could say that it was Ludmilla's fault. She had always wanted children, you know. And when she married him, she imagined a house full of adorable babies. But it wasn't to be, and as the years went on, she blamed him more often. At some point I supposed she stopped to wonder why—since he was a widower when they met—he never had any children by his previous wife."

"Did she divorce him?"

"His first wife? No," Priscilla said, "she died—I have no idea of the cause. Anyway, Ludmilla began to blame him, which, whether it was true or not, did nothing to keep their marriage together. It could have been her as well, but later events proved that it was him."

"When she had a child by McMonigle," Diane said.

"Yes," Priscilla answered. "She began to accuse him occasionally—even in my presence—of all sorts of things. She told him once, for example, that she was surprised that a man who indulged himself so freely with her person—meaning, they had sexual relations with great frequency, as she had told me on other occasions—why wasn't she pregnant? It was during one of these arguments—more like brawls, really, since Ludmilla was always so physical—that Harold called me on the telephone."

"So it was him?" Warren asked. "I thought it was Ludmilla."

"No," Priscilla said. "Ludmilla, according to him, had gone

completely insane—breaking dishes and that sort of thing. He asked me if I wouldn't come over immediately. Well, it was about twelve miles to their place, so I couldn't get there before she'd locked herself in the bedroom."

"Was that where you found her?"

"Yes," Priscilla continued. "It seems that somehow, in the heat of their argument, he said something about me—and then, from what I gathered later, he let spill the whole story. The story about his encounter with me, that is. So when I arrived, Ludmilla was furious—not only at Harold, but at me as well."

"Why you?"

"At me for not confiding in her. After all, she had married a man who had prior sexual relations with her sister—and of course she jumped to the conclusion (probably correctly, of course) that he'd done the same with other young ladies, and that he never would have married her had it not been for me."

"He's a jerk," Diane stated.

"Was," interjected Warren.

"So there we were," said Priscilla. "He burst in the door of the bedroom, breaking the lock and smashing the door. She was waving a kitchen knife about and swearing in the most awful manner you can imagine. It was so completely unlike her—well, the swearing was, anyway. Then in the process of trying to calm her down, we became rather physically violent. She gave me a solid shove, quite deliberately, and the next thing I knew, I was picking myself up on the front lawn."

"That's when you died?" Diane asked.

"Exactly."

They sat silently for some time. Warren wanted to ask a number of questions, but every time he opened his mouth Priscilla shushed him with a finger to her lips. "We'll talk later," she said, half smiling.

Warren nodded silently, and smiled in return.

"The other question, then," Diane said after a time, "is who killed Jarmsford—or did he commit suicide?"

"Suicide?" Priscilla said incredulously. "Of course not—

Ludmilla did him in. I didn't see it of course, but I saw the aftermath, and there's no doubt in my mind that she poisoned him."

"Everyone seemed to think it was McMonigle," said Warren.

"He would have been a primary suspect," said Priscilla, "but I'm quite sure it was Ludmilla herself. You see—she was either pregnant then, or suspected she was. It might have been later— I'm a bit hazy on that. But she did believe she was."

"By who?"

"By Joshua McMonigle. She'd been seeing him for some time, and their relationship took quite an intimate turn. I witnessed them having sexual relations on several occasions—even in Ludmilla's own house when Harold was absent."

Diane smiled. "Wicked Ludmilla!"

"She was," insisted Priscilla. "First she killed me, then her husband. What a shock it was when Joshua married her!" She clapped her hands. "Now I remember. Ludmilla only thought she was pregnant when she killed Harold, because the week after she had her period. And it wasn't until four or five months later that they were married. And about six or seven months after that Katherine was born."

"Katherine?" asked Warren.

"That was Ludmilla's daughter."

"What happened to her?" asked Diane.

"Eventually—I mean about twenty years later, Katherine married a mechanic, and I believe they moved to Oregon. The middle boy—Josh's middle boy Erik, I mean—ended up in Alaska, and did quite well for himself. Jake stayed right here. The youngest boy—who was three, I believe, when Ludmilla married Josh— went to Wyoming or maybe it was New Mexico."

"So except for Jake McMonigle they're all gone?"

"As far as I know," said Priscilla.

"Maybe I should tell him the truth sometime," Diane said.

"It's not worth it," Priscilla said, shaking her head sadly. "There's no reason to do so—let him just forget about it all."

Warren agreed with her that it was best left alone, and Diane nodded with a sigh. It was late, and she let Priscilla and Warren talk while she watched, not wanting to go to sleep; afraid to sleep lest they disappear without saying good-bye. At some point, she slid into a dream.

To Diane's surprise, when she awoke the morning after pouring the ashes of Warren and Priscilla together and watching them consummate their marital union, neither of them disappeared. For days they all spent cozy evenings together. Diane was thankful that school was almost out, so she had little homework to worry about, but Warren insisted she study for her finals. It was more than a week later—during which time they lived and made love, all three together in her room after her evening studies—that she began to notice they were fading.

Diane turned sixteen at the end of June, and felt joyous— immensely happy and filled to bursting—that Warren and Priscilla were still with her. Her relationship with Peter began to blossom as well during the interim, and they had naturally proceeded from good-night kisses to more physical intimacy. Diane usually left Priscilla and Warren at home when she went on dates, and when she returned, delighted in telling them all about the evening.

"I let him finger-bang me tonight," Diane announced one evening in July.

"Wonderful," Priscilla agreed, having been long since apprised of Diane's conviction to give herself to Peter. "Did it feel really nice?"

"It was great," Diane whispered. "He made me come, even. God, it was wonderful."

"I'm glad for you," said Priscilla. "But you must take care you don't spend too much time at it—make sure Peter continues to take you real places, not just to bed."

"I will," Diane said solemnly, at that moment not really caring whether he did or not.

Later Priscilla told Warren that soon Diane would be strong enough, confident enough, and well-enough involved with Peter that they could finally leave. It had been only for her that they managed to hold themselves to Earth for so long, and Priscilla was certain that she and Peter would have sexual relations very shortly. Warren thought himself able to wait for that event, and in early August, it finally happened.

[35]

Diane was supposed to meet Peter at the corner of Miller and Fourth. She had told him she was taking him to see something special—a place she really liked, but she would not tell him where it was, or what it was called. Before leaving, she showered and put on clean clothes. Over a pair of button-fly cut-offs she wore a short-sleeved cotton shirt, but instead of tucking it in, she folded the tails in back, then undid the bottom buttons and tied it in a bow below her breasts.

"If that doesn't seduce him," Priscilla commented, "nothing will."

In her pack, Diane carried the thermos containing Warren and Priscilla, but she warned them strictly before leaving the house that if they wanted to watch—which she had practically begged them to do—they could not utter a sound. Warren agreed, and Priscilla tried to say she would only comment if absolutely necessary, but Diane swore her finally to silence.

Peter waved from across the street when she stopped at the corner to wait for the light. He was in a T-shirt and cut-offs. After they met and discovered to their amazement that they were wearing nearly identical shoes, they pedalled down Jefferson in the great afternoon heat.

"So where is this place?" Peter asked when they had gone almost to the end of Jefferson Street. The neighborhood was unfamiliar to him, and he glanced around at street names he had never heard of.

"Just a block further," she said, puffing. "On the left." She turned in to the main gate of Ace Storage and Peter followed, jumping from his bicycle right behind her.

"A storage locker?" he asked.

"It's mine," she answered brightly. She popped her head into the office and said hello, then turned quickly and pulled Peter along beside her.

"Which one?"

"Number fifteen."

"It's her lucky number," whispered Warren to Priscilla as they strode along behind.

In front of the door Diane stopped and took the key from her pocket. "Wait 'til you see it," she said, fumbling with the lock. After she opened the lock, Peter pushed up the door.

"Wow!" he exclaimed. "All this stuff is yours? You mean your parents' stuff, right?"

"No," she said taking his hand. "It's all mine."

"Where'd you get it?"

"Someone gave it to me," she said.

"Come on . . . Who'd give you a bunch of antiques?"

"An old guy who didn't want it all," she said. "It's a long story. The only problem is paying for the locker. Shit, it's going to take almost my whole allowance."

"It must," he said looking around. "What did you want to show me?"

She stood near him and put her arms around his arm. "Just—everything. Want to see some of the stuff in boxes?"

"Who did all this belong to before you got it?"

"It used to belong to a lady named Ludmilla McMonigle," she said. "But she was in a nursing home. She died, and her stepson didn't want it—so he gave it to me."

"He must be crazy," Peter said, looking through some newspapers on top of the nearest box. "Look at this—1947." He leafed through half of the stack. "Here's one from forty-five. Thirty-eight. Cool—you could probably get a lot if you sold these."

"Want to help me price it all?"

"Sure," he said. "Have a garage sale?"

"I might," she replied. "How much do you think I could get for the piano?"

"He gave you a fucking *piano?*"

"No, just an ordinary one," she said.

He laughed and turned toward her. She bit her lip and tossed her head. With a smile, he kissed her and put his arms around her. "Love you," he said.

"Love you, too," she replied, kissing him. "Let's close the door."

He grinned. "Is that what you had in mind? A place to make out?"

"It'll be private," she said, "even if we're just looking at stuff."

He walked over to close the door, and seeing the light switch, flipped it on. After the door closed, it was not very bright, but they could see well enough and their eyes adjusted quickly. There was a heavy blanket on one of the boxes, so Diane spread it on the floor, then sat down and pulled a box forward. "This one has postcards," she said. "Want to see some of them?"

"Sure," Peter replied sitting down next to her. Together they began to look through postcards. Diane held them, and told him she had seen them already. The day before she had expressly put them within easy reach, too, but did not mention that.

"This one's from Florida," she said of one, then of the next, "and this one's from Italy."

"The Dolomites. Uh huh." Peter turned it over. "1948. Cool stamp, too."

She slowly drew out a card from the pile and held it up. "This one's not a postcard . . ." Peter smiled shyly when he saw the picture—a woman with long black hair who held open her blouse to reveal a large pair of breasts. "How do you like her?" Diane asked.

"Fine," he said, swallowing. "How come it's double? Hey—is this one of those stereograms?"

"Uh huh. There's more, too. I don't have a viewer though. Want to see them anyway?"

"Sure," he said shrugging.

"Doesn't this look like fun?" she asked, cheerily pulling out another. She set it on her knee and they both leaned over to look.

It showed a man and a woman naked and embracing, their lips locked in a kiss.

"It does, doesn't it?" he whispered, and pulled her toward himself, softly kissing her lips. She pulled her hair away with one hand, and put her arms around his neck.

They kissed for a long time, and Peter's hand found its way downward to brush against Diane's breast, covered by a thin bra beneath her shirt. When his hand touched her, she took her own hand and pressed his palm against her breast.

"Can I feel you up?" he whispered in her ear.

She almost giggled. Did he still need to ask every time? "If you want to," she whispered back.

Still kissing, he began to unbutton her shirt, sliding his hand in and touching her neck and collarbone after each button, and when he could, he put his arm around her again, inside her shirt, feeling for the clasp of her bra.

"Not there," she said, pulling his hand forward. "Here." She put his fingers on the clasp in front, between her breasts.

"Cool," he whispered. "That's sexy."

"You like it?"

"Uh huh." He tweaked it open and let it fall aside, then slowly brought both palms against her warm breasts. Beneath, he could feel her heart beating.

Diane wanted him, desperately wanted him to touch her and slide his fingers into her—but took it slowly, savoring the kisses and the smooth feel of his palms on her nipples. He smiled, and bent down, almost lying in her lap to kiss her breasts, then laughed when they became tight and hard in his mouth.

"It means I'm ready," she whispered, and let her hand slide down his T-shirt. She tugged the shirt gently from his pants, then slowly wiggled her fingers inside. Kissing him still, she unbuttoned his pants and reached down for his penis. "Can I feel it?"

"Uh huh . . ."

It was hard and terribly warm. Diane pulled it upward, feeling its length and weight in her hand. Its rigidity fascinated her. Soon, she would have it inside her, and longing for that, she ran her fingers around the swollen head. "God, you have a big cock," she said.

"Not really."

"It's big enough for me," she said, and bent to kiss it, having never kissed one before. There was moisture on the tip, glistening, and she let her tongue come out to touch it. It tasted salty and slick. "Is this sperm?" she asked.

"No," he said, wrapping his hand around hers, which lightly held his penis. "It gets like that when I—when I have a hard-on." She began to move her hand slowly up and down the shaft.

"Show me how," she said.

"How what?"

"How to rub it. Does it feel good?"

"Yeah," he said. "Here, like this," and wrapping her hand carefully showed her how to pull and push it so it was not too sensitive. "If you just slide your hand over it, it's sometimes uncomfortable 'cause it's not lubricated like a cunt—I mean vagina."

"Cunt's OK," she said.

"But when you do it like this, it feels really great."

"How about this?" she said, and bent down to draw it into her mouth. She tried to work it around and kept her teeth away, like she had seen Priscilla do—and was thankful she had some idea of what to do with her tongue. She could hardly imagine what the first time would have been like for someone who had never even seen anyone having sex. And she felt lucky that Priscilla and Warren had been quite patient enough to teach her some things.

"Oh, shit," he said, and leaned back on his elbows. Presently, he straightened his legs and let her straddle him, sucking slowly. "I'm going to come," he said suddenly.

"No wait," she said releasing his penis. "It looks funny like that," she added, poking it and laughing at the way it bounced back.

"Look," he said, "I can make it move, too." He clenched himself to make it bob up and down while she laughed, then sat up suddenly and reached for her. Her shirt had fallen completely off, and he slid her bra down over her shoulders, then kissed her breasts and stroked them. Into her eyes he gazed, smiling, and began to unbutton her pants. "Want to do it?"

She nodded and whispered to him, "Yeah. I want to do it with you." She lay on the blanket and arched her hips while he pulled her cut-offs down, then wriggled out of them while he slowly pulled down her panties.

"It's beautiful," he said looking at her pubic triangle and stroking her thighs. She spread her legs slightly, letting him run his fingers down her labia. They were wet to the touch and bumpy—he knew the feeling, but had never both seen and touched them simultaneously, unconstricted by panties. Usually he was finger-banging someone and only had their pants unbuttoned—but he had read 'The Sensuous Man' which his brother recommended as essential. He kissed her legs and her breasts, then her stomach, and slowly worked toward her hips, loving the look and feel of her skin. "Can I eat you out?"

"Sure," she whispered, then when his tongue dipped into her cleft cried, "It feels good."

He licked quietly, and pushed her thighs further apart. "Do you like it?"

"It's great," she whispered. "Oh, shit—here—right here," she said, guiding his hand. "My clit's right here. Rub like this slowly—oh, shit it feels good—oh, jeez. Eat me out, Peter."

He stabbed lightly with his tongue, flicking it across her clitoris. "Yeah," she whispered, "just like that. A little faster, but not much—oh, man . . ." Taking his head in her hands, she wound her fingers in his hair, pulling him forward and back in the rhythm she wanted—just a little faster—and when she was almost coming, pushed his face closer. "Really fast, now," she said, panting heavily. "Yes—" and she dissolved into a moan.

He scrambled forward and lay full length over her, his penis halfway hard between her legs. "Did you come?"

"Uh huh," she said hugging him.

"I love you," he whispered, embracing her tightly, then ran his tongue around the edge of her ear, whispering, "I love you. I love you."

"I love you, too," she said, and near his ear whispered, "Let's do it."

"Diane," he said, rolling onto his side. "Uh—"

"Oh yeah," she said laughing, then sat up and reached over to grab her purse. "I have a rubber."

He had been about to ask whether she wanted to go through with it, because he had no protection. "You do?"

"Yeah—my *Mom* gave it to me a long time ago."

"Your Mom?"

"You know, when we had our big 'Facts of Life' talk."

"Cool," he said accepting the package from her hand.

"I'll put it on, OK?" she said, and took back the package to tear it open.

He lay down, and let her stroke and kiss his penis until it was hard as a cucumber again, then she paused to unroll the condom over it, all the way to the base. When she had finished, she lay down and opened her legs.

"Diane—" he whispered. "Are you a virgin?"

"Yeah," she said, then seeing his look of concern, "But hey—I love you. I really want this—I mean, I want to give myself to you."

"Yeah," he whispered. "I love you too. I just don't want to hurt you—isn't it supposed to hurt?"

"Don't worry," she said.

When she felt the head of his organ pressing against her, though, she wondered if it would be all right. He pushed harder, and she felt the urge to back away. "You have to push," she said. "That's what I've heard. Just—shove it in, and then it'll be all over."

"But it's hurting you . . ."

"Diane," Priscilla said softly. Diane looked at her, but did not answer. "Try sitting on top of him, and take it at your own speed."

"Here, let's try this," Diane said, suddenly sitting up. She made Peter lie on the floor and straddled over him. His penis seemed slightly less solid than before, and she rubbed carefully, letting it play against her vaginal lips. "Does it feel good?" she asked, rotating the head against herself. "It does for me."

"Yeah," he whispered.

Holding him steady, she started to sit down, and felt the huge head pressing and pressing, then suddenly, it popped inside.

"Push," she said, and tried to sit down.

"Now that you've got him that far," Priscilla suggested, "if you can turn over, he'll probably be able to go all the way in."

"No, you'll have to be on top," Diane whispered to Peter. She lay atop him, then rolled over, trying to keep his penis inside. Settled on her back, she urged him onward.

"Doesn't it hurt?"

"Yeah. But it feels good, too. Especially my clit . . ."

The pleasure of having his penis squeezed just inside the entrance excited him, but still hesitant, seeing that it hurt her, he tried not to move too quickly. The urge to thrust his hips was too strong to resist, and finally, pressing forward harder and harder, then pulling out a little, he got everything lubricated enough to eventually slide completely into her.

"Oh shit, that feels so good," he said, then shuddering, ejaculated and shivered.

"Bravo!" Warren cried, and clapped his hands. Priscilla joined him for the applause, and then they both fell silent.

"Did you shoot it?" Diane asked, laughing and hugging him.

"Oh yeah—I came." Peter let himself down softly on top of her.

She loved the warmth and pressure—even his huge penis, which had seemed too big a thing to ever be inside her, gradually ceased to sting, though it was still big. She felt it growing smaller until finally it slipped out altogether.

"Tie the rubber in a knot," she suggested. "So we don't have little Peters running all over the blanket."

He laughed and tied it off, then put it into his pants pocket.

They sat together, his back against a box, and hers against his chest, nestled in his arms.

"Was it OK?" he asked. "I didn't hurt you too much?'

"No," she said. "It was great. Next time it'll be even better."

"And it only gets better from there," Priscilla said, whispering in her ear. Diane started

"What's the matter?" Peter asked.

"Oh, nothing," she said. "Want to look at some other stuff? There are some photo albums, too. And a bunch of old magazines. There are a few National Geographics and stuff. A bunch of Ladies' magazines, too, and some of them have really hilarious ads."

"OK," he said. "Maybe we should put our clothes on first?"

"Later," she said, hugging him again. "I just want to be naked with you for a while."

"OK—let's see some magazines, then."

They lay down side-by-side on their stomachs and leafed through magazines.

[36]

In late August, Warren and Priscilla lay with Diane on their bed after making love—the three of them, very long and very passion-ately—sat naked and beautiful talking in whispers. As delicately as he could, Warren explained that they could feel themselves grow-ing fainter.

"It's like something pulling at us," he said. "Like I've told you before, it's pulling us from behind, and I think we're being slowly drawn away."

Diane nodded, and finally admitted to herself that it was really so. They were fading. "I've noticed it too. Can't you stay somehow?"

"We'd love to," Priscilla said. "The both of us, really. But—it's too overpowering. We're hanging on now only by power of will."

"If we really let go," Warren said, "we'd be gone, I think."

Priscilla concurred. "But we had to say a proper good-bye, first."

"It's all right," Diane answered, her eyes filling with tears. "I knew it couldn't last." With trembling lips, she began to cry. "I wish you could stay."

Priscilla reached out to embrace the air around Diane. "We both love you dearly," she said.

"We do," agreed Warren.

"I know," Diane said, barely able to talk with her throat constricting.

"And it's not forever," Priscilla whispered, looking deeply into Diane's eyes. "Always remember that, dearest. It's not forever—and we'll be—we'll be *there*, where ever we go, waiting for you."

"We will," whispered Warren. He took Priscilla's hand, and they embraced each other tightly.

Priscilla smiled, her own lips trembling. "Good-bye."

"Good-bye," Warren said.

They seemed to relax completely, then faded so abruptly that Diane gasped and they were gone. Nothing could hold back her flood of tears, and she cried quietly all night. In the morning, she felt too wretched and lonely to go to school. Nancy came to her room and after checking for fever, gave her two aspirin. She tried to ask what the trouble was, but Diane maintained her silence, only crying harder, burying her face and pulling the covers over her head. Seeing that something had terribly upset her, Nancy pulled the covers from Diane's head and sat simply stroking her daughter's cheek while she cried herself to sleep again. There was nothing Nancy could do. She felt strangely helpless, but hoped Diane would talk about it when she was ready. It was funny, too, Nancy thought as she stood up to leave—that Victoria had been sleeping badly as well. She stood over Diane's bed, then sat down again. A while later, Victoria woke up crying, and she went to feed her.

[37]

By the time Warren and Priscilla left, Diane was deeply in love with Peter, and this eased her transition in the way they had both hoped it would. She relied heavily on having Peter's shoulder to cry on, and him to make love with, for the first weeks after their departure. She even started to think about trying to collect her thoughts to tell her mother all about it. Sometimes before going to sleep she dramatized the story: "When I was fifteen, I moved in with a much older man; and from him I learned the depth and breadth of love . . ." That seemed like a good beginning, but she was not quite ready to tell the rest. She knew she would have to get over it first, if there was any such thing as getting over that sort of love. It seemed impossible then. She would remember Warren always; and she had her diaries to remind her of anything about him that she might accidentally forget.

Though her youthful love for Peter lasted little more than a year, she found great intimacy with him, and never in later years did she regret taking him as her first lover—after Warren, she always added silently. Warren was really the first.

Every time she made love she would dissolve into a sea of absolute bliss that seemed to go on forever. The waters of pleasure would envelope her at the brink of orgasm, and wash her up a lifetime later on the shore, gasping in her lover's arms. Then she would cling and fondle, comfortably laying her head against his chest. Sometimes in the back of her mind in her exquisite tiredness she would begin to wonder how Warren fared with Priscilla in heaven, where she imagined they had gone.

To Warren and Priscilla she attributed all the happiness of her life. In a way, they had left her pregnant with a seed that continued to grow more wonderful as the years passed. Through them she had learned to love, to make love, to let go; and had accepted satisfactory answers to all of the greatest questions of life—questions so many people never stopped asking. She had no fear or wondering of what lay beyond life, and came to enjoy all its aspects in perfect serenity. There were times when she believed that faintly she heard their voices, still whispering to one another nearby.

"She turned out all right, don't you think?" Warren would ask.

And Priscilla would always answer in her enthusiastic way, "Oh, Warren—she's marvelous!"